DEAD MAN'S DIVE
A CORNISH CRIME THRILLER
BOOK 2

BERRICK FORD

HARVEY BERRICK PUBLISHING

COPYRIGHT

DEAD MAN'S DIVE

Copyright © 2024 by Harvey-Berrick Publishing
All rights reserved.
No part of this book may be reproduced in any form or by any electronic or mechanical means, including information storage and retrieval systems, without written permission from the author, except for the use of brief quotations in a book review.

Cover photo Adobe Photostock
Editor: Coby Llewelyn

For Coby Llewelyn
More inspirational than she knows

CONTENTS

Foreword	vii
Cornish Crime Thriller Series	xi
Prologue	1
Ten days earlier...	5
Chapter 1	7
Chapter 2	18
Chapter 3	27
Chapter 4	36
Chapter 5	45
Chapter 6	58
Chapter 7	65
Chapter 8	72
Chapter 9	82
Chapter 10	88
Chapter 11	103
Chapter 12	110
Chapter 13	115
Chapter 14	123
Chapter 15	130
Chapter 16	138
Chapter 17	147
Chapter 18	165
Chapter 19	176
Chapter 20	181
Chapter 21	198
Chapter 22	216
Chapter 23	229
Chapter 24	241

Chapter 25	252
Chapter 26	260
Chapter 27	269
Chapter 28	281
Chapter 29	290
Chapter 30	298
Chapter 31	304
Chapter 32	319
Chapter 33	326
Epilogue	346
What to read next...	355
The Cornish Crime Thriller Series	357
Acknowledgments	359
Forensic File	361

FOREWORD

Dead Man's Dive is the second book in the Poldhu & Rego crime series set in West Cornwall, a place I call home.

These two police officers, one a student PC, the other a Detective Inspector, are ordinary people doing an extraordinary job. They're not superheroes, just the everyday kind of heroes that you'd pass in the street.

If you enjoy this book — and I hope you will — **I'd really appreciate if if you'd leave a review** on the site where you bought it. It really does make a difference.

Thank you!

B.F.

PRAISE FOR BERRICK FORD

"Authentic and gripping"

"Accurate when it describes how policing works. Any current or ex-police officers, as well as anyone interested in crime, will love this. No one is a superhero and the plot twists and turns until an unexpected climax."

"A window into a darker world"

"The characters had some very powerful emotions and the villain was a real surprise in what was a page-turning twist of plot."

"A cut above most crime novels."

DEAD MAN'S DIVE
A Cornish Crime Thriller #2

It started as a date with a diving instructor, but when Tamsyn finds a body during a wreck dive off the Cornish coast, her work-life balance is in serious jeopardy.

Who is the mysterious diver with the Cyrillic tattoos, and why has no one reported him missing? Is this an accident or evidence of organised crime, and why are fingers pointing towards the military naval air station of *RNAS Culdrose* a few miles away?

Tamsyn is just a student constable so Detective Inspector Robert Rego is brought down from Devon to take over the case. He's missing his family in Manchester and gets seasick just looking at a boat.

But this crime is bigger than both of them, and the pressure isn't just to solve the case ... but to forget about it completely.

Cornish Crime Thriller Series

#0.5 *Dead Start*
#1 *Dead Water*
#2 *Dead Man's Dive*
#3 *Dead Reckoning*
#4 *Dead Shore*

PROLOGUE

Tamsyn used the staff entrance at Penzance police station, wondering why she'd been called in on her day off.

Her path was blocked by two plainclothes officers.

"Tamsyn Poldhu?"

"Yes?" she said smiling politely, but not recognising either of the men.

The taller one stepped forward immediately.

"Tamsyn Poldhu, I am Officer 6943 of Counter Terrorist Command South West, and I am arresting you on suspicion of the threat of action under the Terrorism Act 2006."

"What? No! That's not..."

"You do not have to say anything. But it may harm your defence if you do not mention when questioned something which you later rely on in court. Anything you do say may be given in evidence."

Her smile was slow to disappear because Tamsyn

couldn't take in what the officer was saying, only that it was *wrong*.

"What?" she gasped. "No, this is a mistake!"

The man ignored her.

"It is necessary to take you into custody immediately to obtain evidence by questioning and to allow for a prompt and effective investigation."

Tamsyn could not speak, could not comprehend. Her mind spiralled, making no sense of the words that she was hearing.

Inspector Maura Walters, Tamsyn's boss, strode down the corridor towards them, her face a stern mask.

"Tamsyn, you are immediately suspended from duty. I need your Warrant card, also your Captor spray, baton, work phone and entry fob. You will be taken from here and interviewed by these officers. *If* you are released from custody, you will not come back into this police station and won't have contact with any officer that works here. Do you understand?"

Tamsyn stood there blinking, confused, uncertain. It was a prank, some sort of joke. But the officers were serious, determined.

"What? N-no!" she managed to stammer at last. "No! This... No! This isn't what was supposed to happen!"

Their expressions didn't change even by the slightest flicker.

"This is a mistake," she said again, her voice shaking. "Ask DI Rego! Detective Inspector Robert Rego. Ask him! He'll tell you everything."

She might as well have been talking to the granite cliffs of Land's End.

In shocked silence, she handed over her Warrant card and key fob, and was escorted to her locker so that her baton and incapacitant spray could be collected.

Tamsyn saw several officers that she recognised and they all watched her, their faces grim and hostile.

One of the plainclothes officers took her arm as she was marched back along the corridor and out to a waiting police van.

"Tamsyn!"

She turned her head as the man she knew as 'Tank' shouted her name, but the officer who had her arm didn't slow his pace.

"Don't say anything!" Tank ordered. "Don't talk to anyone, don't trust anyone!"

His eyes narrowed as he glared at her, and all she could do was stare back.

"Tamsyn!" Tank yelled again. "Don't say fuck all until you've spoken to your Fed rep! Nothing! You hear me?"

The plainclothes officers loaded her like cargo into the van and slammed the door shut. As they walked around to the front, she heard one of them talking into his radio.

"I've just arrested Poldhu."

Not even her first name: just 'Poldhu', as if she were a known criminal.

"Yes, sir," he continued. "We're leaving Penzance now."

She heard the sirens, and the van began travelling at speed, blue-lighted all of the 115 miles to Exeter, the HQ for Devon & Cornwall Police.

Her body was shaking with shock and fear, and her mind kept somersaulting through the events of the last few days. *This isn't right! It's a mistake! It's all a terrible mistake! I can fix this. I just need to speak to Inspector Rego – he'll tell them, he'll tell them that they've got it all wrong!*

And then other thoughts, other voices started to worm their way into her mind. It had felt weird, the operation. Why hadn't protocol been followed? Why was there no backup? She'd been told it was covert, that only *she* could help them; only *she* could save the op, their case, the country. But why? Why only her? *I'm just a student officer – why me? Why me? Why me?*

Because you're naïve, the voices replied. *Because you're stupid. Because you trusted the wrong people ... the wrong person.*

Her body became numb.

It's a mistake.

He'll fix it.

It's a mistake.

She nearly wept with relief when she saw the tall silhouette and broad shoulders of her boss, Detective Inspector Robert Rego, standing in the corridor as she was brought through the doors of Exeter police station.

"Sir!" she screamed, her voice piercing. "Inspector Rego!" The crowd of officers surrounding him cleared.

Her heart stopped.

He was handcuffed.

Her mind swam and she felt faint. She'd trusted him. He'd promised her...

If he spoke, she couldn't hear him, but his lips were moving, and she thought he mouthed the words,

"I'm sorry."

TEN DAYS EARLIER...

CHAPTER 1

Tamsyn sank slowly through the water, suspended in a silence so profound that her own soft breaths roared in her ears.

She hadn't thought she'd feel safe with the vast weight of water above her, but she did. She felt peaceful. She felt content. She listened to the sound of her breathing and watched the colourful shoals of fish darting around. She felt at home in the element in a way she hadn't in months.

Adam drifted closer, signalling to her, his bare hands eerily white in the half-light. He brought his thumb and forefinger together to make a circle: *Are you okay?*

Tamsyn ran through a mental checklist: breathing, regular; ear pressure, equalised; bubbles showing that her dive set was working correctly. She took another slow breath, then returned the 'okay' signal. He responded with a thumbs down, indicating that they should continue their descent.

Tamsyn controlled her breathing the way she'd been

taught and a slow stream of bubbles trickled from her regulator, the only clue which way was up.

She followed the shot-line, sinking slowly. At ten metres the water began to change from turquoise to green, darkening below, and Adam checked again that she was okay. Then he pointed downwards again, the light muted now, and they began their final descent, the sense of isolation complete.

It felt so strange to stand on the seabed looking up, up, up towards the sky, the sun sparkling on the surface so far above her.

The thought was unnerving, so she concentrated on admiring the silvery pilchards swooping past her like starlings of the sea. Ferns grew in clusters, roots clinging to rocks, their green fingers waving gently.

A sea slug, the size and shape of a cucumber, idled past, making her gasp in surprise. The sudden rush of bubbles was a reminder to stay calm, to breathe evenly.

Adam finned towards her, checking on her again.

He was an experienced diver, the club's instructor, her dive buddy and maybe boyfriend, but at that moment, Tamsyn wished she were alone in this silent world: no words, no talking, no responsibilities, just drifting on the current.

Adam signalled, pointing in the direction of the dark, hulking shadow behind her.

For more than a hundred years, the SS *Mohegan* had lain at the bottom of the sea, broken across the treacherous Manacles rocks, within sight of the spire of St Keverne's church on Cornwall's Lizard peninsula.

In just 27m of water, the *Mohegan* was a popular diving spot and often used by sub-aqua clubs to give learner divers their first experience of a wreck dive.

Adam had been excited for Tamsyn to see it and promised that there were souvenirs to be had. Divers regularly brought up crockery and pieces of pottery. They'd been planning this dive for weeks, waiting for the right weather that coincided with one of Tamsyn's days off.

"And I've got a friend who says it's haunted," he'd laughed, just before they left the dive boat.

Tamsyn had returned his smile because that's what he expected, but the thought made her uneasy. People had drowned here and not all the bodies of crew and passengers had been recovered: essentially, they were diving a grave site.

Moving slowly through the water, weightless and at peace, she had her first glimpse of the huge wreck, the brass portholes drifting into view. Tamsyn felt as if she were travelling back in time, wondering who had looked through these small windows and whether they'd felt death hovering the night of the shipwreck.

The huge cargo hatches were empty eye-sockets in the massive vessel and Tamsyn paused as the outline of the ship's hull stretched into the darkness, visibility decreasing quickly as their swim fins stirred the silt around them.

Slowly, keeping her breathing at a normal rate, she followed Adam as he finned the length of the wreck, pointing out the engine and massive boilers resting on rocks encrusted with maerl, a red seaweed with a hard, chalky skeleton.

When she saw bright anemones swaying alongside a family of sea urchins, she wanted to smile. With the mouthpiece in place, she couldn't, but she wanted to.

The feeling of contentment lasted until Adam reappeared out of the gloom, holding something in his hands. She couldn't see what it was, but he seemed pleased and placed it in his mesh dive bag, then pointed back the way they'd come toward the shot-line, telling her to start her ascent.

As she followed him, she ran through the calculations: how many times she needed to decompress at 6m intervals, and at the correct pace.

She almost swam into Adam when he suddenly reared back, his legs and arms thrashing wildly as blood bloomed in the water. An enormous conger eel darted from the wreck, latching onto Adam's left hand. Bubbles spewed from his regulator as he screamed in pain. The needle-sharp teeth sank deeper, and Tamsyn could see the pain and panic in his eyes. She reacted without thinking, grabbing a rock and hitting the creature as hard as she could. Again and again, she used every ounce of strength, but her blows were slowed by the water. Adam punched the creature with his free hand and smashed its body savagely against the crumbling hull.

Finally, the eel let go, gliding backwards into its underwater lair, the unblinking eyes seeming to stare sullenly at Tamsyn as it retreated.

Something brushed past her arm and she wheeled towards it, the rock still clenched in her fist.

But it wasn't the eel and it wasn't Adam.

Another body was suspended inside the wreck: lifeless, dead.

And then she did scream, or tried to.

She spun in the water, gasping, stirring up more silt until the world disappeared. She was hyperventilating now and no longer knew which way was up.

Her brain was in neutral, unable to function. Just a single certainty: *I'm going to die.*

When something grabbed her arm, she thought her heart would stop. But it was Adam, the puncture wounds visible on his hand, his little finger hanging by a thread.

He signalled upwards with growing urgency.

Tamsyn finned too fast, shooting up, using too much air. Adam followed, his damaged hand trailing blood behind him.

He was still holding her arm, and it felt as if he was dragging her down – she was desperate to shake him free. He signalled urgently with his damaged hand, and she remembered that she had to stop, had to decompress, had to wait five, agonisingly long minutes until it was safe to continue.

Adam's movements became slower, almost lethargic, and she realised he was going into shock. She grabbed his cylinders' harness and towed him upwards to the final decompression stop: waiting, counting and praying that she was doing it correctly because their lives depended on it.

When Tamsyn's head finally broke the surface, she tore her facemask away, gasping fresh air in heaving lungfuls. Adam was beside her, his face contorted and his eyes glassy.

But they weren't safe yet.

The weather had changed in the short time they'd been underwater, and the dive boat rocked from side to side, the waves growing rougher as the seconds passed. Tamsyn cursed Adam's cavalier decision to continue the dive with just the two of them after his friend cancelled, and her own weakness for going along with it. She knew better. For God's sake, she knew better than to trust the sea.

She yanked off her fins and hurled them onto the deck, struggling to hold onto the boat's dive ladder as she was dunked into the sea, then whipped back as the small boat bucked and reared, her ribs slamming painfully against the metal rungs.

It took three tries before she managed to clamber aboard and flopped onto the deck. She rolled onto her belly, and tried to find Adam in the surging water. He'd managed to shed his weight belt and swim fins and was holding onto the bottom rung with his good hand, but didn't have the strength to pull himself up. She stretched out as far as she could over the boat's side, but she couldn't reach him. She needed a rope or...

Her eyes fastened on the boathook used for docking. If she could just hook it around his harness without smacking his skull...

The hook clanged off Adam's cylinders five times before she managed to hook her prize. The dive boat tugged against its anchor, lurching wildly, and Tamsyn fell to her knees, but she didn't drop the boathook.

Using the last of her strength, she heaved Adam onto the deck, a neoprene-clad tuna.

His skin was pale under the tan, his lips blue, and his

breathing fast and shallow. She didn't know if it was shock or hypothermia.

"Adam! Where's the first aid kit?"

He mouthed something, but she couldn't hear him and he looked as though he was on the verge of passing out.

The first aid kit must be in the boat's wheelhouse. She lurched towards the small cabin, saw the the plastic container with the white cross on a green background, and pulled it open. Grabbing a bandage and foil blanket, slipping and sliding across the deck, she managed to strap his hand tightly.

Adam groaned faintly and blood oozed through the white cotton. She wound the emergency blanket around his shoulders and positioned him so he couldn't be thrown out of the boat.

It would have to do.

Tamsyn ran back to the wheelhouse and picked up the radio, turning to channel 16.

"Pan-pan! Pan-pan! Pan-pan! Falmouth Coastguard, Falmouth Coastguard, Falmouth Coastguard. This is Tamsyn Poldhu with the dive boat *Heart of Lowenna*. We're two POBs, anchored 50m southwest of the *Mohegan* at 50.02.38 degrees north, 05.02.26 degrees west. I have an injured man – conger eel attack – and he's bleeding heavily from his hand. One finger is... in bad shape. Can you send the rescue helicopter? Over."

The reply was almost immediate.

"Pan-pan *Lowenna*, pan-pan *Lowenna*, pan-pan *Lowenna*, this is Falmouth Coastguard, Falmouth Coastguard, Falmouth Coastguard on channel one-six. Message received. That is negative on the rescue helicopter, negative on the rescue helicopter. We'll send the lifeboat from Falmouth. Over."

"Falmouth Coastguard, this is *Lowenna*. There's a lot of water moving about here for a safe transfer and I'm only nine minutes from Porthoustock. Can the lifeboat meet me there on the quarry side? I've started the engines and am *en route*. Over."

"*Lowenna* this is Falmouth Coastguard. Understood. The lifeboat is on way to Porthoustock. Over."

"Understood, Falmouth. Over and out."

Tamsyn gripped the wheel and pushed the throttle forwards, increasing the speed as much as she dared in the choppy waters.

The little boat bounced and skittered across the waves, slamming down into the trough then lurching up into the next set. She couldn't risk looking over shoulder to see how Adam was doing.

Wind whipped her wet hair across her face and she shivered uncontrollably. Nine minutes seemed to take a lifetime.

As she neared the shingle beach, two elderly fishermen waved to her from the wharf, ready to grab the lines as soon as she could throw them ashore. She guessed that they'd heard her emergency call and had rushed to help.

She was coming in fast and knew she should slow the engines, but a quick glance told her that Adam was unconscious.

The little boat roared into the harbour, breaking the five knots speed limit, then she slammed the throttle into reverse, and tossed a rope to the waiting men. They caught it skilfully, quickly securing *Lowenna* as she bumped against old tractor tyres that had been suspended from the harbour wall instead of buoys, and boarding the boat.

"Poldhu? You Ozzie's granddaughter?" one of them asked as they both clambered aboard and squatted down next to Adam.

"Yes, that's right. I'm Tamsyn," she said, her voice tight with strain.

"Thought so," the other one nodded. "I'm Jack and that there is Clemo.'"

"'E's awright, maid. The boy just fainted. Nasty bite though, bleeding like buggery – 'e might lose that finger."

The man sounded philosophical: life at sea was a dangerous business. Tamsyn could hear her grandfather's voice in her head: *the ocean gives and the ocean takes away.*

She crouched down next to Adam, taking his uninjured hand in hers, feeling its icy coldness.

His eyelids fluttered as the men undid his harness, removing the rest of his scuba equipment, and the faintest colour returned to his cheeks.

"Sorry," he whispered, giving Tamsyn a wry smile. "More exciting than I'd planned."

Tamsyn leaned closer, so the two men couldn't hear her.

"Did you see the body?"

His forehead wrinkled.

"What?"

"Another diver. He was dead."

"What?"

"You didn't see him?"

"No, nothing." Adam gave her a faint smile. "I told you it was haunted."

Tamsyn didn't reply and was relieved when she finally heard the sound of the lifeboat's engines.

"The lifeboat is here, Adam."

"Come with me?" he asked weakly.

"I'll look after *Lowenna* for you then meet you at the hospital. I'll only be an hour behind you."

"But..."

"I'll be fine," she said, deliberately misunderstanding him. "I've been around boats my whole life. I'll be okay. And I'll bring your stuff so you've got some dry clothes when I pick you up at the hospital."

She suspected that his hand would need surgery, but she didn't tell him that.

The lifeboat crew took over then, climbing aboard the boat and stretchering Adam across onto the lifeboat.

"I'll see you later," Tamsyn called reassuringly, but Adam didn't reply.

She waited until the lifeboat had left the harbour, then turned to the two old fishermen.

"I really appreciate your help."

"Don't you fret, maid. Regards to your grandfather."

They waved away her thanks and brought one of the waiting tractors down over the shingle, tying *Lowenna*'s lines to it and dragging it up the beach to beyond the highwater mark.

She collected Adam's phone and dive set from the boat but decided to stow it all in her own car. They'd both parked on the shingle beach, as all the locals did, but she didn't want to leave expensive equipment in Adam's car for several days – that would be an invitation for someone to help themselves.

It was a forty-minute drive to the large hospital in Truro, but first she had to make a call.

She tried to phone her boss but only got his answering service.

"This is DI Rego. Leave a message and I'll get back to you."

"Sir, it's Tamsyn Poldhu. I've found a body."

CHAPTER 2

DI Rego had turned off his phone to attend his daughter's sports day. When Tamsyn tried to call him, he'd been running in the parents' race, coming a respectable third behind an ultra-competitive man wearing Lycra, and a woman who'd warmed up with burpees and lunges.

His wife laughed and cheered, and eight-year-old Maisie gave him a big hug. He knew it would only be a couple of years before she became like her elder brother where everything Dad did was an embarrassment. But for now, he enjoyed the hug.

He didn't pick up his messages until they were leaving Burger King sometime later: one from Tamsyn and two from his DS at Penzance police station.

"Work?" his wife asked, raising an eyebrow. "I thought you had the weekend off?"

"Sorry, love," he sighed. "I have to go."

She gave him a lopsided smile. "I don't suppose there's

any point in asking if it can wait till Sunday so we can all drive down together."

"I'm sorry, Cass, it can't wait."

She raised one shoulder.

"Guess we'll see you on Sunday evening then. Drive safely."

At least Maisie's sports day hadn't been added to the long list of family events he'd missed since becoming a detective.

Rego left Manchester behind and headed toward the setting sun, knowing the journey would take a minimum of six hours.

When he'd taken a promotion to Inspector with Devon & Cornwall Police four months earlier, his family had stayed behind so the kids' schooling wouldn't be disrupted. It was hard on everyone, but it wouldn't be forever. Once he had a couple of years as DI under his belt in the more rural community, he planned to apply for a transfer back to Greater Manchester Police.

Rego would be the first to admit that he'd had a city copper's mentality, thinking that life would be slow down in the southwest, but so far that had proved to be very far from the truth. At Easter, he'd led a team that brought down a major organised crime network which had been using small harbours up and down the coast to bring in quantities of illegal drugs.

He frowned at the memory: his student officer, Tamsyn, had nearly died on that operation. And now she claimed to have seen a body while diving off the Lizard peninsula.

He'd made it as far as the M6 when his sergeant phoned again.

"Sorry to interrupt your leave, boss."

"Don't worry, Tom. I would have been driving back the day after tomorrow anyway. What's the status?"

"The search team haven't found a body, so there's not much to report. We've got the Coastguard out there and the helicopter from Newquay, as well as two RNLI lifeboats. The professional dive unit were in the water 30 minutes ago, and we've asked leisure divers to stay away from the wreck while the recovery effort is underway. Nothing so far."

"Have you spoken to Tamsyn?"

"Yes, boss."

"What exactly did she say?"

"That she saw a body close to the seabed, wearing a wetsuit, facemask and dive tanks."

"And she's sure the person was dead?" Rego asked. "Not just another diver?"

"She says there was only the two of them out there that day." DS Stevens paused before continuing, picking his words carefully. "Unfortunately, the man she was diving with was injured at the scene in an unrelated incident, but according to the officer who spoke to him, he was unable to corroborate her sighting and sceptical that she'd seen anything at all. Mind you, he'd just about had his hand bitten off by a conger eel..."

"Bloody hell!" Rego shuddered.

"It happens, but he was just unlucky – congers have poor eyesight so it probably thought it had smelled a tasty snack. Anyway, I don't reckon the lad was in the best shape to say what Tamsyn did or didn't see."

Rego heard the protectiveness in his sergeant's voice and smiled to himself.

"Thanks, Tom. Well, keep me updated. I'll be at the station by midnight. I *don't* expect to see you there."

Rego flipped down the sun visor and continued southwest.

Adam had been taken to a specialist unit in Plymouth, so by the time Tamsyn had safely beached Adam's boat, had it towed above the high water mark by tractor, then driven 60 miles to the hospital, he'd already been in surgery for an hour.

The hospital staff wouldn't tell her anything because she wasn't a relative, but one of the nurses had taken pity on her and given a quick thumb's up as she'd stepped out of the operating room.

She felt useless; she couldn't even phone his parents because she'd never met them and didn't have their numbers. Adam had once told her that his parents were divorced. Thankfully, one of Tamsyn's colleagues from the station had promised to take care of contacting the family.

Tamsyn checked her phone for the umpteenth time but there were still no messages. She glanced up when a woman in an expensive business suit rushed into the waiting room. She looked enough like Adam to be his mother, Tamsyn stood to speak to her.

"Hi, are you Adam's mum?"

"I'm his mother, yes. Who are you?"

"I'm Tamsyn."

There was no recognition in the woman's eyes, so Tamsyn continued quickly.

"I was with Adam when he was injured."

"What happened exactly? They didn't tell me anything on the phone."

"We were diving the *Mohegan*, a wreck off the Lizard, and he was bitten in the hand by a conger eel. His little finger was ... damaged and..."

"Dear God," the woman held her hand to her chest. "Who are you exactly?"

Tamsyn hesitated. Clearly, Adam had never mentioned her to his mother or that they'd met at the dive club earlier in the year and had been dating since her 21st birthday last month.

"We met at the dive club and he said he'd take me down for my first wreck dive," she answered at last.

"So, he was out there with just a student?"

The woman sounded as if she blamed Tamsyn, but whatever response she might have made was left unsaid when the nurse from the operating theatre reappeared, her gaze bouncing between the two women.

"Are you the family of Adam Ellis?"

"I'm Julie Kurl, his mother."

The woman had turned her back on Tamsyn.

"The procedure went well and we're taking Adam into recovery now. Dr Barnes will be out to talk to you shortly, but it's good news."

"Thank God," said Adam's mother, following the nurse, then remembered Tamsyn was still there and glanced back at her. "Thank you for your help, Tarryn. You don't need to stay now."

"Oh okay," she said, feeling dismissed. "Of course, no problem. This is my number – perhaps you could call me later and let me know how Adam's doing?"

Adam's mother nodded distractedly, her gaze on the door to the operating theatre.

"I brought his clothes, phone and car keys," said Tamsyn as she placed the piece of paper with her number in Adam's sports bag next to his mother. "So ... I'll hang onto his dive kit and cylinders. I didn't want to leave them on the boat." Tamsyn waited a moment but there was no response. "Um, well, tell Adam I said hi and ... I'll message him later."

On the way to her battered old Fiat, Tamsyn stopped to buy a takeaway coffee from the self-service machine in the hospital's café. She felt exhausted and needed the caffeine to make the 80-mile journey home. After the initial rush of adrenaline, her mood had swung between shock and numbness, and now she was crashing. The coffee would wake her up, but it was scalding hot, so she sat in her car with her eyes closed, sipping it slowly. There was no law against drinking a soft drink or coffee while driving, so long as the driver wasn't distracted by it. Odd pieces of law often swam through her brain at the weirdest moments.

It felt like the day had gone on forever and all she wanted to do was go home and have a hot shower, but she wanted to know what the dive team had found, too.

She picked up her phone to send Adam a text, although it seemed unlikely that he'd read it tonight. She wrote and rewrote it several times before she finally sent it.

Then she leaned back in her seat, eyes closed again, the coffee balanced precariously in her lap.

Had her mind been playing tricks on her? Had she really seen a body down there? A shudder ran through her and she had to grip the paper cup with both hands.

The image of the faceless man had begun to fade from her mind, superimposed by the eel's attack and the memory of Adam's blood in the water, the rush to the surface and the battle to drag him into the dive boat. She wasn't even sure how she'd managed that. She was strong, but he was a 13 stone rugby player.

Adrenaline was a hell of a drug.

She wondered if she'd be in trouble if the police divers didn't find anything. Then she remembered the Go Pro camera that Adam had clipped to his harness, saying he wanted to record her first wreck dive. But then again, if he hadn't seen the body, it was unlikely the camera had caught it.

Her phone rang, interrupting her thoughts.

"Hey, Jess," she said faintly.

"Hey, yourself, you hag! I've been waiting all day to hear how the big date went. So, was it snog, marry or avoid?"

Tamsyn gave a shaky laugh. "Zero on the snog front, unlikely on the marry part, and he'll probably want to avoid me after today."

"It can't have been that bad," Jess said, congenitally prone to look on the bright side. "Where are you?"

"Derriford."

There was a short pause. "The hospital? Oh my God!

Are you okay? Shit! What happened? You're okay, right? Please tell me you're okay!"

"Jess, I'm fine. Honestly, I'm fine. But, um, Adam, not so much. He was bitten on his hand by a conger eel and he's just had surgery."

Jess's voice dropped several decibels. "Oh, my days! I'm so sorry. That sounds frickin' unbelievable! But he's okay, right?"

"I think so. He nearly lost his little finger and he's just come out of the operating theatre. I think they've managed to sew it back on."

"That is ... fucked up!"

"I know. I guess I wouldn't blame him if he wanted to avoid me after all that."

"Seriously? How is any of this your fault? It isn't. It was some monster eely thing. Ugh. I hate those things. Remember when we saw one washed up on the beach? You screamed like a girl."

"That was you."

"Only because you were chasing me with it."

Tamsyn grinned at the memory, then her smile faded.

"And that wasn't the worst thing that happened today," she said quietly. "I saw ... I saw a body by the wreck ... a dead diver. The Dive and Marine Unit are looking for it now."

There was a long silence where all Tamsyn could hear was her friend's shocked intake of breath.

"You're sure he was dead?"

Tamsyn closed her eyes, remembering the eerie way the man had hung in the water, unmoving.

"Yep, pretty sure."

"When will you be home?" Jess asked. "It sounds like you need a hug and a bottle of vodka. Not necessarily in that order."

After Tamsyn finally agreed to meet Jess later, she ended the call, finished her coffee and started the engine, but she had to wait until her hands stopped shaking before she put the car in gear.

CHAPTER 3

Rego was still two hours from Penzance when DS Tom Stevens phoned to tell him that the body of a male wearing a wetsuit and scuba equipment had been recovered from the wreck site, exactly as Tamsyn had described.

"Whoever he is, he's been in the water a while, boss."

"Days?"

Stevens hesitated. "Maybe even weeks."

"And there are no reports of missing divers?"

"None that we've found yet, and no missing dive boats either, but we're still looking."

"So where did he come from? Could he have swum from the shore?"

"I spoke to Sergeant Nate Tregowan – he's Dive Supervisor from the Dive and Marine Unit at Plymouth. He said it's an easy swim from Porthoustock – the nearest harbour – or even Porthkerris which is the next bay round – and there's a big dive school there ... but I sent uniform and there's no unclaimed car at either place or anywhere nearby. And you wouldn't want to carry scuba gear far on foot – it must weigh thirty to forty pounds or more. So, it's not likely he walked far with all that, and anywhere else would have been a heck of a swim, so right now, we don't know who he is or where he came from."

An uneasy feeling slithered down Rego's spine. It definitely triggered alarm bells that a diver hadn't been reported missing – at the very least it would be unusual, but then again there were always nutters who would dive on their own.

"Okay, Tom. Identifying him and the cause of death is a priority. Is the body being taken to the mortuary at Truro?"

"I'll check, boss. He might be on his way to Rose Cottage."

The whimsical name was used for the mortuary of a hospital by police and other emergency services to avoid alerting members of the public to a fatality – in reality, this Rose Cottage was the mortuary at Penzance hospital, but Rego wanted the body at the main forensic lab.

"No, I want Truro for this with a forensic PM. See if Dr Manners is available. And I want everything photographed – everything. Do we have any divers at the station?"

"Well, there's Tamsyn, but she's still learning, far as I know. Probably someone at Camborne. But Nate is the man you want for anything dive related. What he doesn't know hasn't been written yet."

"Okay. So, key questions: are there any serial numbers or tags on the diving equipment that might identify where the kit came from? If it's been hired, a dive centre will be missing it. If it's private, I want to know where and when it was bought. Is there anything unusual about the kit or is it bog standard? Is it all in good working order? How much air was in the tanks? Was it air? Or a gas and air mix? What does that mean? How long could he have survived? He must have been wearing a dive watch, but I've no idea what information dive watches record: find out. Was he wearing a wet suit or a dry suit? What does that tell us? And look for any obvious damage. I think our first assumption would be that he's a solo diver who got snagged or had some medical episode that caused his death," Rego paused. "But we'll have to wait for the *post-mortem* to establish the cause of death."

"I think all diving equipment has serial numbers, but I'll check. Anything else, boss?"

"Missing person reports: any males of the approximate age and build of our vic, or anything on social media. And speak to Tamsyn. It must have been a hell of a shock. Make sure she's okay – but I want her in first thing to give a statement."

"Got it."

"Okay, thanks for the update, Tom. I'll see you in the morning."

Rego ended the call and reached for a cigarette, then remembered that he'd given up smoking. He had to settle for opening the window and listening to Radio 1 to keep him awake. He didn't recognise any of the bands. God, that made him feel old.

When he finally parked outside Penzance police station just after midnight, the moon was high in the sky. He yawned widely, then groaned as he stretched. His knees creaked and his backside felt like it had been welded to the car seat, but as he opened the driver's door and breathed in the salty sea air, he smiled to himself. Crazy how quickly the place had begun to feel like home.

He wondered if his wife and the kids would feel the same way when they visited. Perhaps that was asking too much: Cornwall was so white and Rego's mother was a black Bermudian woman; Cassie's folks were Jamaican.

To be honest, he'd expected to experience more racism than he had, but apart from a number of second glances, it had all been surprisingly silent. So far.

But as his DS put it, "We do have telly, boss."

The station was eerily quiet. The night shift had already gone on duty and Rego only saw one uniformed officer who was scowling at vomit staining the legs of his trousers.

Rego raised his eyebrows and the young man straightened up.

"Sorry, sir. I bloody hate Friday nights."

Rego nodded in sympathy – they'd all been there.

CID was empty. There was only one detective to cover the night shift and Rego saw from the call log that his youngest DC, John Frith, was attending a serious incident of sexual assault.

He glanced around the office for signs of what he'd missed during the three days he'd been upcountry. As usual, DC Jen Bolitho's desk looked like a bomb had hit it, then come back to detonate again. It was a mystery to everyone how she ever found anything, but she always did. By contrast, DC Jack Forshaw's desk was so tidy, his pens were lined up by order of height. Rego was tempted to shuffle them, but when he saw the towering piles of folders on his own desk, the urge left him.

He logged onto his laptop, catching up on everything that had happened on the case over the last few hours. He scrawled some notes to himself, then he took one last look at his overwhelmed desk and went home to grab a couple of hours sleep.

For the first two months he'd been in Cornwall, Rego had stayed at the Premier Inn close to Penzance town centre, but six weeks ago, he'd finally found the time to scour the local rental market – what was left of it after Airbnb had taken the lion's share – and he'd signed the lease on a small cottage in Newlyn. The granite walls were a foot thick and the rooms were dark, but it had an open fireplace, a millionaire's view over the harbour, and came with its own parking space in a nearby car park.

Rego stripped off his clothes, dumping them on a chair, and collapsed into bed. His brain continued to whirl with questions until he fell into an uneasy sleep as the moon travelled across the sea outside his window. Tamsyn's image swam before his eyes, along with the nameless, faceless man, floating in the darkness.

Rego had forgotten to draw his curtains, so dawn woke him shortly after 5am. He lay with his eyes shut against the light and debated whether he'd be able to go back to sleep for a couple of hours. But the moment he had that thought, his brain coughed into gear, stirring up the list of questions he had about the dead diver, which actions were urgent and immediate, and most importantly, whether his favourite café would be open yet. He could murder a bacon sandwich.

It was slim pickings in the kitchen when he finally dragged himself out of bed. He dunked the lonely teabag in some hot water and drank it black.

In Manchester, coppers could always rely on an early morning bacon sarnie in a cabbie's café; down here in Cornwall, it was the fishermen who were awake before dawn.

Rego strolled down to the *Fishermen's Rest* and took his favourite seat outside on a bench in the sunshine.

On one of his first visits to the café, he'd tried the Fisherman's Breakfast of pilchards mashed with onions and tomatoes with a poached egg on top, and had never looked back. His DS had tried it once and said it repeated on him all day. Light weight.

Then with two black coffees under his belt, he felt equipped to face what he knew would be a long day on just three hours sleep.

He was at the station by 6.45am but it was already busy with uniformed officers coming off the night shift and others arriving for the day shift. In CID, John Frith was yawning over his desk and looked like hell.

Most people hated working lates, and shift work played havoc with your body clock as well as your social life.

Rego listened to his DC's report of the serious sexual assault callout that had taken up most of the night, made a few comments, but overall, it sounded like the young officer had coped well in a difficult situation.

Frith smiled tiredly and started to tidy his desk before going home. Rego booted up his laptop and logged in. He wanted the report from the underwater search team but nothing had appeared in his inbox.

DEAD MAN'S DIVE

"Hello, sir."

Rego looked up to see Tamsyn standing in front of him. She'd grown in confidence from the new student officer he'd met on his first day at Penzance nick, but she still looked young, especially out of uniform.

"Tamsyn, how are you? Have a seat."

He pointed at the chair on the other side of his desk and she sat down.

"I'm fine, sir."

Rego nodded, not entirely believing her. "And your friend..." he glanced at his notes, "...Adam Ellis. How's he doing?"

"Okay, I think. I was there when they were bringing him out of surgery and apparently it went well. I think they managed to reattach his finger, but I googled it and it says there could be some loss of movement. He's probably more worried about getting back in the water," she said with the ghost of a smile.

"How are you enjoying learning to dive?"

Rego couldn't quite hide the lack of enthusiasm in his voice. He wasn't a fish; he preferred to stay on land.

"I've done my Advanced Ocean Diver course and Nitrox training, but if I want to get Sports Diver, I'll have to do a lot more dives – maybe do the Wreck Appreciation course – although it can get a bit expensive."

Rego only vaguely knew what she was talking about, but nodded as if he did, practising his 'active listening' skills.

"Are there a lot of wrecks here about?"

Her eyes widened perceptibly.

"Yes, sir. Hundreds, probably thousands. The waters around here are really dangerous, lots of submerged reefs."

She seemed to be checking how much of this he was taking in, because she continued immediately.

"I guess that's where all the stories of Cornish pirates and wreckers come from. That's why we've got lighthouses at Lizard Point, Longships, Tater Du, Wolf Rock, Pendeen – and some of the wrecks are really old. Adam has dived the *Saint Anthony* that went down at Gunwalloe in 1527. It was carrying copper and silver. Adam says the cargo was worth about ten million in today's money."

Rego sat up straighter. "Ten *million?*"

"Yes, sir. You have to get a licence to dive there – Protection of Wrecks Act 1973," she smiled shyly. "I looked it up."

Rego drummed his fingers on the desk. "And how far is this wreck from where you were diving?"

"It's the other side of the Lizard, sir. About ten miles by land, twenty by sea."

"Is the *Mohegan* a valuable wreck?"

"Not really, sir, I don't think so. She went down in 1898. You don't need a licence to dive it or anything."

"What about other valuable wrecks in the area?"

"There's a Shipwreck Index, but I don't even think the site of the *Saint Anthony* is valuable now. Most of the goods were recovered at the time. Three of the big landowners sent their men down to recover all the cargo washed up on the beach at Gunwalloe, and it kind of disappeared." She gave him a conspiratorial look. "They say it paid for the building of Pengersick Castle at Praa Sands."

Rego raised his eyebrows. "I see! Well, thank you for the history lesson, Tamsyn."

He was still smiling, but in all seriousness, he made a note to find out if there'd been any recent illegal salvage attempts on important wreck sites, or maybe even recent wrecks that were valuable. He vaguely remembered seeing on the news some years back that a container ship off the Devon coast had lost a batch of BMW motorbikes which locals had helped themselves to.

"Tell me what happened yesterday," he said. "With as much detail as you can remember."

"Yes, sir. And I need to show you this, too."

She handed over the object that Adam had tucked in his dive bag just before he was attacked.

"What the hell is that?"

CHAPTER 4

At first glance, the object looked a bit like a police issue ASP baton. It was the same length but twice as thick with a torpedo-shaped nose and something that appeared to have been snapped off or damaged in some way at the other end. Rego couldn't tell if the casing was metal or a sort of heavy-duty plastic, maybe shellac. It was smooth, sleek and deadly-looking, and Rego had no idea what it was.

He didn't touch it, instead rummaging in his filing cabinet for an exhibit bag, then pulling on a pair of forensic gloves.

Tamsyn pulled a face, obviously realising that these two actions were something she should have done.

"I don't know if it's important or anything," Tamsyn said hesitantly. "But because of the body ... Adam found it near the wreck of the *Mohegan*. He's an instructor at my dive club. It was just before the eel attacked him."

"I think you'd better tell me the whole story."

Rego listened intently as Tamsyn described everything that had happened.

"And it was just the two of you? There was no one else driving the boat? Is that even safe?"

Tamsyn flushed red. "Adam's friend was supposed to be there…"

He stared at her grimly and her gaze dropped to the table.

"Who else saw you? And how did you end up with this…" Rego waved his hand at the object on his desk without touching it.

"The two old guys at Porthoustock Harbour helped me take off Adam's harness which had his dive bag attached to it before the lifeboat arrived. Everything was still on the deck, so they could all have seen it. Nobody mentioned anything, and honestly, what with Adam bleeding all over the place, I don't think anyone would have noticed. But I took everything with me because I didn't want to leave his set or his GoPro in his car because I knew he wouldn't be able to collect it for a while. So, I put it all in my car. And this was with it."

"He had a GoPro camera? Where is it now?"

"In the boot of my car, sir," she said, her cheeks turning pink.

"Have you looked at the footage?"

"No, sir. I forgot about it. Do you want me to go and get it?"

"Yes, PC Poldhu," he said firmly. "It's evidence."

She mumbled an apology and hurried from the room. Three minutes later, she was back – and she'd taken the time to put on a pair of forensic gloves as she handed the GoPro to Rego.

"Where exactly were you when your friend found the object?" Rego asked, continuing his questioning.

Tamsyn squinted. "We were about two or three metres from the *Mohegan*'s boiler room. He was out of sight for a few seconds – I assumed that he'd picked it up from the seabed, although I can't be sure. Our fins were stirring the silt by then and it was getting a bit murky." She paused. "What do you think it is?"

Something that hasn't come from a 130 year-old wreck.

Rego didn't know if it was relevant evidence or not, but something felt off. The object could even contain a hazardous substance, although as at least two people had handled it already, so it probably wasn't toxic, all the same...

The strange object couldn't be linked to the body yet, but it was clearly newish and didn't look like it had been in the water very long. He considered the possibility that it was a marker beacon to direct someone to a drug drop, although he'd never seen anything like it before. And if the GoPro didn't pinpoint the exact location where the object was found, he needed to speak to Adam Ellis: if he'd found it on the seabed, then it could have fallen or been dropped from a passing boat; if it had been found inside the wreck, then someone had deliberately placed the item in that position.

He didn't say any of this to Tamsyn.

"I don't know what it is. Could it be off a fishing boat?"

She looked doubtful, which meant that if she didn't recognise it, then it probably wasn't fishing-related because her whole life she'd been around the fishing industry.

"Have you told anyone about it? Your grandparents? A friend, perhaps? Someone at the dive club?"

"No, sir. No one. Well, I told my friend Jess about Adam, and that I'd seen the dead diver, but I didn't tell her about the ... thing. I'd forgotten about it until I took everything out of the boot of my car this morning. I've put the rest of Adam's set – his cylinders, harness, and all that – in the garden shed." She gave an awkward shrug. "There's no room in the cottage."

"Was there anything else in Adam's things that seemed out of place?"

"No, I don't think so."

"And did either of the men at Porthoustock comment on it at all?"

"No, sir. I don't think they saw it. It was in his dive bag and everything was full on at the time."

Rego nodded. "Okay, thank you, Tamsyn," and he took a second exhibit bag out of his filing cabinet and slid it towards her across his desk along with the weird object. "Just in case."

"Sir?"

"It's your exhibit, Tamsyn, so TP/01 on this case, and TP/02 on the GoPro. Make a pocketbook entry describing exactly what happened on the dive; include where you think your friend found the object and how you came in possession of it."

Rego didn't know whether or not a crime had been committed, but the cylinder could be evidence and needed to be recorded properly.

"Go and write up your notes." He pointed at the object. "But we'll keep this between you and me for now, okay."

"Yes, sir." She stood up, then hesitated.

"Is there something else?"

"It's not important."

"Tamsyn?"

"Gran and Grandad want to invite you and your family over for tea when they're down this summer," she said in a rush.

"Really?" Rego was surprised. "I thought your grandad wasn't too keen on me after I brought him in for questioning back in March."

"Oh, he isn't," Tamsyn grinned. "But you also saved my life, so that puts you in the plus column." She shrugged, obviously embarrassed. "You don't have to come, but Grandad thought your children might like to come out on the *Daniel Day* with us." She sent him a sly look. "Unless they get seasick like you. Sir."

"I didn't actually throw up when I went out with the Coastguard."

"Oh, okay ... although that's not the way I heard it," she said under her breath.

Rego leaned back in his chair, smiling. "Please thank your grandparents for me, and I'll ask the kids when my wife brings them down."

She returned his smile and left the small office.

As soon as the door closed behind her, Rego's smile evaporated and he picked up the strange object, examining it closely. A diver who was unreported, days or even weeks after he'd gone missing with no evidence of where he'd come from; and a strange object that didn't *fit*, all within a few miles of a valuable historic shipwreck. He frowned.

And all within a few miles of the major military base of *RNAS Culdrose*, as well.

It was probably nothing. He was probably being unduly cautious, maybe even paranoid, but his gut was telling him otherwise.

Before he talked himself out of it, he picked up his phone and dialled. He waited impatiently for the call to be answered, drumming his fingers on the desk.

"Rob, mate! How's life in the land of the Cornish Pasty?"

Vikram's rich, Brummie accent was unchanged, and he sounded happy to hear from Rego.

"Hey, Vik! How's life at the Circus?"

"I could tell you, but then I'd have to kill you," he laughed.

Rego and Vikram had started at Greater Manchester Police the same week, back in the day, but Vikram's enormous brain and affinity for computers had taken him in a different direction. From frontline policing, he'd gone to work for the National Crime Agency, the UK's FBI, specialising in organised crime gangs; and more recently, he'd been seconded to MI6 – Rego had no idea what he was doing there these days.

They spent a couple of minutes catching up then Rego got to the purpose of his call.

"So, during the dive where the unknown victim's body was eventually found, the friend of one of my PCs picked up this weird thing. I'll have to talk to him to find out whether it was on the seabed or inside the wreck, but the guy has just had surgery, so that'll have to wait a bit. I've no idea what it is, Vik, but it's definitely not over a hundred years old. For all I know, it's been dropped over the side of some freighter but ... I don't know. I'm thinking maybe some sort of homing beacon for a drug drop? I thought I'd ask my egg-head friend if he knew what it was before I kick it up the line and risk embarrassing myself. I'm sending you a photo on WhatsApp now."

Rego waited while Vikram studied the photograph. He honestly expected his friend to laugh it off or make some joke about anal plugs, but he didn't. Instead, his voice was intense and full of concentration.

"How big is it?"

"About 60cm with a diameter of around 7cm. And there's a bit sticking out that looks like something smallish was snapped off, but there's a huge gash in the back section – it's definitely not complete."

"Yeah, I see that. What does it weigh?"

"I've no idea. Maybe, the same as a bag of potatoes?"

"A kilo?"

"More."

"About two or three kilos then."

"Something like that. What do you think it is?"

Vikram was silent for several seconds.

"And this was found somewhere off Lizard Point?"

"Yes."

"Where exactly? Near Goonhilly Downs?"

"Uh, well, that's only a few miles away. Apparently near an old shipwreck from the last century, the SS *Mohegan*. I've got some footage that might help pinpoint it."

"Footage from where?"

"The diver, Ellis, he had a GoPro. We should be able to see the moment he picked up the ... whatever it is."

"Good, email that to me, too."

"What are you thinking, Vik?"

"Not sure. I have some ideas I want to check out first. I'll send a courier to pick up both items."

"I can get them on the overnight transport and—"

"No!" Vikram interrupted sharply. "Don't hand them over to anyone unless you talk to me first. No one! I'll be in touch."

And the call ended so abruptly that Rego was still staring at his phone wondering what the hell had just happened.

Vikram was usually pretty laidback and not the kind of guy to go off the deep-end. Rego picked up the GoPro and decided to download the video onto his laptop. Pulling on another pair of forensic gloves, he used his phone cable to power up the GoPro. A minute later, he emailed the file to Vikram, and began to watch the entire dive footage, his screen angled away from his office door.

He saw Tamsyn's excitement as she fitted her dive mask into place and the quick smile she flashed at Adam Ellis before they both went off the side of the dive boat. He watched their slow descent, the footage becoming grainier with the loss of daylight. He saw Ellis turning toward Tamsyn, then moving into the body of the wreck and reaching down, returning with the device in his hand, obviously studying it. He saw the chaos and confusion when Adam was attacked, blood blossoming in the water. He saw glimpses of Tamsyn hammering at the giant eel with a rock, and he saw her panicky movement as she towed Ellis upwards to safety. He watched her heroic efforts to lift the much heavier man onto the boat, and her first aid treatment.

She'd obviously forgotten about the camera completely, because there was ten minutes of footage from the deck of the boat as she took it into the harbour, a brief glimpse of the boots of the two old men that she'd mentioned, followed by nearly 27 minutes of footage which must have been from the boot of her car, until the battery died.

Rego felt clammy just watching all that, and the respect he had for her grew. In his mind, there was no doubt that Ellis wouldn't have made it without Tamsyn. The woman deserved a medal.

He touched the smooth surface of the object again. Whatever it was, it had Vikram worried. And if he was worried, Rego was pretty sure that a shit storm of epic proportions was about to drop in his lap.

CHAPTER 5

Tamsyn still hadn't heard from Adam. She'd texted him when she got home the night before and again first thing that morning. If he hadn't replied by lunchtime, she'd have to pull up her big girl's panties and call him.

She sat at an empty desk, one eye on her phone, the other on the report she was supposed to be writing of what she'd seen – God, was it only yesterday? And then there was that weird torpedo-thingy that Adam had found, but as Inspector Rego had told her not to mention it, she'd have to leave it out of the report. She wondered if she should have told him that she had a picture of it on her phone.

The room was starting to fill up as more members of E-team arrived for the morning shift. Mitch, one of the older officers, told her that shifts used to start with the Inspector reading out incidents that they needed to be aware of, but briefings were all electronic now. Tamsyn was already self-briefing by reading the updates on her MDT work phone. It sounded like the night shift had been kept busy with a fight at the Yacht public house in Penzance that had resulted in multiple arrests.

Jason was another student officer who'd started at the same time as Tamsyn, and he stopped by her desk to talk about their individual portfolios which listed the incidents they'd attended and ensuing actions. He was a former Royal Marine and Tamsyn had been slightly intimidated by him at first, but as they'd worked together over the last few months, she'd grown more comfortable with him.

"Sounds like it all kicked off in town last night," he said, sounding almost wistful.

"Does it bring back memories of your bootneck days?" Tamsyn teased, raising an eyebrow.

He grinned back. "No comment."

Other officers crowded around to discuss the brawl, most taking the view that there'd be a few more of those before the summer was over. It was the start of the school holidays so the towns and villages were filling with tourists. More people meant more work, especially as people on holiday tended to consume levels of alcohol that weren't always sensible, plus parking spaces were at a premium in places like St Ives, with road rage incidents on the rise, and locals didn't always appreciate being squeezed out of their pubs and cafés even though most of them depended on tourists for their livelihoods. It could be a combustible mix.

The only member of E-team who didn't stop by to chat with Tamsyn was Jamie. He was a few years older than her, already an experienced officer, and they'd been on their way to becoming friends. But his attitude towards her had cooled since he'd started dating Chloe Rogers, a nasty piece of work in Tamsyn's opinion. Chloe loathed Tamsyn, and the feeling was mutual. Privately, she called her 'Bitch Tits'.

Rogers was a civilian investigator based at Camborne police station but unfortunately, she seemed to spend more time at Penzance.

Tamsyn had no idea what had sparked the initial dislike; they'd never been friends at school but since Tamsyn had come to work at Penzance station, Chloe had taken every opportunity to be a raging pain in the ass.

Tamsyn also suspected that Chloe had been the one who'd given her address to a local lowlife, leading to Tamsyn's car being vandalized. Since she couldn't prove it, Tamsyn kept her mouth shut and her eyes on a swivel when it came to the other woman.

Jamie gave Tamsyn a cursory nod but turned his back on her when Chloe walked in. When he began enthusiastically examining his girlfriend's tonsils with his tongue, Tamsyn rolled her eyes and shut off her computer, heading to the locker room to change into her uniform, then heading to the briefing room with the rest of E-team.

Sergeant Carter updated them on an incident that had just occurred.

"Porsche versus a surfer's van at Chiverton. The van won. Looks like the Porsche went the wrong way at the roadworks by the new roundabout and is currently parked over a set of cones with the van up his backside – no serious injuries. Officers from Traffic are on scene and there's a tow truck with a winch on the way, but it's slow going."

Several people chuckled – the on-going roadworks on the A30 were the bane of their existence with minor prangs almost every day.

"Next up: the summer Lift Legend Campaign has started so we're working with pubs and clubs to reduce drink and drug driving. We've got more than 100 participating venues who offer free soft drinks to designated drivers, so this is my one and only reminder to the shift to be careful yourselves to maintain the highest of standards, as the consequences if you don't will be severe." He glanced up. "Right, that's it: Mitch, you're Charlie Mike 1, refs at six; Jethro, Charlie Mike 2, refs at 5; Ky, you're the designated taser officer..."

And he carried on handing out their assignments and patches so they all knew where they'd be patrolling for their shift.

When he'd finished, Sergeant Carter peered over the top of his glasses.

"What else? Oh yes, Jason, Tamsyn, you have a meeting with Sergeant Terwillis at 4.30pm back here to go over your portfolios. Right, everyone else, you know what you're doing."

She'd only just sat down at her desk to work through the mountain of paper and online reports that constituted a modern-day copper's lot, when Control called from D&C Police's HQ in Exeter, sending her to a dispute between two drivers on Paul hill.

Tamsyn drew in a deep breath – she could pretty much guess what had happened there. The half-mile from Newlyn to the top of the hill leading to Paul village was very steep, and so narrow that in several sections only one car could pass at a time. It relied on drivers' common sense and courtesy to keep the traffic flowing, neither of which seemed to be in abundance some days.

So, she headed to the car park behind the station to pick up her patrol car.

The Vauxhall Astra assigned to Tamsyn had seen better days and at ten years, was one of the oldest cars in the fleet with over 200,000 miles on the clock. A few of the new automatic Peugeots were coming through now, but only one had reached Penzance station.

There was a rumour that they'd be getting electric vehicles to test soon. Camborne had two, but the station didn't yet have a proper charging point, so they were having to make do with the charger cable being plugged into an ordinary socket and being hung out of the window to the car below.

Police cars were always thrashed – when there was an incident, there was no time to warm up the engine, you had to go: a cold start to 110mph in a few seconds ripped the guts out of a vehicle.

Tamsyn wasn't yet convinced that police EV's were a good thing. She worked in a largely rural area and didn't want to get caught without charge in the car – and so far, there were very few high-speed chargers in West Cornwall. With the standard-issue patrol cars, she used the pin-lock system which meant that when the car was stationery for any length of time, she could still access ANPR or blue lights without draining the battery – all things you needed at an RTC or assisting a broken-down vehicle. She hadn't even sat in one of the electric cars yet.

Some of her fellow officers had their favourite cars, but Tamsyn didn't care much. Even the oldest, most knackered car in the fleet was a massive upgrade on her ancient Fiat Uno.

The vehicles were supposed to be left as found, fuelled up and hoovered, but Tamsyn already knew that occasionally the lazier officers left crisp packets, drinks tins and half eaten pasties under the seat.

Mitch had shown her how to fully search a car before going out on patrol, especially under seats and in crevices.

His weathered face had folded into a frown as he'd explained it to her.

"The thing is, Tam, you've got to know that your ride is pristine, because if you bring a druggie in and you later find something stuffed in or under a car seat, at least you can say you searched the car after transporting a prisoner back to custody and what's found must be theirs as you had searched the car beforehand." He examined her face and nodded. "It's a good habit to get into."

Thankfully, the police garage workshops at Camborne were excellent and kept the patrol cars on the road. They even gave them a good clean once a week unless the car was filthy and your sergeant moaned that the car needed a wash, in which case you had to do it yourself. Although, if a detained person bled, puked or pissed in the car, for health and safety reasons it got cleaned straightaway by a contractor with special kit.

There would always be a spare car available, and the one that needed some extra work would be taken off the road and isolated, then shipped to Camborne where a professional valeting company would clean it.

Mitch said that it used to be a joke that the sergeant got the new car, and the most recent recruit would get the old banger. Tamsyn didn't mind having an older car. She'd only been driving four years and as far as she was concerned, having an old car where she didn't have to worry about every scratch and bump while driving along the narrow Cornish lanes – well, it wasn't a problem.

Tamsyn checked the car thoroughly, then followed the cockpit drill, adjusting the seat and wing mirrors, then saw that the petrol gauge was on half-full. She made a note to fill it up later, checking that the debit card which went with the car was in place. She pulled out her RFID key fob which automatically added her time start and the car's current mileage to the log. At the end of her shift, she'd record the mileage again and sign off.

As it happened, she couldn't even get to the scene: traffic was backed up in every direction at the four-way junction by a granite bridge in the centre of Newlyn, and she had to abandon her patrol car outside Jelbert's ice cream shop with the blue lights flashing, cone off a section of the road, and make her way on foot.

It was a steep climb in her dark uniform, hi-vis jacket, and 12kg of kit: heavy stab vest and all the equipment draped over her utility vest: baton, torch, leg restraints, handcuffs and key, evidence bags, police notebook and pens, Mobile Data Terminal (her Force-issued smartphone/tablet), rough-cut scissors, tourniquet and surgical gloves, spit hood, gloves, body-worn video and Airwave police radio.

She soon arrived at the nub of the problem: a face-off between an irate woman in a Mercedes SUV going up the hill and a double-decker bus coming down.

"Officer, thank goodness!" the woman cried out as soon as she saw Tamsyn. "Tell this ... this Neanderthal to move his bus and stop blocking the road! He only has to go back a few feet! I'd have to reverse halfway down the hill, not that I can do that now!" she spat.

"I'm not allowed to reverse on a public road with passengers on board, everyone knows that!" said the bus driver heatedly.

"I know the Highway Code! The person reversing uphill is the one who has to make way!"

The woman wasn't wrong, but safety came first – apparently with common sense trailing a long way behind.

"She's only got to reverse back a short distance," the bus driver huffed, "but she expects me to back up 50 yards or more!"

"Okay," said Tamsyn. "One at a time. Madam, would you stand over there, please," and she gestured to the woman driver.

"No! I want to hear what he says!"

"Over there, please, madam," Tamsyn said firmly. "I'll be talking to you in a moment. This way, thank you."

The woman grudgingly moved a few feet away, and Tamsyn led the bus driver a short distance from the scene of the altercation.

"Sorry about that," said the bus driver wearily. "Don't tell her I said so, but us bus drivers say that buses aren't allowed to reverse with passengers on board for a very good reason ... when we meet Hugo in his BMW or Sharon in her Audi on a narrow country lane and they expect me to reverse my bus a hundred yards when they only need to go back a few feet, it don't half come in handy to be able to convince them that I'm legally forbidden to reverse. But honestly, you can see that she only had to go two foot!"

He saw the look on Tamsyn's face.

"Okay, maybe twenty foot. But I reckon she don't know how to reverse that Chelsea tractor of hers. I'd have had to reverse halfway up the hill!"

Tamsyn could see the truth of what he was saying and it certainly seemed that the woman was not helping the situation.

"Right, I'll need the bus's vehicle registration, reference number, and your name please, sir."

The driver sighed but gave her the information straightaway.

Then Tamsyn returned to the woman with the Mercedes.

"No!" said the woman emphatically when Tamsyn spoke to her. "I am *not* moving my car. *He* has to move."

Tamsyn was hot, and irritated by the woman's attitude – it was clear that she only needed to reverse seven or eight metres at most.

She started to write down the Mercedes' number plate number.

"What are you doing?" the woman asked angrily. "I haven't done anything!"

"I'll need your name please, madam," Tamsyn said calmly.

"This is ridiculous!"

Tamsyn just waited as the woman huffed and puffed. She was tempted to give her a ticket that meant she'd have to drive to the nearest station and present her driver's licence, insurance and MOT within the next seven days.

The woman was still ranting at Tamsyn, but after three months as a student officer, it was water off a duck's back. She wasn't even the newest recruit anymore.

Tamsyn's face was neutral, but internally, well, that was different.

If you keep pissing me off, I'll go over your vehicle looking for Construction and Use offences. Is that tyre looking a little worn? I wonder if you have enough fluid in your washer bottle?

But really it was more important to get the traffic flowing.

"It will be safer to move your car," said Tamsyn reasonably, ending the woman's angry words, "and we need to get the traffic moving as quickly as possible."

The woman glowered at her and looked like she was going to argue.

"I'm going to create some space behind you so you can reverse your car," Tamsyn prompted, "...or I can do it for you. Whichever you prefer."

"I don't see why I should," the woman repeated, but less forcefully. "Fine," she snorted as Tamsyn continued to stare at her. "You do it!"

It took a fair bit of shuffling of cars and squeezing them onto pavements while onlookers gawked and videoed the scene on their phones.

Tamsyn was sweating freely by the time she climbed behind the wheel of the Mercedes and reversed it far enough to allow the bus to pass.

The bus driver gave her a thumb's up as he squeezed past and the passengers gave a ragged cheer.

"I've made a note of that driver's details," said the woman with the Mercedes, her face flushed bright red. She stared at Tamsyn. "I shall be making a complaint."

Tamsyn didn't bother to ask who the woman would be reporting.

She walked back to her own car, overheated and feeling the full weight of her hot and sweaty hi-vis and the rest of her equipment.

She collected her traffic cones and stood in the shade of Jelbert's ice cream shop, drinking down half a litre of water to cool off.

She was glad that she'd sorted out the stand-off and got the traffic flowing again, but really? Was that going to be what the rest of her day would be like? She shook her head tiredly and smiled wryly to herself.

"Would you like a free ice cream, officer?" the shop owner asked, looking at Tamsyn's bright red face.

"That's really nice of you, but I have to get going," she said, her spirits lifting with that small kindness.

"Do I know you? Are you related to Ozzie Poldhu?" the woman asked.

"Yes, that's right. I'm Tamsyn, his granddaughter."

"Thought so. Can always tell a Poldhu – it's the eyes. You say hello to your grandparents for me."

"I will! Thanks again!"

She sat in her patrol car and quickly checked her personal phone; there was still no word from Adam, so before she lost her nerve, she dialled his number. The call went straight to voicemail. She didn't know what to think as she left a short message. Was his phone out of charge? Was he ghosting her? She hoped he was okay and that there hadn't been any complications with the operation.

Adam's mother hadn't called either, and Tamsyn didn't have her number. Maybe she should go back to the hospital? But the thought of driving nearly two hours to Plymouth after a nine-hour shift wasn't tempting either, and she didn't even know if she'd be allowed to see him. Maybe she should wait until he'd been questioned.

She shoved her private phone in her back pocket and got on with the job of being a police officer in a busy holiday resort in July: sunburned tourists trying to find A&E, one lost child recovered at the games arcade in Wherrytown, a surfer's car parked in a passing spot on a backroad near Pendeen so a tractor couldn't get by, and a cow on the road near St Buryan.

And just when she thought about heading back to the station for the meeting with her tutor, she had to call a Code Zero emergency when she attended a jewellery shop in Penzance where the owner recognised a stolen necklace that someone was trying to sell. The person who'd been burgled was a friend of the shop owner, and the police had been called.

Before she walked into the shop, she activated her body cam so all the interaction would be recorded. It was standard procedure but she had a feeling she'd be needing it.

From the outside, the shop looked quiet, but the moment Tamsyn walked into the shop, everything kicked off.

"You fucking cunt!" yelled the thief.

It wasn't clear whether he was talking to her or the shop owner, not that it made any difference.

"Calm down, sir," Tamsyn said, keeping her voice quiet but authoritative. "I just need to have a word."

He launched a punch which Tamsyn managed to duck,

but she fell heavily against the display cabinets, sending a torrent of jewellery raining down to the floor. Wincing, Tamsyn grabbed her Captor spray and managed to get him to back away, but he wasn't giving up.

Swearing violently, he threw a large mirror at her which glanced off her police hat. This time, Tamsyn did use the spray. She shouted a warming, then sprayed him in three sharp bursts. He was on his knees in a second, screaming and swearing as his eyes watered from the stinging spray.

Breathing heavily, Tamsyn sat him up and cuffed him as he thrashed his legs and swore at her, clicking the handcuffs up one more notch to make them uncomfortable, hoping this would get him to stop lashing out. Then she followed standard procedure to double lock them, using the handcuff key to push in a small button which locked the cuffs so that they couldn't be compressed anymore. Then she called Control for transportation and a medical examination.

He'd need to be monitored now to make sure that his breathing wouldn't be compromised by the spray. She asked the shopkeeper to open the door allowing fresh air to circulate.

"He didn't want to be arrested, did he?" said the owner shakily.

Tamsyn dusted off her uniform trousers.

Just another day on the job.

CHAPTER 6

By late morning, Rego still hadn't heard back from Vikram and he didn't know what to make of that. So, he put it out of his mind and carried on doing his job – he had a couple of hours to catch up with paperwork before the *post-mortem* of the unknown diver which the Coroner's Office had scheduled for 4pm.

No matter how many of these he attended, the smell always got to him. He had no idea how long the diver's body had been in the water so he made a strategic decision to skip lunch.

He'd also taken his sergeant's advice and called Nathan Tregowan, the Dive Supervisor whose team had recovered the body. But so far, the man hadn't called back and hadn't emailed his report either. Being a police officer taught patience, but it didn't come naturally to Rego.

He was halfway through the hundred-odd emails in his inbox when his phone rang.

"Good morning, sir. Nate Tregowan returning your call."

"Thank you for calling back, Nate. I haven't received your report yet."

"I'm still working on it, sir."

"When will I have it?"

"Today, sir – I just need to check a couple of things first."

"Okay, but I have some questions about the victim you pulled out of the water yesterday before the PM."

"Yes, sir. I have some questions, too. I was wondering if I could attend the autopsy with you."

Rego raised his eyebrows. It wasn't a completely unusual request, but Rego hadn't been expecting it.

"I don't see why not, but is there something in particular you're looking for?"

He could sense the man's evasiveness when he answered.

"I'm not sure, sir, but I was hoping that the pathologist could clear up a few things for me." He cleared his throat. "It's probably nothing."

That was the second time this morning someone has said those words to Rego. He *really* didn't like coincidences.

"Well, I don't know anything about diving so it will be useful to have you there," Rego began. "The *post-mortem* is at Treliske at 4pm. You're welcome to attend."

"Thank you, sir."

"Did you learn anything from the victim's equipment now that you've had a chance to look at it? Were there any identifying marks? Anything that might tell us where it came from or who he is?"

Tregowan's tone was neutrally polite, addressing a

senior officer that he didn't know ... although he still had that air of evasion.

"There's a couple of ways to answer that, sir. Maybe a bit of background information would help?"

Rego glanced at his watch.

"Sure, fire away."

"We didn't retain the dry-bag – his dry-suit – that's with the body. I just collected the external set, cylinders, harness and so on. I didn't remove the facemask either, sir."

"Okay, and...?"

Tregowan exhaled slowly.

"Scuba diving equipment is designed to keep you safe underwater. The essential parts of the set include masks, fins, cylinders, and BCDs – that's buoyancy control devices. It's expensive, and every piece of gear has its own unique serial number in the event of theft but also, more importantly, in case there's a manufacturing fault, it can easily be traced back to the manufacturer. So, when a diver buys new gear, the first thing they should do is register the serial numbers. Most people do it, probably 99% in my experience – and there are instructions with the kit when you buy it on how to complete the registration."

Rego perked up at this information, feeling like his job had just got a whole lot easier.

"But," Tregowan continued, "I made a cursory inspection of the dive set on scene and took the cylinders and BCDs to examine more closely, like I said..." he paused.

"Go on?"

"...and I couldn't find any serial numbers – if there were ever any in the first place."

"Wait, what are you saying? Didn't you just tell me that all scuba gear is individually numbered?"

"Usually, sir, yes. But this set didn't have any numbers that I could see and there weren't any file marks either – and I've examined every inch with a magnifying glass."

Rego's mind was racing, trying to understand the significance of what Tregowan was telling him.

"And the other thing, sir, this kit has a top-quality rebreather."

He paused again and Rego guessed this was significant.

"A rebreather? What's that?"

"It recycles the gas exhaled by the diver, removing carbon dioxide and adding oxygen, to form a closed loop. There are no bubbles, low noise, and constant buoyancy. You can stay under up to five times longer than for an equivalent weight of Open Circuit. And gas consumption on a rebreather is independent of depth. Professional divers use them."

So maybe the victim wasn't just a recreational diver.

"I'm told there are potentially valuable shipwrecks all around the area near where our victim was found," Rego mentioned casually. "Could he have been a professional diver looking for gold doubloons or whatever the hell they look for?"

"It's possible, sir," Tregowan said dubiously. "Although the ones that you need a licence to dive aren't that close to the *Mohegan* – he'd have been way off course or drifted a fair bit. But there's no sign of tearing on the dry-bag which would have happened if it had bumped along the bottom of the seabed for any length of time … and the crabs would have been at him."

Rego had already been put off seafood for life – that wasn't what was worrying him.

"So, you're saying that the body *hasn't* been in the water that long?"

"No, sir, that's not what I mean. The victim had been trapped *inside* the wreck and floating."

"Because his buoyancy aids would have stopped him from sinking?"

"No, those would have leaked over time, sometimes it can take just an hour or so. But the diver didn't have a weight belt, and you need one of those to take you underwater in the first place. So, he either lost it or shed it deliberately."

"Why would he do that?"

"The short answer is if he panicked. There's a thing called 'oxygen toxicity'. It varies from person to person, but at 2-bar, oxygen can become lethal – and the first signs of it would be a seizure, a bit like an epileptic fit. If he'd panicked and dropped his weights inside the wreck, he'd have just bobbed up to the ceiling and got trapped inside."

"And that's what you want to ask the pathologist about?"

"Yes, sir, it's one possibility."

There was a longer pause and Rego's patience ran out.

"Nate, I can't help feeling there's a lorry-load of things you're not telling me and I don't have time for that."

"I'm sorry, sir, it's just ... weird."

Rego rubbed his forehead. "Give me an example," *before I die of old age.*

He heard the man draw in a deep breath.

"All the equipment was non-ferrous, nothing magnetic:

brass zips, stainless steel cylinders, the works, and all expensive, very expensive – the kind of kit that someone working in mines or bomb disposal would wear..."

"Mines? Bloody hell!"

"And the rebreather – well, they're not necessarily designed for operation with a full facemask unless a diver-communication system is also a requirement."

So, who was the diver communicating with and why didn't this person or persons report him missing?

Rego's questions were piling up.

"And the rebreather also has some modifications that I don't recognise. I was a Navy diver for fifteen years, sir, and I've never seen anything like this. I'm thinking military quality – experimental military grade."

Rego immediately thought of *RNAS Culdrose*, a key part of Britain's frontline defences, and just a short distance from where the body was recovered.

Tregowan was still talking and obviously thinking along the same lines as Rego.

"But we'd have heard if Culdrose had lost one of their divers – maybe not officially – but I know people in the trade there. I'm sure I'd have heard something. I could ask around? I mean, that set – there's nothing standard about it, sir. It must be military."

Yes, but whose military? Having recently talked to Vikram who was working for the spooks, and thinking about his strange reaction to the mystery object that Tamsyn's friend had found, Rego's mind was racing – and he really didn't like the direction it was going.

"Okay, ask around – see what shakes out of the tree." He paused. "Anything else I should know before the PM?"

"Not at this point, sir, but I'll have time to look at the dive watch before I meet you. That'll tell us the max depth and no-deco dive-time; it would be linked to his cylinder to tell him about remaining gas, and the watch should have an alarm and be pre-programmed for a rebreather." He paused, "But I can tell you that it's a top of the range piece worth a few grand."

Rego was interested. Very interested.

"And I've sent the cylinders to the lab, sir, so they'll be able to analyse the gas."

Rego made a decision.

"Okay, Nate. Make some discreet enquiries at Culdrose, but keep it unofficial for now. I'll see you at the mortuary this afternoon."

Rego ended the call and stared again at the strange object on his desk. The uneasy feeling was growing stronger.

CHAPTER 7

Tamsyn was drooping with tiredness.
She'd arrested the man from the jewellery shop on suspicion of theft, and had cautioned him. When he'd spat at her, it had taken both her and a colleague to cover his face with a spit hood. The man hadn't stopped swearing since.

She'd gone to Camborne, the nearest police station with a custody suite, to book in the prisoner with the custody officer, and he'd reminded her to submit a 'use of force' form. Every time an officer drew their incapacitant spray – even if they didn't use it – the paperwork had to be done.

The rest of her shift was spent getting a statement from the shopkeeper and securing the CCTV, then in the police station dealing with the prisoner.

She'd been running late for her meeting with her tutor and then had to complete the rest of the paperwork, so by the time she got home, her nine-hour shift had turned into 11 hours.

And Adam still hadn't been in touch.

At least Morwenna was waiting for her when she got home, and jumped into her arms the second the front door was open enough for her to squeeze her small, hairy body through the gap.

"Hello, scruffalicious," said Tamsyn, burying her face in the little dog's warm, wiry fur. "How's your day been? Better than mine, I hope. I suppose you want to go for a walk?"

The small dog snuffled with happiness, and Tamsyn dumped her bag on the floor, then clipped on Mo's lead and headed back out into the evening sunshine.

She'd gone no further than the garden gate when her elderly neighbour called her name.

Tamsyn groaned inwardly.

Nellie Gwinnel had been born in the cottage next door and planned to be taken out boots first, as she'd told Tamsyn on more than one occasion. She'd reached her ninth decade a few years back, and was tiny and stooped, with sharp eyes and sharper tongue. She was also a one-woman neighbourhood watch who saw and heard everything.

"That dog o' yous been barking' 'is head off! Couldn't hardly hear me telly!"

Tamsyn looked down at Mo who gazed up, her soft brown eyes wide and innocent – which meant exactly nothing.

"Sorry about that, Miss Nellie," said Tamsyn, stroking Mo's head. "She probably saw a squirrel in the garden or something."

"No, it was a man from the council 'bout the rats," said the elderly woman.

"In our back garden?"

"Well, it warn't mine! I put pizen down reg'lar, see."

Tamsyn frowned. They didn't have a rat problem because Mo liked nothing better than to hunt through the compost heap and take on any rodent stupid enough to stray into her path. A quick shake and their necks snapped. Tamsyn's grandfather disposed of the bodies on a frequent basis. Anyway, her grandparents would have told her if they'd called in pest control – even assuming they could afford them, which they couldn't.

"What time was this?" Tamsyn asked.

"D'you think I've nothin' better to do 'an watch out my window fer rat catchers?" the old woman asked indignantly, sucking in her hollow cheeks. "Musta been about three o'clock. I heard the church bells a few minutes afore."

Tamsyn smiled. "Thanks, Miss Nellie. I'd better go and see what they were doing."

"You feed your dog too much!" Miss Nellie called after her. "'E should be rattin' for 'is own supper!"

Tamsyn withheld a shudder. True, Mo wasn't the most discerning of diners, but she didn't want the little dog eating the rats she killed which probably carried diseases ... or might have been poisoned.

But when Tamsyn looked in the back garden, she saw immediately why Mo had been barking.

Someone had broken into her grandfather's garden shed.

The door was hanging off its hinges and the contents had been tossed about haphazardly. Although the thieves appeared to have left behind her grandad's powered hand tools, and that was odd – Tamsyn knew that these were the most popular tools to be stolen: easily sold on eBay and passed on.

Then she realised what was missing – there was no sign of Adam's diving equipment.

"I don't think he was a rat catcher, Mo," Tamsyn said quietly to the dog. "Any chance of a description of that pest controller?"

Mo wagged her tail.

Tamsyn checked through the mess but she didn't think anything else had been taken even though tools were strewn about so it was hard to be certain.

Miss Nellie was still peering over the fence.

"What's up, maid?" called the elderly woman, her narrow face full of interest.

Tamsyn straightened up. "Could you give me a description of the man you saw, Miss Nellie."

The old woman's shrewd eyes tightened.

"He had a grey b'iler suit," she said grudgingly. "Van was grey, too. Is summat wrong?"

"Did the van have a name on the side of it or a logo?" Tamsyn asked.

The old woman shook her head. "None as I could see. Mind, I was watching my programme so I didn't think nothin' of it. Are you saying 'e were a wrong 'un?"

Tamsyn forced a smile. "Probably nothing to worry about, Miss Nellie, but I'm going to phone Grandad, just to be on the safe side."

Tamsyn was a hundred percent certain that neither of

her grandparents had ordered pest controllers; she was less sure about whether the theft was deliberate or opportunistic. But if the man was an ordinary burglar, he'd have taken her grandfather's power tools; if he wasn't an ordinary burglar...

She wasn't looking forward to telling her grandparents about the break-in. Or Adam. *Crap!* She needed to tell him about his dive set, then considered that wasn't the sort of news a person recovering in hospital would want to hear. But she did need to speak to him. Reluctantly, she dialled his number but the call went to voicemail again.

Then she tried her grandmother's mobile but the call went unanswered and Tamsyn remembered that she'd gone to a meeting with her friends about planning the Lughnasadh festival. Tamsyn left a vague, rambling message, the gist of which was that Miss Nellie had seen someone messing around with the garden shed and that the door was broken, but nothing seemed to be missing. She hated lying to her grandparents, but hated worrying them more.

Tamsyn stood and stared at the mess around her.

Adam's dive set had been in the shed for less than 24 hours after finding a dead diver – and the only person she'd told about it was DI Rego. She was glad that she'd taken the GoPro off the harness and given it to her boss.

She thought about phoning the Control room to report the theft but Rego's words from earlier that morning held her back.

Her mind was ticking through what she should do when she saw tyre tracks on the bit of grass in front of the gate. They were too wide for her grandfather's car – they looked more like tracks from a van. Of course, it could have been the postman, and Tamsyn made a mental note to ask Miss Nellie if and when the postie had been by.

Even so, she went back to the shed and picked up an old bucket, placing it over the tyre tracks to preserve the tread.

Mo watched with her tail drooping, seeming to realise that a walk wouldn't be happening anytime soon.

Tamsyn tried Rego's phone but the call went to voicemail, too. She left a short message then wondered what to do next. She should probably see if her neighbour could give her anymore details about what she'd seen and heard.

"I tole you everthin' a'ready," said Miss Nellie crossly when Tamsyn knocked on her door. "It warn't no postman that time o' day. This 'un parked 'is van outside your 'ouse 'bout half an hour or so after your grandmother went to the shops. Your dog made a right racket so I watched fer a bit. But then my programme started." She looked abashed. "What did he do, maid?"

"It looks like he broke into Grandad's garden-shed," said Tamsyn reluctantly.

Miss Nellie pulled her cardigan tightly across her thin shoulders. "Can't trust no one these days. When I was a girl, we never locked our doors, never!"

"Well, if you think of anything else, Miss Nellie, just let me know."

The old woman nodded, then rummaged around in her enormous shopping trolley that was leaning by the entrance to her front door.

She thrust a piece of paper into Tamsyn's hand.

"What's this?"

"The number plate, o' course," said Miss Nellie with a defiant stare.

Tamsyn couldn't believe her luck and grinned at the old woman.

"Miss Nellie, you are a *legend!*"

The old woman beamed.

CHAPTER 8

Rego had never seen so much activity in the morgue before, especially on a weekend, and for once, there were more live people than dead ones.

He'd met the Home Office forensic pathologist, Dr Manners, before, but he'd never seen the straight-talking woman with the ramrod posture so flustered.

The mortuary assistant was unknown to him, a woman in her early thirties, currently slumped in a plastic chair sipping water from a paper cup, and the photographer was standing to one side looking shocked.

A stocky man with a military haircut quietly introduced himself as Nate Tregowan.

All eyes turned to Dr Manners as she began speaking.

"Inspector Rego, I'm so glad you're here," she said briskly. "We have something of a situation – quite unprecedented. I've only seen this once before in my career..."

The pathologist's words died away as she gathered her thoughts, turning on the video camera before resuming.

"Vicky began the process of removing the dry-suit," the pathologist began again, nodding toward the mortuary assistant. "She is our anatomical pathology technologist. She carries out the eviscerations of the deceased: removes the organs, weighs and measures them, conducts internal and external examinations such as looking for bruising, tattoos, scars, anything unusual, then she restores the organs to the cadaver after." She cleared her throat. "But when Vicky began to remove the deceased's dry-suit, we found this."

Dr Manners drew the sheet back and Rego saw that the corpse was still clad in the dry-suit but with scissor marks up the front where the mortuary assistant had begun her job.

Rego peered closer, his eyebrows shooting up.

"What the hell? What is that?"

"Adipocere," said Dr Manners. "Also known as 'grave wax' ... or you might simply say soap."

"Soap? You're telling me that the body is made from soap?"

"The fat in the body has turned to soap, yes," said the pathologist gravely.

Rego was almost waiting for someone to jump out shouting 'April Fool', but no one so much as drew a breath.

"You see," said Dr Manners, "saponification requires a cool setting and poorly oxygenated water, and this dry-suit has seals at the neck, ankles and wrists. Over time, the seals have failed, allowing water to seep in, but very, very slowly, keeping marine life out, and ultimately creating an anaerobic environment. This organic substance," she continued, indicating the browny-grey colour of the corpse, "is formed by the anaerobic bacterial hydrolysis of fat in the body's tissue. Putrefaction has been replaced by a permanent firm cast of fatty tissues, extending to the internal organs, and the face: the adipocere."

Dr Manners' voice became animated.

"When you see a body with adipocere, it is absolutely clear it is not a fresh body – it could be months or even years old. There's a documented case from the mid-nineties when a headless body, fully encased in adipocere, was found floating in a lake near Interlaken in Switzerland. This torso baffled police and scientists for more than a decade because they had no idea who this person was or how long the body had been in the water. Then about ten years ago, researchers from the University of Zurich used radio carbon dating and published the results of their investigation – the man had drowned in the lake more than three hundred years earlier."

She didn't look at her audience but down at the body on the table.

"The researchers concluded that after he drowned, the body drifted down to the lake bed and was covered by sediment, where adipocere formed and coated the torso in much the same way we see here." She waved her hand at the body. "It requires an environment that has high levels of moisture and an absence of oxygen, such as in wet ground or mud at the bottom of a lake or a sealed casket – in this case the dry-suit. Formation begins within a month of death, and, in the absence of air, it can persist for centuries, as I've explained."

Rego stared at the corpse, remembering what Tregowan had said about the unusually high quality of the diver's equipment, about the possibility of it being experimental. It definitely hadn't been down there for centuries.

"How long, Dr Manners?" Rego asked. "How long has the body been down there?"

"At least a year," Dr Manners said thoughtfully. "Perhaps two or three – maybe even longer. I'll need to do some thorough research on it."

This was not good news.

"However," continued Dr Manners, "Since adipocere represents unusual preservation of soft tissues, we do have the external morphology that can contribute to identification. Additionally, soft tissue preservation can also preserve evidence of injury or lack thereof and thus contribute to interpretations of foul play."

Rego looked at Tregowan who was speechless, and then at the photographer.

"Document everything," said Rego. "I want every millimetre of the body photographed; everything on video, as well."

"Yes, of course," said Dr Manners, glancing up. "This will be an excellent teaching example."

She stepped back and her assistant picked up the scissors and continued to open the dry-suit with some difficulty, cutting from bellybutton to throat, peeling open the thick membrane and insulating all-in-one suit underneath.

Rego peered down at the waxy corpse. It was one of the strangest, most eerie things he'd ever seen – the man, long dead, encased in a soapy residue, his features still vaguely recognisable.

"Get a close up of those tattoos," Rego said to the photographer, stepping to one side and snapping a picture with his phone as everyone peered at the black lines of tattoos under the waxy surface of the skin.

Rego didn't speak any foreign language except some Bermudian patois he'd learned from his mum, but he recognised Cyrillic writing when he saw it. His bad feeling about this case intensified, and he had his doubts that the body's secrets would ever be shared with Dr Manners' students.

There was a sudden commotion outside and the door flew open. Four men in suits strode into the room.

One of them put his hand over the video camera.

"Stop recording and step away from the table."

"What the hell? On whose authority?"

Rego's voice was loud – everyone else froze in surprise.

"This is now a case of national security," said the man who appeared to be in charge. "Don't ask any questions – it's on a need-to-know basis and you don't need to know. Thank you, Inspector Rego. We're taking over now."

"Not until I've seen some authorisation to remove evidence from this mortuary," Rego snapped.

Instead, the man held out his phone to Rego with a FaceTime call.

"Rego," barked the vaguely familiar voice of a senior police officer with a shock of red hair, "this is Assistant Chief Constable Gray. You are to cease with this investigation and hand over all paperwork and digital records to these officers. All data pertaining to this case must be sealed and handed over – arrangements are in place for IT to isolate this record."

"But sir..."

"I don't like it any more than you do, Rego, but we all have our orders. No arguments – it's happening. Understood?"

"Yes, sir."

There was nothing else Rego could say.

They all stood in silence as the body was zipped into the body bag and the memory cards were removed from both the video and the stills camera. The names of everyone present were taken, and each person was reminded that talking about what they'd witnessed would breach the Official Secrets Act and could lead to their prosecution. They all had to sign a form to that effect.

When the four men left with the body, everyone seemed to breathe again.

Rego was furious at the way the team had been treated but reined in his own anger.

"Thank you for your time, Dr Manners, everyone," Rego said at last. "I'm sorry it was wasted."

He exchanged a look with Nate Tregowan and they left the morgue together.

"That pisses me off," Tregowan said to Rego as they headed toward the car park.

"Yep," said Rego, quietly fuming.

"So, that's it then?"

"Looks like it." Rego's voice was clipped.

If he'd known Tregowan better, Rego would have been tempted to vent to a fellow officer, but he didn't, so he kept his mouth firmly shut.

Tregowan gave him a long, hard look, nodded once, and headed for his car. Then he stopped, turned, and walked back towards Rego, glancing around him as he did so.

"Sir, there's something I need to tell you." He still looked uncertain. "I didn't say anything before because I wanted to speak to the pathologist but now that's not happening..." he took a deep breath, clearly knowing that by talking to Rego he was ignoring a direct order from ACC Gray, and potentially risking his career.

He hesitated, hoping for a sign from Rego.

It looked like trust was going to have to be a two-way street, so Rego nodded.

"Go on."

"I analysed his dive computer and..."

"Wait, where was there a computer?"

Tregowan gave him a look that was slightly pitying.

"His dive watch, sir. They're mini computers processing huge amounts of data the whole time you're on the dive. The victim had a Shearwater Petrel 3, a top of the range computer that would give information on air, Nitrox, Trimix, CCR, up to five gases, decompression, dive planning, vibration motor alerts, dive logging, Bluetooth and comms, and a Bühlmann GF algorithm."

"It has Bluetooth? Who was he communicating with?"

"I'd really like to know the answer to that as well, sir, because Bluetooth only has a short range so it would be unlikely to transmit to the surface."

"Another diver then?"

"It's possible, but it's the Bühlmann algorithm that really caught my attention."

He paused as if Rego should know what he meant, then continued quickly.

"Bühlmann created this algorithm, a model using maths, to show the way inert gases enter and leave the body as the ambient pressure changes. These are used in personal dive computers to compute no-decompression limits and decompression schedules for dives in real-time, so you can plan the depth and duration for dives and the required decompression stops."

"Okay?" Rego was beginning to see where this might go.

"Diving can be dangerous, even when you're not at depth." Tregowan inclined his head to one side. "If gases are wrong, you can taste it quite quickly, especially if it's Helium, for example."

"So, it was the wrong gas in his cylinders?"

"I'll get to that, sir, but the thing is, his dive computer was wrong."

"Wrong how?"

"The algorithms were wrong – his decompression stops would have been all over the place."

"But that's not what killed him," Rego said slowly. "You told me yourself that he was inside the *Mohegan* and when he released his buoyancy device, he was trapped inside."

"That's what I thought," Tregowan agreed, nodding vigorously, "but when we started analysing his dive tanks, the mix of gases wasn't quite right either but not wrong enough that he would have noticed right away."

Rego frowned. "But wouldn't this all-singing, all-dancing dive computer have told him that?"

Tregowan smiled grimly.

"Yes. Except his dive computer had been manipulated pre-dive."

"You mean...?"

"Someone close to him changed the mix of gases and then the settings on his dive computer. Either one of those things could have killed him, but by altering both?" He stared at Rego. "Someone wanted him dead."

He shrugged uncomfortably.

"And you're sure it couldn't have been an accident?"

Tregowan shook his head and explained further.

"The dive computer is an independent system, so there'd be no way for anyone on surface to know what was happening to the diver."

"But you said it had Bluetooth. He was transmitting to someone. Could someone have altered the computer from the surface?"

"He had Bluetooth capability but I don't know if he was transmitting on that dive. If I had more time, I might have been able to analyse the data and find out. Either way, sir, he was murdered ... and the government is trying to shut us up."

Rego agreed that the evidence was pointing in that direction, but what he didn't know was whether the spook squad were following the same lines of inquiry.

Tregowan's phone beeped with an incoming message and he glanced down, his lips thinning as he read the message on his screen.

"Fuck," he swore softly. "That was the Super – the men in black have already taken everything from our investigation team: cylinders, dive watch, isolated our IT records, the lot – every piece of evidence has gone from the lab, too." He shook his head. "Bastards."

Then he looked up at Rego.

"I've been a diver a lot of years and I can tell you that poor bugger on the slab would have had some awareness of what was happening to him. That's why he took off his buoyancy device – he knew he was dying and he was trying to escape."

Rego put his hands on his hips, stared up at the sky, then turned to look at Tregowan.

"I appreciate everything you've told me, Nate, and I appreciate your trust, but at this point, the Security Intelligence Service officers know more than us, and we've been ordered to stand down."

"I could still make some discreet enquiries," Tregowan said hopefully. "Call some of my old buddies."

Rego shook his head.

"No, Nate. There's nothing more we can do. This is one we won't win."

Tregowan's shoulders sagged. "Yeah, I know. It's just ... thank you for listening, sir."

They shook hands, and Tregowan strode towards his car.

Rego waited until he'd gone then called the one person who might have answers: Vikram.

The phone rang once before it was answered and Rego expressed himself vociferously.

"What the fuck is going on, Vik?"

But a recorded message played over him: *"This number is unavailable."*

The call ended and for the second time that day, Rego was listening to dead air.

CHAPTER 9

Rego drove back to Penzance in a vile temper, full of frustration and tension until a headache began to pulse behind his eyes.

He'd run up against the spook squad before, although he'd never had a case, *his case*, completely removed from his control. But as Assistant Chief Constable Gray said, they all had their orders, and if it was about national security, there was nothing he could do about it.

Still, he wondered. Did that mean they already knew the identity of the dead diver? Did they know who had killed him? Had the killer been caught or was he still out there? When had he gone missing? Had the man's family been notified, having already waited years to find out what had happened to their loved one? Or maybe they'd never be told; maybe they'd never know.

Then he thought about the weird device that Tamsyn's friend had recovered from the wreck, the device that was currently locked in his desk drawer awaiting Vikram's courier. Finding the device and Rego's subsequent call to

Vikram, that's when the investigation had gone pear-shaped. At least, that's what he'd assumed, but maybe it wasn't about the device – maybe it had been about the body all along. It was frustrating not knowing.

He wondered if the weird object would still be there when he returned to the office. It should have been checked into evidence along with the GoPro, but Rego hadn't followed protocol because of Vikram's reaction, and as he'd told Tamsyn not to write about it in her report, it was possible that ACC Gray didn't know about the object or the camera. He should tell him immediately.

Although it would be interesting to look at the object again. And Vikram had said not to hand it over to anyone without his express permission, so if Rego took his time returning to the station and if the intelligence agents couldn't find him, well, that might annoy MI6. What a pity.

Rego rubbed his aching temples: curiosity could be a killer, and he was playing games with people who didn't have a rule book.

His in-car phone rang and Tamsyn's name flashed up.

"Yes, Tamsyn."

"Uh hello, sir. I'm sorry to bother you…"

"Get to the point, PC Poldhu."

Rego's temper had already been shortened by several country miles today.

"Sorry. Um, so … someone broke into Grandad's shed and they stole Adam's dive kit. They didn't take anything else, just the diving things. I thought I should tell you first, sir, because of … you know."

"When did this happen?"

"Today, about 3pm."

Rego's irritation rose another notch. First his case had been hijacked, now the spooks were damaging the property of his young officer's family.

"Are you certain the dive equipment was all that was taken?"

"Not a hundred per cent," Tamsyn replied, "it looked like Grandad's power tools were still there though, so I didn't think it was an ordinary burglary. I might be wrong."

Rego didn't think so, but he did have a few questions for her.

"Did your grandparents see or hear anything?"

"No. Grandad was out on the *Daniel Day*, and it's Gran's afternoon for her, um, women's group. Then they were meeting at the Mack Shack, the pub, so they probably wouldn't have gone home, but even if they had, you can't see the shed from the kitchen window. They don't know yet, and I didn't call it in either."

"Was there any damage to the property?"

She paused. "Well, the lock is broken and the door is hanging off. But I think that's all."

"I'll look into it."

"Oh, okay. Thank you, sir."

"Anything else?"

"My neighbour saw him – Miss Nellie. She thought he was from the Council, setting rat traps or something. She didn't see his face and she's really old. But she did get the van's number plate."

And she read it out to him.

Rego sent up a prayer to the patron saint of Neighbourhood Watch, possibly named Nellie.

"Okay, Tamsyn. We'll keep this between us for now. I'll give you £20 out of petty cash to pay for a new lock."

"You don't need to do that, sir."

"Yes, I do. And Tamsyn, you have to let this go because you can't talk about it."

"What do I say to my grandparents? And Miss Nellie? They're bound to ask me about it."

"Tell them it was probably some local scrote and that your neighbour scared him off before he could do anything. I'll be in touch."

Rego pulled into a layby and punched the number plate information into the ANPR database. The registered keeper came up as B&G Engineering Ltd from Hemel Hempstead. There was a website but no landline, just a mobile phone number and a PO Box. With no physical location listed and very little information, it looked like a fake website to Rego. And he was fairly sure that the van Tamsyn's nosy neighbour had spotted was a vehicle belonging to the security services. There was, however, the possibility that another player could somehow be involved. He hoped like hell he was wrong about that. Everything came back to the device Tamsyn had found and the phone call that Rego had made to Vikram.

Even though their friendship went back years, Vik wouldn't have had much choice in passing on the information to his MI6 bosses.

But that made no sense. If Vikram had told them about the device, why would they bother taking Ellis' dive kit from Tamsyn's back garden?

Unless they were after the GoPro.

Rego thought about the day he'd met Vikram, starting

at Greater Manchester Police the same week, two wet-behind-the-ears young coppers, Rego with a Bermudian mother, Vik with an Indian father. They'd faced the same casual racism every day, they'd been friends, as close as brothers...

Rego felt the sting of disappointment.

As for the removal of the victim's body, all Rego could do was put in a formal complaint which would go nowhere but possibly make him feel better.

The spooks would just spout 'national security' and maintain plausible deniability.

Rego slammed his hands against the steering wheel in frustration.

He decided to go back to the station, take one more look at the device – assuming it was still there and hadn't already been seized – and then go home and forget about the day. There was a fish and chip supper with his name on it.

After navigating the on-going roadworks on the A30 and cursing at the buildup of holiday traffic, Rego's temper hadn't improved as he parked behind Penzance police station.

But as he climbed out of his car, the hairs on the back of his neck stood up – it was the eerie feeling of being watched.

Glancing around casually but seeing nothing, he used the car window's reflection to scan behind him. Yep, there he was: white, early thirties, short hair.

Rego spun around and met the man's eyes. The stranger didn't even try to hide but instead inclined his head to one side in a 'follow me' gesture, then turned and walked in the direction of the large, semi-tropical gardens of Penlee Park, framed by towering palm trees and giant echium.

Rego made no attempt to catch up with the man until they reached a heavily wooded area with evening sunlight slanting through the trees.

The man sat on a bench and pulled out his phone. Rego sat at the other end of the bench, gazing into the distance.

CHAPTER 10

"Thank you for coming, Inspector Rego," the man began, still not looking at him. "My name is Paul Jameson and I'm a Leading Hand in Comms with the Royal Fleet Auxiliary at Culdrose."

Rego's interest was piqued but he waited in silence.

"The RFA is the merchant navy, so technically I'm a civilian – although the RFA is fully integrated into operations around the world," Jameson continued, "and the merchant navy provides support on everything from high-tempo combat and counter-piracy campaigns, to disaster relief and emergency evacuations."

He spoke like he was reading from a recruiting brochure.

Rego waited for more, but the man's eyes were fixed on his phone. As an experienced police officer, Rego knew that few people were comfortable with silence, preferring to fill it with words, so he leaned back on the bench, gazing up at glimpses of sky above the dense foliage.

"I heard a rumour, well, more than a rumour," Jameson

continued at last, "I heard that you found the body of a diver near the *Mohegan*."

Rego didn't answer, simply waiting for the man to tell him what he'd come to say.

"I know who it is," Jameson said quietly.

Rego carried on staring upwards, but he was listening intently.

"The body you found..." Jameson cleared his throat. "His name is ... was ... his name was Fedir Kuzma. I knew him as Freddie."

"What makes you think that the victim is Fedir Kuzma?" Rego asked.

Jameson didn't look up.

"Five-ten, 75 kilos, brown hair, brown eyes," he paused. "You probably can't see his eye colour," he said quietly. "He had beautiful eyes."

Jameson glanced up at Rego.

"We were together for six months."

Rego simply nodded.

"Being gay in the Navy is the punchline to a joke, right? Able semen – I've heard them all. The RFA is supposed to be inclusive but for a lot of people, they're just more comfortable not knowing. You definitely don't go into the Mess holding hands. If you want to get promoted, stay in the closet and don't let anyone know that you're queer." His voice was soft and bitter. "There's a reason I'm still only a Leading Hand after 13 years in the job."

Rego nodded slightly to show he was listening.

"When I met Freddie, it was love at first sight." Jameson's lip curled. "He was on attachment from the Ukrainian Navy. But it took me three weeks to get up the courage to talk to him. We had to be careful, sneaking around, hiding what we felt. No one knew we were together."

"Did the vic— did Freddie have any distinguishing marks or tattoos?"

Jameson didn't reply to the question, but he scanned through his phone then passed it to Rego. The picture was of a heavy-set man from the waist up, his face turned away from the camera and his coarse body hair almost obscuring the swirl of tattoos on his left arm, shoulder and pectoral muscle.

It matched the tattoos Rego had seen on the victim's body.

"It's him, isn't it?" Jameson asked.

"How long has it been since you last saw Freddie?" Rego asked, taking a copy of the photo to compare with his own later, then sliding the phone back across the bench.

"One year, three months and 22 days," Jameson intoned. "He was getting ready for another training mission, at least, that's what he told me. I never really knew what he did. His English wasn't great and my Ukrainian was non-existent."

He gave a hollow laugh.

"That night – our last night – I waited for him to come to my room, but he never came. I assumed that the training had run over or he'd been dragged out for team drinks or something. But then he didn't come the next night either, and then I heard that the Ukrainian team had gone home."

He paused, and glanced at Rego again.

"I know what you're thinking, Inspector. You're thinking that Freddie wasn't really that into me and just decided ghosting me was easier. And to be honest, I thought that, too. Except nine months ago, I received this."

He pulled a crumpled envelope out of his back pocket and handed it to Rego.

The stamp was in Cyrillic and the handwriting was awkward with some letters the wrong way round, but Rego could see that it was addressed to Jameson at *RNAS Culdrose*.

"It's from his sister, Kateryna. He must have told her everything, because I don't know how else she would have known about me. You can read the letter if you want – it says that she hasn't heard from him in months and do I know why because he hasn't been in touch with her. At first, she thought he was just busy, and then she thought the letters weren't getting through because she'd been evacuated from Mariupol, but when she started asking questions, the Ukrainian Navy told her that there was no record of anyone by the name of Fedir Kuzma, past or present. That's when she wrote to me."

"Can I take a copy of this?" Rego asked.

Jameson shrugged. "Sure."

"What did you do with the letter afterwards?" Rego asked as he photographed the note.

Jameson frowned at him.

"What did I do? Her letter freaked me out. Why were they denying any knowledge of Freddie? He was here training with a detachment of the Ukrainian Navy, for God's sake! It was part of a deal that our government had with Ukraine."

His mouth tightened into a thin line.

"I've been researching it in my own time, but I

haven't got very far," he sighed. "We had a load of fundraisers and clothes drives to support Ukraine when Russia first invaded. And as far back as 2020, our government gave the Ukrainian's a 10-year loan of £1.25 billion for the re-equipment of the Ukrainian Navy, as well as an agreement to train their personnel. Everyone at Culdrose knew about it – we were proud to help. That's why Freddie was here: to train with some of our divers, I think. So why did the Ukrainian government lie about having no record of him? It doesn't make any sense."

Rego could hear the frustration in his voice, overlaid with something darker.

"I wrote back to Kateryna and said I hadn't seen him but that I'd ask around." Jameson's head drooped. "No one at Culdrose was admitting anything except that the Ukrainian team had gone home. I wrote to Kateryna twice more, but I never heard from her again. I don't know if my letters reached her – I don't even know if she's still alive because of everything that's going on in Ukraine. I didn't know what to do and no one seemed to know anything about a missing diver..."

"Until now," said Rego.

"Until now," Jameson agreed. "Is it him?"

It was a compelling story, but there was still a possibility that Jameson wasn't who he said he was.

"Do you have a picture of the two of you together?" Rego asked.

Jameson nodded and handed over his phone again.

Rego looked at a selfie Jameson had taken with the swarthy man with the tattoos. The sea was behind them and they were both wearing sunglasses and smiling. The man had his arm slung around Jameson's shoulders.

Rego swiped left and right without asking, just in case the photo was staged or a fake, but the picture was one of a series which convinced Rego they were genuine. There was a photo of the men kissing and several that were indoors and far more intimate.

When Rego glanced across at Jameson, the man's cheeks were flushed, but he met Rego's gaze head on.

"Do you have any ID with you?" Rego asked as another check.

Jameson pulled out his wallet and showed Rego both his driving licence and Culdrose pass.

Rego studied the documents, photographed them, then slid the wallet back to Jameson.

"I'm very sorry for your loss."

Jameson nodded but didn't speak for several seconds.

"Thanks," he said shortly, tapping his wallet against his knee.

"Did Freddie have a phone while he was over here?"

Jameson shook his head.

"No, he said an international SIM was too expensive and that the Ukrainian Navy didn't want any of them posting photos of training ops in the UK."

"How did you communicate with him?"

Jameson gave a faint smile.

"Old school: we sent notes to each other. It was … exciting … getting a note pushed under my door with a time and place to meet up." He sighed. "Once, we went to the Premier Inn at Helston."

"Can you remember the date?"

Jameson nodded, scrolled through pages of old emails, then slid his phone over so that Rego could see the booking information.

Rego wanted to be absolutely certain that Jameson was who he said he was. Rego knew that all Army, Navy and Airforce recruits had their fingerprints taken when they got their medical examination for entrance, taking their entire handprint and each individual finger in several different angles on both hands, and he suspected it would be the same for all personnel working on the base. A quick call to the Ministry of Defence Police at Culdrose would confirm it.

Rego passed his phone to Jameson.

"If you could put your number in my contacts," Rego added casually.

Jameson didn't hesitate to take Rego's phone, adding his details and handing it back. Rego discreetly slipped it into a pocket so he didn't smear the fingerprints.

Jameson didn't seem aware of what had just happened; his gaze was fixed to the ground when he took a deep breath.

"Look, Inspector, something happened to Freddie, something no one wants to admit to. I don't know if there was an accident or what happened. But someone is covering it up. It could be the Ukrainians or..." he shook his head. "I know that a gay, foreign sailor isn't exactly anyone's priority, but it matters to me. *He* matters. All he wanted was to serve his country and see a free Ukraine. He deserves better than what happened to him. And if it's all swept under the carpet, then we're no better than the Russians."

He stood up and stared down at Rego.

"You have my number. If you find out anything..." he paused, searching Rego's face, then his gaze shuttered. "Thank you for your time, Inspector," and he walked away, disappearing amongst the lengthening shadows.

Rego sat on the bench for several more minutes, mentally constructing a timeline of events. He wasn't sure he put much credence in the sister's letter by itself – Ukraine was in chaos, records could be incomplete, lost, or destroyed. But when he factored in the UK government's urgency in claiming the body and appearing to clean house at the same time, well, that definitely concerned him, and he didn't like where his conclusions took him.

Rego was a copper's copper, joining the force young and working his way up through the ranks.

But his route to joining the police hadn't been a direct one; in fact, there'd been a time when it looked likely that he'd end up on the wrong side of the law. Petty theft, drinking, smoking spliffs, hanging out with a dodgy crowd on the edge of Manchester's gangland scene – it would have been a very different story if not for the influence of one man. Winston Deleon was born in Kingston, Jamaica, and joined Greater Manchester Police in the early seventies, at a time when there were very few officers of colour. One of the last acts of a long career had been to give the young Rego a second chance and a third chance, then read him the riot act about the direction he'd been heading:

"Wake up and live, boy! Dat what my man Bob Marley say. Because you go hanging wit dem crowd, you put your han' in de debil's mout' – careful tek it out."

He'd never forgotten the advice which had spoken to

his younger self. Becoming a police officer a few years after had completed the realignment of his moral compass which street life in his teenage years had confused.

He felt strongly that Jameson and Kuzma's sister deserved to know the truth, but determining what that was would not be easy or straightforward. He'd also received a direct order to let it go, even saying the same words to Nate Tregowan and Tamsyn less than an hour ago.

Disobeying a direct order would definitely be the same as sticking his hand in the devil's mouth. But investigating Jameson's phone number would give details of billing, calls, cell site information and much more. Although, the risk was that if the security services knew as much as Rego – which was entirely plausible – then they would also have Jameson's number and they would have already pulled all the phone records. And key intel would also be more than 12 months old, which would make it difficult to get, although not impossible. If Rego followed the same method of investigation, the data could be flagged, which would then alert others to the fact that Rego hadn't dropped the case.

Which I have, he reminded himself.

Still, it was a low-level hum of irritation that chafed at his detective's brain.

He shook his head and stood slowly. It rankled, but the decision had been made by people well above his pay grade. He had his career to think about: his career and his family.

Rego walked back through the park, absentmindedly taking in the beauty of the gardens at twilight, letting his subconscious steer the direction of his thoughts.

When he reached the police station, it was between shift changes and almost empty. He didn't see a soul as he headed to his office, although he could hear people talking in another part of the building.

He unlocked his filing cabinet, almost surprised to see that the object was still there. He turned it over in his hands, wondering why it had triggered alarm bells at MI6's HQ in Vauxhall. If it was so important, why hadn't the security service agents accompanied him back to the station to collect it. In fact, they hadn't even mentioned it when they'd said that all evidence had to be handed over to them. Maybe it had been implied, maybe they hadn't wanted to mention it in front of the others. But then again, they'd had the opportunity to speak to him in private: they hadn't taken it. Which left him wondering if Vikram had told anyone about it.

What are you playing at, Vik?

Normally, Rego would have simply called his friend, but that route was currently unavailable to him. He vacillated for a whole minute before he decided to call Vik's wife, feel her out, see if she had any insight.

She answered cheerily.

"Hi Rob! How are you? It's been an age. When are you and Cassie coming to see us – the kids must be getting so big now."

Nothing had changed in her rapid-fire delivery and Rego felt himself smiling despite everything that was going on.

"I'm okay, thanks, Kamla. Cassie and the kids are coming down soon and staying for the summer."

"Oh, your mum won't like that," she laughed. "She thinks none of you can manage without her."

Rego winced at the reminder that he still needed to tell his mother about the family's summer holiday plans.

"You're probably calling for Vikram," she said. "He told me that his phone has been playing up. But he's away on some work thing – don't ask me, I'm always the last to know. He's been calling me every evening on the house phone. Do you want me to pass on a message?"

"Nah, that's okay. I just called to say hi," Rego lied.

"Okay, I'll let him know. Good to talk to you, Rob. Ugh, gotta go, I can hear carnage in the living room. Why did we have kids again?"

And the call ended.

But Rego had learned two more pieces of information: Vikram was missing in action and lying to his wife.

He sat at his desk, wondering what to do next.

He felt uneasy leaving the object in his desk along with the GoPro, knowing what he knew or thought he knew. He was also aware that not recording either item in the detained property book was breaking a lot of rules which could rain fire and brimstone down on his head.

From his first day in the job, he'd known that there were the three Ps that could bugger an officer's career: policewomen, piss, and property. Shagging a female officer and ruining your marriage; drinking to help you sleep at night; or getting distracted and putting a piece of evidential property in your pocket/lunchbox/drawer, then being deep in the shit when someone came to claim it.

In the end, he dropped the device into his messenger

bag – used in preference to a briefcase which most other DIs used – and relocked the filing cabinet.

Then, gingerly, he retrieved his phone from his pocket and closed his office door so he wouldn't be disturbed. Using a portable forensic kit, he dusted black carbon powder onto the phone's surface where Jameson had touched it, sticking to the sweat left by the friction ridges of his fingerprints. He then photographed the marks and lifted them using DCF tape, fixing it to a plastic sheet so it could be stored as evidence, recording the date, equipment used and context in which he'd retrieved the prints: all of which he had no intention of putting into evidential property.

And then he hesitated.

Up until this point, he'd toed the line – he might have stepped right up to the line and leaned over it for a better view – but he hadn't crossed it. Besides, Jameson had come to him; Vikram's reaction had taught him to be cagey, and his instincts screamed that the whole thing stank. But he hadn't gone over the line.

The thing was, DIs had quite a lot of freedom to act. And if he filled in a form requesting confirmation of Jameson's identity from the MoD police, well, as authorising officer, it would go straight through. It didn't need to be a big deal.

Just for curiosity's sake.

And no one would be interested if he checked to see if Jameson came up on the Police National Computer which listed criminal convictions and those pending. And once Rego had done that, he thought he may as well check the

Police National Database which fed in intelligence from across the country.

There was nothing about Jameson on that either.

Just to be sure, he checked the Niche database of local intel. Still nothing.

He tapped his fingers on the desk, the form requesting information on Jameson from the Ministry of Defence Police displayed on his laptop's screen.

It only took a couple of minutes to fill in the form and send it off, and seeing as he'd gone that far, he emailed his contact at Culdrose, Bronze Commander, Sergeant Ed Bladen, and asked for access to Jameson's service contract.

MDP were a civilian special police force and part of the United Kingdom's MoD. They provided armed security and counter terrorism services to high-risk areas, as well as uniformed policing and some investigative services to MoD property, personnel, and installations. The Military Police, or Royal Naval Police as they were at Culdrose, they investigated crimes committed by soldiers/sailors. Rego hadn't met any RNPs yet, but hoped they were used to cooperating with the MoD plods – it would make his casual enquiries more ... casual.

And with that decision, Rego crossed the line.

He mulled over whether or not to request Call Data Records for Jameson's phone. If he put a rush on them, the information could be back in two or three weeks, otherwise they'd end up joining the very long queue of phone records waiting for analysis. Rego was well aware that there was an eighteen-month backlog in forensics across many Forces; 24 months or more in some cases, and that included analysis of phone downloads. Of course, in the event of a murder or serious crime, work could be bumped to the top of the queue: priority one for murders or other serious offences where the phone companies were contracted to turn the data around in 24 hours. Unfortunately, the cost of this service was quite high. Rego considered asking for the data on a priority two – a seven-day turnaround. He definitely didn't want to wait 28 days for a priority three.

It was the same for forensics as well. Each submission would be allocated a priority: the higher the priority, the quicker the turn-around, the higher the cost.

It was frustrating that doing so would trigger questions that Rego didn't want to answer. Even entering the numbers on the occurrences database would leave a digital trail.

So, he took another risk, and put a rush on obtaining the CDR for Jameson's phone. Depending on what came back, he'd then decide if he needed to allocate an officer to analyse it, because that would be a lot harder to explain away.

He pondered the fact that Kuzma hadn't had a phone ... or at least if he had, Jameson wasn't going to give him the number – or didn't have it. Either way, Rego would soon know how long Jameson had kept his current mobile number, and whether it included any messages to a Ukrainian code. His instincts told him that Jameson had been on the level, but he still needed to check it out.

Rego typed up a report on his laptop of everything that he'd done, made some notes about his thoughts, suspicions and concerns, then ensured it wasn't being stored anywhere but there, password protected, which was as far as his familiarity with technology took him. He knew that someone like Vikram would bypass that in minutes. But it was something.

Uneasy with his role in all this, Rego closed his laptop and slid it into his messenger bag, then headed back to his cottage, stopping only to pick up cod and chips with a portion of mushy peas.

Tomorrow was Sunday, a day off, and he'd promised Cassie that he'd go shopping at Tesco to stock the fridge and freezer for her and the kids so they'd have some food when they arrived that evening.

He also had to undertake the hazardous job of telling his mum that the kids would be staying with him for the summer … and that there was no room for her. Certainly not in the cottage, although it had occurred to Rego to find her a B&B somewhere nearby. But then again, Cassie wanted a break from his mother's constant interference – or helpful assistance – depending on which woman was bending his ear at the time. Rego very much wanted to stay married, so it was a simple choice.

It was time to forget about secrets, spooks and spurned lovers; time to forget about bodies that turned to soap. Time to forget about the job for a few precious hours.

Although, now he thought about it, there was one other person who might be able to help him … maybe.

CHAPTER 11

Tamsyn lied to Miss Nellie and then she lied to her grandparents when they came back from their sea shanty evening at the Mack Shack. Even though it wasn't the first time she'd been ordered to hide the truth from her family and friends, it wasn't any easier. And they all believed her without question, which made her feel worse.

A guilty conscience hadn't let her sleep well, so she was more than happy to lounge around in bed the next morning watching stupid TikTok videos with Mo next to her. She wasn't on shift until 4pm and if felt good to just be Tamsyn and not PC Poldhu for a few hours.

She caught up with Jess at lunchtime, and they ate ice creams on Penzance prom, dodging the seagulls, and watching the skateboarders and tourists.

"You haven't mentioned Adam, so I'm assuming you haven't heard from him," Jess said at last.

"No, nothing. I was a bit worried at first but now I just think he's being a dick. He can't even say his phone died because I took the charger from his car and put it in the bag I left with his mum. God, I hope he's okay."

"Maybe she took the bag home with her," Jess said, crunching on the end of her 99 and curling her tongue around it lasciviously, laughing when a teenage boy tripped over his own feet.

"Stop being a ho-bag," Tamsyn smiled as Jess winked at her.

"Fine, I'll stop damaging teenage boys if you promise to stop blaming yourself. Adam is a dick, quite a hottie, but a dick all the same – we both know it. I have no idea why you decided to give him the benefit of the doubt in the first place."

"Because you told me to," Tamsyn pointed out.

"More fool you for listening to me," Jess grinned, tossing the bottom part of her cone to Mo who hoovered it up eagerly.

The time passed quickly and Jess had to leave to show a potential client around a property in Porthleven, so Tamsyn and Mo walked down seaweed-slick steps to the small beach below the prom where Tamsyn threw a ball for Mo until the little dog was a hot, panting mess.

On the way home, she bought a new padlock for her grandfather's garden shed, and spent ten minutes fitting them and replacing the screws where they'd splintered the door. It was the best she could do.

Then she had to rush, making sure she'd packed a couple of clean uniform shirts and trousers.

"Tammy, shall I make you a sandwich for later?" her grandmother called from the kitchen. "Or I've got some pasties just come out of the oven?"

DEAD MAN'S DIVE

It was no contest, and Tamsyn's stomach growled in appreciation as her grandmother wrapped the still-warm pasty in greaseproof paper.

"God, that smells great! Thanks, Gran."

It was something to look forward to, although, many shifts went by when she didn't have a chance to drink a cup of coffee, let alone eat the food she'd taken with her.

She gave her grandmother a huge hug, then waved as she rushed out of the door.

"I'm on till midnight – don't wait up!"

She was halfway to the station when her phone rang, a mobile number that she didn't recognise. Tamsyn accepted the call without speaking, knowing that automated calls were usually dropped if she didn't talk first.

"Hello?" A woman's voice, brittle and anxious. "Hello? Tarryn?"

Tamsyn realised it was Adam's mother calling her ... and still hadn't bothered to get her name right.

"Hello, Ms Kurl," she answered evenly. "This is Tamsyn. How are you? How's Adam?"

"I don't know!" the woman wailed. "He's disappeared! Have you heard from him?"

Tamsyn was taken aback.

"No, I haven't. I called a couple of times but his phone went straight to voicemail. He didn't reply to my texts either."

"Well, where is he?"

"You've tried his place in Falmouth?"

"Of course I have! And I've called all his friends. No one has heard from him since yesterday."

"Might he have gone to another family member?" Tamsyn asked gently.

"You mean his father! Why would he go to Derek?"

Tamsyn didn't reply to that.

"Anyway, he hasn't; I checked," the woman said bitterly. "And that was *not* a fun conversation, I can tell you. He's still an arrogant pig."

"When did Adam leave hospital?" Tamsyn asked, diverting the woman's rant before it gained momentum.

"He didn't just leave! Your lot took him. That's why I called you. Honestly, Tarryn, I thought you'd know all this."

A cold feeling crept over her.

"Ms Kurl," said Tamsyn, using her police voice. "The police don't take people from hospital beds even if they're arresting them, and Adam is not under arrest."

"But..." the woman said, sounding confused. "But the nurses told me that the police came and took him away for questioning."

"What time did this occur?" Tamsyn asked, reaching into her bag for her notebook and pen.

"The nurse said it was before lunchtime. Two police officers came in and talked to Adam this morning, then he left with them."

"Did the officers give their names?"

"No, I don't know. The nurse didn't say."

"Were they in uniform?" Tamsyn asked patiently.

The woman hesitated before replying in a small voice. "I don't know."

"Okay," Tamsyn said soothingly. "Did you happen to take the name of the nurse you spoke to?"

"No, why would I?" She paused, thinking. "She was short and tubby, you know, fat."

Tamsyn raised her eyebrows but made a note all the same.

"I'm sure we can find out which nurse you talked to and perhaps get a description of the men that Adam left with. I'll call the station to see what I can find out. Leave this with me, Ms Kurl, and I'll call you back. It might not be straightaway though."

"What? That's it? I'm just supposed to sit at home and twiddle my thumbs? For God's sake! My son is *missing* and he should be in hospital. Haven't you listened to a word I said? God, this is such a bloody waste of time!"

"Ms Kurl, Adam is an adult and you said that he left of his own free will. I'm going to make some calls but that's all that I can do for now." Tamsyn cut off the woman's irate reply. "If you could text me a list of all the people you've spoken to so far, along with their contact details, that would be helpful. And if there's anyone else that you haven't contacted yet, that would be useful, too. And my name isn't Tarryn, it's Tamsyn. Police Constable Tamsyn Poldhu."

The first thing Tamsyn did was to call Camborne Police Station and speak to the custody officer to find out whether Adam had been interviewed or arrested. But there was no Adam Ellis on record. Not even pertaining to the dive where they'd found the body. Nothing at all.

Perhaps the information hadn't been entered yet, although it should have been by now.

Could it be because DI Rego had told her not to talk about the dive or what they'd found to anyone? Maybe that's why it wasn't on the system. And the weird thing they'd found – something else that she wasn't supposed to talk about. And then Adam's dive equipment had been stolen from her grandfather's shed. Surely, it must be linked; surely, it must have something to do with Adam going missing.

Or am I being paranoid?

But she knew in her gut that it was all connected, she just didn't know how or why.

She really wanted to call DI Rego, but he'd been short with her and told her she had to let it go. Although that had been to do with the shed burglary not a missing person.

She tried Adam's phone again, just to check, but as before, it went straight to voicemail.

Nope, time to grow a pair and call her boss.

When he answered, his voice sounded distracted, and Tamsyn winced, worried that she was annoying him by calling on a Sunday.

"Sir, it's Tamsyn. I'm sorry to bother you again, but Adam Ellis has gone missing."

She relayed his mother's call and her conversation with the custody officer at Camborne.

"Adam's mum is really worried. I told her I'd make some calls," she finished lamely.

Rego was silent.

"What should I tell her?"

"Tell her that you've reported to me and that I'll call her tomorrow when I've looked into this. Email me all the information you have."

"Thank you, sir," said Tamsyn, relieved to have the responsibility lifted from her shoulders.

As a police officer, she needed to be able to respond to reassure people when the public requested her help, but with Adam going missing, the answers seemed to be racing away from her.

CHAPTER 12

Rego's day was going from bad to worse.

He knew that he'd have to tread carefully with Ellis going missing. This could easily turn around and bite him. The mother's vague description of the men Ellis had gone with had more than a whiff of security services about it, despite her belief that they'd been police officers. But Vikram's reaction gave Rego the feeling that there might be other players in the game that he knew nothing about. The truth was, anyone with an interest could have told Ellis that they were from His Majesty's government and the guy would have gone with them.

Of course, if Ellis turned up dead somewhere, the shit would hit the fan, especially as Ellis had a link to the murder victim. From what Tamsyn had said, the security services had no reason to detain Ellis after they'd put the fear of God in him. Unless...

Rego frowned. Why had Ellis chosen to dive the wreck at all? And why with a novice diver? One who happened to be a police officer. Was he trying to line up some sort of alibi where Tamsyn would take the fall? It wasn't an impossible scenario, but having to consider it didn't make him feel any better.

He really wanted to be able to talk this all over with someone – the one thing he wasn't allowed to do. He could have done without Adam Ellis going missing. He wanted to believe that the man had just left hospital of his own accord, but then he'd have to believe in faeries and unicorns, too.

His immediate boss, DCI Finch, would listen but have to kick any concerns up the chain of command, so Rego debated whether or not to go straight to ACC Gray. The problem was that Gray would most likely order Rego to stand down when he heard how Ellis was connected to the case, and disobeying him would stall Rego's career at best – at worst, it could end it.

He toyed with the idea of talking to one of Vikram's colleagues at the NCA in the hope that someone could get a message to Vik with his new team of spooks; he even considered calling the contact number on the Secret Intelligence Service website which he'd googled shortly after midnight.

Is that really the best I can do? What the hell is that gadget that Tamsyn's friend found?

So, after Rego had verified that no one from Devon & Cornwall Police was involved with removing Adam Ellis from Treliske Hospital, he decided to call DC John Frith, and send him to the hospital on the pretext of taking a statement from Ellis.

He planned to text Frith shortly before he'd get there, saying that Ellis had gone missing and passing on all the information Tamsyn had given him. Slightly underhand, but it wasn't exactly breaking Gray's orders. Frith would be able to interview the doctors and nurses who had been treating Ellis, and get a description of the men who'd taken him.

After that, Rego spent a busy afternoon making up the kids' beds and cleaning the cottage. Cassie had standards, and they were significantly higher than his own.

He still hadn't heard back from Frith, so with nothing else to do, Rego headed to Tesco, his brain fuzzy as he tried and failed to remember which breakfast cereals Maisie and Max ate, so he bought four packs of mini variety boxes and hoped for the best. He definitely wasn't going to win Father of the Year when he couldn't even remember what his kids liked to eat. Living away from them was shit.

He tossed in bread, cheese, fruit and frozen vegetables then realised that there was no fresh fish counter. An assistant told him it was because of 'lack of demand'. He thought of Tamsyn and her grandfather's struggle to carry on the family fishing business, and promised himself to stop at a fish shop in Newlyn on the way back.

Frith called when he was unpacking his shopping.

"It's bizarre, boss. Ellis left in a hurry with two men believed to be police officers but the nurse who saw them didn't remember them giving their names or showing their Warrant cards. They weren't in uniform either. She didn't think Ellis looked particularly worried even though he didn't know them, but she said that he was surprised. He took everything with him, so he definitely didn't leave his phone behind but it's still turned off."

"Have you spoken to the mother?"

"Yes, boss. Got an earful from her, but she's certain he's not with any work colleagues, friends or girlfriends, and not with his father either. I thought she was a bit hysterical but Ellis's car is still parked at Porthoustock, and I can't find a single record of anyone from anywhere in D&C talking to Ellis." He paused. "Are we looking at impersonating an officer and kidnapping, boss?"

Rego didn't say he thought that would be the least of their worries.

"Let's hold off on the Hollywood script for a moment, John," he said, trying to sound unconcerned. "But just to be on the safe side, get the CCTV from the hospital security camera and see if you can track Ellis' movements into a car park. You might be able to get the VRM of the car taking him away. Also, the hospital car park is fee paying, so if you track Ellis or the men on camera to a ticket machine, find out their payment method – and we can track a credit card, if we're that lucky."

"On it, boss."

Privately, Rego thought that the pseudo cops would be smart enough to blag their way out of the car park by pressing the button on the barrier and saying they were police. Most car park staff wouldn't even question it and just raise the barrier. But having the vehicle registration mark would be useful. VRM was accessed by the DVLA database which gave cars and motorcycle registrations; data included make, model, Euro status, mileage, engine size, fuel type and colour, as well as extended features to view Road Tax status or MOT history checks.

But it still had to be looked into and analysed. It all took time. He really wanted that CCTV footage.

He opened his laptop and added Frith's findings to the case-he-wasn't-working-on. While he was updating the file, his email pinged with an incoming message.

MDP and the RNP had come through with the information on Jameson. He'd joined the Royal Fleet Auxiliary 13 years ago at the age of 20 as an Apprentice and trained in communications. He'd moved swiftly through the ranks of Seaman Grade 1 and Seaman Grade 2, becoming a Leading Hand eight years ago, since which time, his career appeared to have stalled.

Was that because he was gay, as Jameson had told him, or for some other reason? Rego read on.

All of his fitness reports were positive if somewhat lukewarm, which could fit with the homophobia as Jameson had suggested.

Jameson had worked at both a ship-wide level and multi-ship task-force level, reporting to the Area Services Manager as part of an onboard IT Networking team. Although he'd started by managing the Global Maritime Distress and Safety System to ensure that his ship always remained ready to respond to an emergency, his work at Culdrose for the past four years had been to do with Military Integrated Communications Systems. Rego's spider senses were tingling.

Jameson had worked on top secret military communications.

Oh, shit.

CHAPTER 13

The cottage was clean and tidy, the fridge and freezer stocked with food, and Rego was using the 'Find My' app to watch Cassie's slow progress down the A30.

He was looking forward to having her and the kids for the whole summer, even though his mother had decided to have a full-blown meltdown and all but disowned him when he'd told her about their plans. She'd called him ungrateful and selfish, and then she'd started to cry. She'd fumed, berated him for being an uncaring and unfeeling son, cried some more, insisted that the children would miss her, and then she brought out the big guns, imploring God to help her errant son see the error of his ways.

Rego hadn't been unmoved and had promised to spend time with her at the end of the holidays. Patricia Rego had not been appeased or impressed.

Rego was made of tough stuff, but having his mum sobbing over the phone had almost broken him. It had been on the tip of his tongue to invite her down, but then he thought of what Cassie would say about that. It was a lose-lose situation, so Rego held firm.

The four months since he'd left Manchester had been hard on the family. Maisie missed her daddy, but Max was turning into a belligerent teenager more and more each time Rego saw him. He had high hopes that this summer would help them to reconnect.

And he missed his wife. Her absence felt like a dull ache that work could not fill.

Immediately he had that thought, his mind pinged back into work mode, a rubber-band snapping back into its natural shape.

Adam Ellis going missing was a loose end he didn't need. And he still had the device that Ellis had found, with no word about who was going to come for it.

Rego saw that Cassie's car had entered Newlyn and he stood outside the cottage to welcome them.

Maisie was first out of the car, throwing herself into his arms and talking a mile a minute. Then Cassie followed, stretching her back out after the long journey and Rego couldn't help admiring the way her sundress clung to her curves.

"I've missed you," he smiled, pulling her into a hug with Maisie still clinging to him.

"You saw them on Friday, Dad," Max added sullenly, walking past them toward the cottage.

Rego grappled his son around the waist and started tickling him.

"Gerroff, Dad!" Max snarled, trying to bat Rego's hands away.

Rego was relentless and soon Max was laughing like the sweet boy he used to be.

Cassie smiled at their antics and when they'd finished, panting and breathless, she pulled an envelope out of her handbag.

"This came for you yesterday. There's no stamp so it must have been hand delivered. It says it's 'urgent' so I think it's from our Neighbourhood Watch team again."

Rego groaned. Ever since the local Neighbourhood Watch where he and Cassie lived had learned that he was a police officer, there had been dozens of requests for help, advice and crimes reported. He'd passed them all over to the Community Officer.

"I'll look at it tomorrow," he sighed, shoving it in the pocket of his jeans.

Max helped his dad unload the car while Cassie and Maisie took a look around the cottage.

"It's good to see you, Maxamillian," Rego grinned.

"It's just *Max*, Dad," said his son, rolling his eyes as Rego knew he would.

"We're going to have a great summer," said Rego.

"In Cornwall?" Max sneered. "Yeah, right."

"Count on it! We've got the beach and the sea, and, um, the beach. How about we hire some surfboards and learn to surf?"

Max showed a flicker of interest which was quickly snuffed out.

"You'll be working anyway," Max muttered, sounding like an older, world-weary version of himself.

Rego tried not to respond to that. He hoped he wasn't going to prove Max right.

"Robert!" Cassie called from the house. "Do you know how much sugar is in those breakfast cereals you bought?"

"Oops," Rego whispered to Max. "I'm in trouble already. Want to come with me and park the car? We can take the long way back."

Max almost smiled.

The family had a loud, fun evening, despite Max trying hard to play it cool. The kids were tired after their journey and hadn't argued (much) over who got which room, seeming happy to go to bed at a reasonable hour proving that miracles do happen. Then Cassie grabbed Rego's hand and took him to bed, reminding him why he loved being married and that he was a lucky bastard.

Despite that, he was awake at 3am, his brain replaying the last 36 hours of the Kuzma case.

Trying not to wake Cassie, he grabbed his jeans and sweater from where he'd tossed them on the floor, and tiptoed downstairs.

He smiled to himself as he surveyed the chaos of the kitchen. God, he'd been lonely without his family.

Filling the kettle and waiting for it to boil, he sat down at the table and heard the crinkling of paper in his back pocket. He pulled out the envelope Cassie had given him and opened it.

Inside was a page torn from a notebook, and one line was written on it:

> *Jah is the gift of existence*

The word 'gift' was underlined, and it was signed 'Bob Marley'.

Rego was wide awake now. What did the note mean? What was the gift? And who the hell signed themselves Bob Marley?

Suddenly, he smiled. He had a strong feeling the note was from Vikram. It made sense that the guy who knew more about cybersecurity than almost anyone on the planet would go old-school and send a handwritten note. Rego would have bet his pension that Vik had used a new notebook and pen, wore forensic gloves when he wrote the message and would never, ever have licked the glue on the envelope.

Vik had known that Cassie was going to Cornwall and that she'd give Rego the letter: hand delivered, untraceable. Rego tore the note into tiny pieces then used his lighter to set fire to them in the grate.

He had no clue what Vikram's 'gift' might be, but he was sure it would have something to do with the Kuzma case.

He finished making his tea and sat at the table, sipping it thoughtfully. He nearly jumped a foot from his chair when someone tapped on the window.

"Rob, open the door!" came a whispered voice.

Rego peered through the window, his heart hammering, and found himself staring at an enormous shadow, a vast bear of a man.

He let out the breath he'd been holding when he recognised a former colleague.

Richard 'Godber' Beckins had left Greater Manchester Police to go into the private security business for himself, and now he was grinning at Rego through the window.

Quietly, praying that he wouldn't wake his family, Rego opened the back door.

"Godber, you nearly gave me a heart attack! How the hell are you?" Rego asked, pumping his friend's arm.

"Knackered. I drove all night to get here. Eh, have you got your mobile on?"

Confused, Rego pointed at his mobile lying on the kitchen table. Godber walked over to it and turned it off.

Then he said, "Happy birthday, mate!"

"What are you talking about? My birthday is in October!"

"Yeah, Halloween, intit? Must be a bit early then, but I've got a gift for you."

Rego's expression cleared as things began to fall into place. He started to speak but then Godber waved him into silence and proceeded to sweep the cottage for bugs, checked Rego's work phone and made sure it was off, then turned on the radio to a low volume.

"Seriously?" Rego said, eyeing him as he finished the sweep.

"Better safe than sorry," Godber shrugged unapologetically.

"So, where's my gift?" Rego asked.

"What makes you think it isn't me?" Godber laughed quietly.

"So, the note *is* from Vik?"

"Who else? He thought it would be a good idea so you didn't shoot me when I knocked on your door in the middle of the night."

"What would I shoot you with? Max's water pistol?"

Godber pulled a face.

"Mate, you don't even have a taser with you?"

"Bloody hell, Godber! Of course I don't. There are rules about the correct storage of tasers. Jesus, you haven't been out of the job that long!"

Godber ignored Rego's rant.

"I take it Vik isn't returning your calls?"

Rego sat back down at the table, suddenly exhausted.

"No, and even Kamla doesn't know where he is."

Godber sat down at the small kitchen table and stretched out his legs, sighing heavily.

"But Vik *has* been in touch with you," Rego pressed.

"Yeah, and he says he's sorry he can't speak to you. They're watching him."

"Shit! You mean people at his work? MI6?"

Godber shrugged.

"He wasn't sure. It was luck that he was able to get a message out to me."

"So, he's told you what this is all about?"

"He's told me some stuff. Mostly, he said you needed your hand holding, ya big girl's blouse."

"Stop being a dickhead for a moment, Godber. I know that doesn't come easy to you. What else has Vik said?"

Godber's smile dimmed as he looked across at Rego.

"Mate, you've got too much of a conscience for this game. You sure you want to play in the mud?"

"A man has been murdered. I just want some answers."

"I want Miss World to give me a private lap dance and ten-million bitcoin, not necessarily in that order," Godber countered.

"A man has gone missing, too. The diver who found the device."

Godber waved a hand dismissively. "I wouldn't worry about him. The spooks are just putting the scare on him so he'll keep his lips zipped. He'll turn up in a couple of days."

"Well, that's something," Rego sighed, relieved that one potential crime had been solved. "But what about the device he found? I don't even know what to do with it now. ACC Gray said everything had to be handed over, but he didn't know about the whatever-it-is, and Vik said only to give it to his courier, but since he's gone dark ... I don't even know what it is."

"Well, hand it over," said Godber. "Let the dog see the rabbit."

Rego opened his messenger bag and Godber's eyes bulged.

"Fuck me!"

"You're not my type."

"Vik was right! Seriously, Rob, you have no idea what this is?"

Rego shook his head.

"Well, I could be wrong ... except I'm not, and neither is Vik ... but I'd say that this is an underwater comms drone. Probably Russian."

CHAPTER 14

Russian spy technology?

Rego felt out of his depth and wished for the hundredth time that he'd never seen the damned thing.

"How do you know it's Russian?"

Godber looked shifty. "I could tell you but then I'd have to kill you."

Rego hoped that he was joking.

"Just give me a broad outline."

"Okay, but you can't repeat this: ever. I've been working for some of Vik's ... competitors across the pond..." he paused.

"Get on with it, Godber!"

"Keep your hair on! The Russians, Chinese and Yanks have all been developing this technology so they can listen in to all those miles and miles of fibre optic cable that have been laid all over the seabed. But it's difficult. Until recently, the technology didn't exist for good underwater communications, remote controlled boats or subs. There were problems with the distances they could travel on one battery and the transmission of data once they were in place. It's improving all the time, so it's becoming a critical part of HM government's defence strategy. And down here, you're in the prime hot spot. You've got *RAF St Mawgan* up the road, *RNAS Culdrose* and Goonhilly Downs to your east, not forgetting the friggin' motherload of Sea-Me-We-3."

" 'See me' what?"

Godber almost chocked with laughter while Rego rubbed his temples. He'd forgotten how cryptic/irritating/arseish the man could be.

"Speak English, Godber!"

"Fine, you muppet! It stands for South-East Asia Middle East Western Europe – the longest optical submarine telecommunications cable in the world."

"The longest in the world? And you think the Russians are listening into that – or trying to?"

"No, I think the Russians are trying to tap into the fibre optic cables that the general public *don't* know about – the cables which send data between us and the Americans, for example. For all we know, the Russkis are trying to hack the launch codes of all those pesky nuclear missiles that our shoulders-to-shoulders in Washington have."

The implications were chilling, and Rego's thoughts flew to his family sleeping upstairs.

"And they're not the only ones. China's policy of state-backed interference that undermines western democracies isn't a new thing, but they're certainly finding more ways to do it. They'd like a slice of what you have sitting on your kitchen table, too. But there are problems with the technology, as I said," Godber continued. "In early 2023, the Ukrainians successfully tested UUVs – uncrewed underwater vehicles – essentially a drone, called the Toloka TLK-150. Pretty nice piece of kit, but at 2.5m long, somewhat noticeable if you're looking for it with metal-detecting equipment. And because it's a big bugger, it uses up a lot of battery power. Since then, they've been testing the free energy reaction of Lithium and water as an energy resource which will give UUVs a much greater useful lifespan." He looked at Rego. "Imagine what the Russians would do to get their hands on that technology."

"Would it look like this?" Rego asked, pointing to the device.

Godber nodded.

"Possibly, but it's a lot smaller than I'd expected, which means HM gov's intel is out of date, something they'd very much like to know." He licked his lips. "The smaller size will make it easier to conceal, and something like this uses a lot less power. Potentially, it could sit on the seabed undisturbed for years listening in to all those digital codes flying around the world. And if they've improved transmission too, it wouldn't even have to surface to transmit." He paused, letting that detail sink in. "Tell me again where it was found?"

"In the wreck of the *Mohegan*, a ship that went down off the coast over a hundred years ago."

"Makes sense. Inside a wreck, it would be protected from currents and marine debris. They probably even thought it was safe from twats in diving clubs, but apparently not."

Rego stared at the device.

"I can see where something has snapped off. Do you think that was the transmitter?"

Godber shrugged. "I've no idea. I'm pretty much tapped out on the theory of UUVs that aren't supposed to exist. But I can't see how this thing runs – there's no propulsion system that I can see. Maybe that's the part that's broken off. I don't know, I'm just guessing." He grinned at Rego. "But there's one way to find out – we could go down to the wreck and take a look. Know any divers?"

Rego immediately thought of Nate Tregowan.

"Yes," he said cautiously. "A guy I met from the Dive and Marine Unit at Plymouth. He recovered the body in the first place."

Godber looked pensive.

"Do you trust him?"

Rego pulled a face.

"He wasn't happy that the case was pulled out from under us. But I don't know him well – although he was so pissed off after the PM, he offered to sound out some of his old dive buddies at Culdrose. I had to tell him negative to that. He wasn't happy – he wants to solve this, too."

Godber nodded.

"We'll shelve his involvement for now, but it could be the reason that MI6 nabbed the diver who found the drone. They'd want to know exactly where he found it."

That gave Rego pause for thought.

"I don't know much about diving but I don't think they'd be able to make Ellis show them because he's just had surgery. Oh, shit!"

"What?"

"Tamsyn – one of our young PCs – she was on the dive with Ellis. They've already broken into her grandparents' garden shed. They were probably after the GoPro that Ellis was wearing. If they can't get him to show them and they don't have the GoPro, they might try and get to her."

"Then we'll have to make sure they don't," said Godber, looking at him speculatively. "That's if you're talking about running a covert op under the noses of HM's security services?"

Rego rubbed his hands over his face, then explained the investigation he'd done on Jameson and the CDR info that he'd requested.

"Man, you're in deep," Godber said slowly. "You've always been by the book, with the odd exception. But this ... why this case, Rob?"

Rego shook his head hoping it would rattle his brain enough to make sense.

"Because it's on my patch; because it's *my* case; because I'm being messed around; because it involves one of my probationers. Take your pick. But the fact is, Vik is worried – and he's never worried. He's told me to hang on in there, so that's what I'm doing."

"Yeah, keep telling yourself that, mate," Godber jeered. "You just can't let it go till you get an answer." He paused. "It just might not be the one you want. And anyway, what will you do with the truth if you get it?"

All good questions. Rego just really wanted to know the truth – and what was on that drone.

He also knew that if it all went wrong, he'd go to jail. It was the biggest risk of his professional career. He didn't owe Jameson anything. Not really. Not at all.

Except...

Maybe he did.

Wasn't helping people the reason he'd become a police officer? Idealistic and naïve as he'd been. Maybe as he still was.

> *I do solemnly and sincerely declare and affirm that I will well and truly serve the Queen in the office of constable, with fairness, integrity, diligence and impartiality, upholding fundamental human rights and according equal respect to all people; and that I will, to the best of my power, cause the peace to be kept and preserved and prevent all offences against people and property; and that while I continue to hold the said office I will to the best of my skill and knowledge discharge all the duties thereof faithfully according to law.*

Of course, that was the old oath that Rego had sworn: it had changed since his days as a raw recruit. There was a King now – something he still couldn't get used to – and the part about 'fundamental human rights' and 'equal respect to all people' having been removed.

And yet ... this was a case of national security, and Rego was considering – had already started – a secret investigation with no official record.

Godber snapped his fingers in front of Rego's face to get his attention.

"I don't know about you, mate, but I really want to know what secrets this baby is hiding," and he ran his hand over the sleek body of the drone. "Maybe you'll decide then if you've got a pair on you."

"Don't tell me you're thinking of…"

"…opening her up, yep. Let's take a shufti."

"No! It's evidence. My career will be fucked ten ways from Sunday if I let you take a screwdriver to an ultra-secret, military-grade, underwater drone."

"Oh, ye of little faith," Godber chuckled. "I don't need a screwdriver; I just need this."

And he held up a small palm-sized black box.

"What the hell is that?"

Godber grinned. "A little gift from a pal."

Then a mobile phone began to ring. Godber pulled it out of his back pocket and handed it to Rego.

"Talk of the devil – it must be for you."

CHAPTER 15

It was one of those shifts where Tamsyn didn't stop. She'd been in her patrol car for less than ten minutes when she was tasked with a run up to a pub fight in Hayle, hitting 70mph on the A30, adrenaline pumping and wishing she'd had her blue-light training so she could go faster, only to get there and find that it had wound down and that the two men who'd been fighting were sitting together at a table, each nursing bruised faces and a pint of Doombar.

"Thanks for coming, officer," said the landlord wearily. "These two were going at it when I called 999. I've made them pay up for the damage to a few glasses and a bar stool."

"What started it?"

He jerked his head at a young woman who was slumped on the floor, too drunk to walk.

"She came in by herself a couple of hours ago and was getting those two idiots to buy her shots. Flirting with both of them, playing them off against each other. I cut her off when I saw how pissed she was; she started getting mouthy, and Sir Galahad over there," he pointed at the man with two black eyes, "he jumped in to help and she clouted him, and his mate got the wrong end of the stick. Couple of wallops and it was all over."

"You said it was an emergency."

He had the grace to look a little sheepish.

"Well, maybe more than a couple of wallops, but little madam over there, she was talking about walking back to her campsite. I was worried she'd get herself run over trying to walk back as drunk as she is."

Tamsyn carried on looking at him, waiting for what he wasn't saying.

"Look," he said at last, his expression tightening. "If I lay a finger on her, she'll be screaming that I touched her up or something – I can't afford that. Even when there's witnesses, your name still gets dragged through the mud. You can't so much as look sideways at a female before you're being accused of all sorts!"

His tone was indignant, almost hurt.

Tamsyn turned her head to the woman who was still motionless on the floor, wishing that the landlord had called a taxi instead of the police. And, to be fair, the two men had both taken a beating. It must have been a nasty fight for a few minutes.

Tamsyn made it clear to the two men that anymore fighting would result in their arrest, and the landlord barred them for a month, although as he obviously knew them, Tamsyn doubted the ban would last that long.

It took several attempts to persuade the drunk woman to get in the back of Tamsyn's patrol car, even with the landlord helping, and even longer to locate the off-grid campsite and unload the woman who, by now, was a dead weight. Tamsyn found her tent, pushed and tugged her into the recovery position and left her with a bottle of water and a request to the irritated site owner to keep an eye on the woman.

The whole thing had taken a quarter of her shift and seemed like a huge waste of resources – and all par for the course.

Then she was called to help Traffic with an RTC between Helston and Penzance, spending several hours in the hot sun, and then an hour before her shift was due to finish at midnight, she got called to a house on the Treneere estate where a man with known mental health problems had started smashing up his own home then progressed to trying to smash streetlamps, and when he couldn't manage that, cars parked in the street. Neighbours had called the police.

The man was also known as an avid collector of martial arts paraphernalia, which included Samurai swords, nunchucks and Shuriken throwing stars.

Control informed Tamsyn that backup was on the way and to stand-by before entering the premises if the man had gone back inside.

She wasn't sure whether or not to hope that was the case. If he was in his own home, he wasn't smashing up his neighbours' property, but then he'd be in a private residence and they'd need a different warrant.

Tamsyn was first on scene, surveying the small crowd of neighbours who had gathered outside as she parked. She could hear a pounding bass, bangs and crashes from inside the property before she even got out of the car.

Every single one of the people standing under the streetlamps looked relieved to see her, and again Tamsyn was struck by the complexity of people's attitudes to the police – even those who disparaged them in public were glad to call them in an emergency.

All the neighbours turned to her, the youngest person there, waiting for her to sort out the problem so they could all go back to bed and get a good night's sleep.

During her four months in the job, she had begun to feel more confident of her abilities to problem-solve, but every day was a challenge.

The man had gone inside, so she took some details from the crowd, finding out the man's name and age while she waited for backup.

"Are you taking him to hospital?" asked a woman in a onesie with panda ears attached to the hood.

"He's gone Bodmin," said another. "Needs the loony bin."

Over the heads of the crowd, Tamsyn saw the flickering blue lights of her backup, turning to greet the officer just arrived on scene, and realised it was Jamie. She stepped away from the crowd to speak to him privately, sharing what she'd learned so far.

"His name is Tom Harris, aged 36 – his neighbours say this happens occasionally, but this is the first time this year, as far as they know."

Jamie nodded, much more pleasant when he wasn't with Chloe.

"I've just been informed that we've got a Section 136,

but that was issued on the information that he was outside. We're supposed to be taking him to Longreach House. If we've got to enter his home, we'll need a 135."

Which meant they had to ask for the new warrant to remove Tom Harris from his home to a place of safety, in this case, a small hospital in Redruth that admitted people with acute psychiatric problems, whether he wanted to go or not.

And that was the tricky part.

Jamie contacted Control to inform them that the man had gone back inside. Louder crashes and thumps started up again, then he appeared in his garden, waving something in his hands, although they couldn't see what it was, but he disappeared inside again.

One of the women who seemed to have been nominated as a spokesperson walked over to where Jamie and Tamsyn were standing.

"Look, you've got to do something. I've got kids who are frightened of him. Last time he was like this, he set his house on fire."

The living room window exploded outwards as he tossed a chair through it, shouting and swearing at the crowd gathered a short distance away. The level of violence was clearly escalating.

Tamsyn blew out a long breath. "Right, let's go and talk to Mr Harris."

"I'll go first," said Jamie.

"No, let me. He might be calmer talking to a woman."

"Are you sure?"

Tamsyn swallowed. *Not really.*

"Let me try," she said, sounding more confident than she felt.

She walked up to the front door and knocked loudly so that she'd be heard over the music thumping through the house.

"Mr Harris, this is the police. Open the door, please."

There was no response, but the crashes seemed to have paused. Tamsyn knocked again.

"Mr Harris, are you okay? This is the police. Open the door."

She pushed the door in case it was open, but it didn't move.

"I'll have a look round the back," said Jamie. "See if the back door is open or if there's a window somewhere."

"Okay, I'll stay here and keep trying to talk to him."

"Tom, my name is Tamsyn," she called loudly. "Your neighbours are worried about you. Will you come out and talk to me? I want to help you."

She heard the sound of breaking glass and a loud scream from the back of the property which made her jump.

Tamsyn took off running, tearing through the back garden full of weeds to the sight of Jamie inside the kitchen grappling with the man who appeared to be holding a sword.

"Code Zero! Code Zero!" she yelled into her police radio, pushing at the backdoor which was now either blocked or locked.

She used her baton to smash a window, clearing the jagged glass so she could climb through.

Jamie had blood running from a cut lip and Tamsyn could see his canister of Captor on the floor.

Tamsyn gripped the handle of her baton as all her training flashed through her mind in less than a second: the areas of the body divided into green, yellow and red target areas: the red areas were a no go unless your life or the life of another was in immediate danger; yellow areas were the joints and should be avoided, if possible, but in a dynamic fight scenario, shit happened.

She took up a stance between Jamie and the offender. Jamie was kneeling up now, but still looked dazed. Tamsyn racked the baton to extend it, resting it on her shoulder and with her other hand stretched out, she created some space between them and Harris. Then she issued the verbal warning.

"Get back!" she said sternly. "Stay back!"

Harris was beyond reason and he lunged towards them. This was the first time Tamsyn had used her baton outside a training room. She didn't hesitate. Aiming for a 'green' area, the major muscle at the top of his left leg, where a full-blown baton strike was really effective, she hit as hard as she could, a single blow that brought the man to the floor, and a few second later, she had him on his stomach, applying restraints to his wrists.

He bucked and thrashed so wildly, he almost tossed her off, but by then Jamie was there, adding his weight and strength until they had him subdued.

By now, the man was howling, an eerie, keening sound that was barely human. It chilled the blood to hear it.

"Are you okay?" she asked Jamie breathlessly.

"Yeah," he said, wiping the blood from his mouth. "Yeah, I'm alright. Thanks, Tamsyn."

She smiled a little shakily, adrenaline still surging through her.

"Poor bugger, eh?" and he nodded at Tom Harris, moaning on the floor.

Jamie might act like a dick when Chloe was around, but he was a good officer, a good man.

It took twenty-five minutes for an ambulance to arrive, and another fifteen minutes until the on-call emergency glazier came to board up the window. Thankfully, D&C Police had a contract that stipulated a glazier or door-repair person would arrive within an hour of being called.

Tamsyn spent the time writing up her notes and wishing she could say goodnight to this shitty, awful day.

But she was worried about having used her baton on a human being. She knew that she'd followed the rules and she knew that she was justified, but still...

Thank God her bodycam would show exactly what had gone down. No one could blame her when they saw the footage.

Thank God she had the next two days off. She planned to do absolutely nothing.

So much for plans.

CHAPTER 16

"Rob, it's Vik."

Vikram's reassuring Brummie accent came clearly through the phone.

"Bloody hell, Vik!" said Rego, his shoulders sagging with relief. "Where the hell have you been?"

"I could tell you but..."

"...then you'd have to kill me, yeah, yeah."

Vikram sighed. "Sorry about all the cloak and dagger stuff, mate, but I can't take chances."

"What the fuck's going on?" Rego asked, his nerves worn paper thin.

"A lot," Vikram answered. "None of it good. Tell me what you know, then tell me what you suspect, and I'll fill in the blanks where I can."

Rego took a moment to put his thoughts in order.

"Twenty-two months ago, a diver by the name of Fedir Kuzma arrives at *RNAS Culdrose* for training with a detachment of Ukrainian Navy. He begins a relationship with Paul Jameson, a Leading Hand in Comms, RFA. No record, apparently as clean as a whistle. Fifteen months ago, Kuzma prepares for a routine dive. He schedules a date with Jameson for that evening but doesn't show, and Jameson never hears from him again. Jameson assumes he's been ghosted. The Ukrainians leave a day later." He paused, making a note. "I need to find the exact date for that."

"Go on," Vikram said quietly.

"Last Autumn, Jameson receives a letter he believes is from Kuzma's sister, asking if he knows what's happened to Kuzma because the Ukrainian Navy are denying all knowledge of him. Jameson asks some discreet questions, but doesn't find out anything. He writes to the sister but there's no further communication. This Friday, PC Tamsyn Poldhu is diving the wreck of SS *Mohegan* with her dive partner Adam Ellis. He recovers an object which I now believe to be an underwater drone, possibly Russian, probably damaged; at the same time, Poldhu sees a body in a drysuit in or near the wreck. The body is recovered, I report the drone to you, and all hell breaks loose: the autopsy is terminated by security service officers, and I'm ordered to stand down and hand over all digital and physical records by my ACC; the Dive Supervisor from the Underwater Search Unit at Plymouth tells me in confidence that before all evidence was removed from his lab by the spooks, he had discovered that Kuzma's dive watch and cylinders had been tampered with by person or persons unknown, which makes it murder. My PC's garden shed is broken into whereby Ellis' dive equipment is stolen; Ellis is removed from hospital by men who claim to be police but are not. Then Godber knocks on my door in the middle of the night to make my life complete. How am I doing?"

"The Dive Supervisor is Nathan Tregowan, right?"

"Yes, what about him?"

"Do you trust him?" Vikram asked seriously.

"Godber just asked me that and I'll tell him what I told you: I met him for the first time at the *post-mortem*," said Rego, his frustration evident. "He seems like a standup guy, but I don't know him, so you tell me."

There was a short pause.

"I hope so," said Vikram, "because we're going to need him."

"For what?" Godber asked, and Rego threw him a disbelieving look.

"I need intel on the Ukrainian dive team, and that's going to have to come from someone who knows about diving. Talk to Tregowan. See who he knows on the dive teams at Culdrose – maybe they'd be up for a little off-the-record chat."

Rego sucked in a breath.

"Vik, what the fuck? Asking a junior officer to have an 'off-the-record chat' with members of the Royal Navy dive team at a military installation that seems to be protecting a lot of secrets? There's no way I can ask Tregowan to do it. This is way over my head. I've been *ordered* to stand down."

"Yeah, but you didn't, did you? You still met with Jameson. And I know why – because you've got a bad case of having a conscience. Some bloke gets himself murdered and you want to find the person who did it."

"What's wrong with that?" Rego asked defensively.

"Mate, really?" said Vikram in disbelief. "You see things in terms of right and wrong, but that's not the way the real world works. Your ACC was ordered to stop your investigation by people a lot higher up than either you or me. Of course, the poor bugger doesn't know what a stubborn bastard you are. You're not stupid, Rob; I'm sure you can think of a few reasons why people didn't want that body identified."

"You're saying he was killed ... assassinated ... by our government?"

"No, of course I'm not saying that," Vikram sighed. "Frankly, we don't know how he died, but we'd like to know *who* he is."

"Fedir Kuzma, Ukrainian national."

Vikram paused. "Possibly. Possibly not."

"I saw the tattoos on the deceased and I compared them to photographs I saw of Kuzma. They looked identical to me."

"Tattoos can be faked," Vikram said dismissively. "But you're missing the point, Rob. The victim and the photographs you saw are probably the same person: but we don't know *who* he is."

Rego couldn't believe what he was hearing.

"Vik, you're telling me that a man who was part of an elite Ukrainian dive team, with access to cutting edge comms technology, who was invited to train with who knows which SBS hotshots at *Royal Naval Air Station Culdrose*, a facility that protects worldwide fibre optic underwater cables, you're telling me *we don't know who he is?*"

"Yeah," said Vikram. "That's what I'm telling you."

"So, fella-me-lad was a spy," said Godber, nodding. "That makes sense."

"Not to me!" Rego said angrily. "Why was my investigation closed down then? Surely, what you've told me is all the more reason to find out what happened to Kuzma or whoever he is?"

"I do want to know what happened to him," said Vikram seriously. "But it must *not* go through official channels. For reasons that I can't go into, I need you to see what you can find out, but discreetly. Talk to Jameson again – do some more digging into his background. Find out who he's been talking to. Get the letter Kuzma's sister is supposed to have sent, or at least get her address. Keep it low key; don't go in all guns blazing."

"Low key?" Rego said in amazement. "Vik, you're talking about an unauthorised covert op on a case of national security involving Russian underwater drones, a technology that's not supposed to exist – all off the books, against direct orders, which could result in the very real possibility of ending my career at best, and at worst, spending a very long time in prison, which would seriously piss off my wife."

"Yep," Vikram agreed. "Would it help if I said your country needs you?"

"It might," Rego grimaced. "But I'm going to need to know why."

Vikram paused, as if choosing his words carefully.

"Tregowan said he'd found evidence that Kuzma's dive computer and scuba tanks had been tampered with. I believe he was right."

"You *believe* or you *know*?" Rego asked sharply.

"Tregowan has ... had ... the evidence," Vikram answered, "but his findings align with a certain scenario that I've been tracking."

His answer was deliberately vague, and Rego could sense his old friend tiptoeing across a minefield of the black arts that made up modern espionage.

"Okay, I'm following you," said Rego, "but what I don't understand is why this is all being done covertly? Why not bring the full resources of the spook squad down to find the rest of the drone or whatever it is you're really looking for?"

"Because I trust *you*, Rob," Vikram said quietly. "And I trust Godber."

His voice fell silent.

"And you don't trust the people you work with?" Rego asked with concern.

Vikram didn't reply, which was enough of an answer.

"I know I'm asking a lot, Rob, and I wish I didn't have to. I wish I could tell you everything, but it's too risky – you're better off not knowing too much: plausible deniability and all that."

"Is this all coming from you?" Rego asked. "Or is someone else pulling your strings?"

Vikram didn't reply immediately.

"Let's just say I'm not completely winging it."

"So, there's a chain of command?" Rego pressed.

"In a way," Vikram hedged, and Rego sensed that he wouldn't get any more out of his friend.

He looked at Godber who grinned and shrugged his shoulders.

"You in?"

Godber gave a lopsided grin with a thumb's up, and Rego sighed.

"Look, Vik, I'm just a boots-on-the-ground copper. All this cloak and dagger stuff is above my pay grade, but if you want my help, I'll do it. Just promise me that you've got my back, yeah? If the shit hits the fan, I have to know that you'll protect Cassie and the kids."

"You got it. Thanks, Rob."

Rego could hear the relief in his friend's voice.

"Okay, so big picture," Vikram continued. "The Cabinet Office has updated the national risk register to help the general public prepare for 'worst-case scenarios' that could strike the UK. One of the threats I'm tasked with looking at is the malicious use of drones to disrupt undersea transatlantic communications cables. You've got a lot of those off the Cornish coast near you, Rob. Your dead diver was part of a Ukrainian team that was trying to recover Russian underwater listening equipment. When he went missing, it was a big stink that was hushed up our end, and the Ukrainians were sent home fast. HM government was concerned that their mission had been compromised, perhaps even infiltrated by unfriendly powers. Nothing was ever proven, but it left a bad taste and cooled relations for a time.

"The drone that was recovered is the first piece of proof that we were right to be suspicious; the dead diver is the second; and what Tregowan found on the dive equipment backs that up."

"What does the GoPro footage show?" Godber asked.

"It shows Ellis picking up the drone," Vikram replied.

"Is he involved?" Rego asked.

"No, we don't think so."

"So, you do have him. Is he going to be released? Because the mother has been blowing up my phone with emails and messages, and she's threatening to go to the papers."

"We're aware of the mother," said Vikram. "She'd already approached *Spotlight Southwest*, but they've had a D-notice slapped on them, and she's been told to keep quiet and her son will be returned to her in due course."

Which confirmed what Godber had told Rego.

"And from now on," said Vikram, "when you talk to me, use this phone. Turn yours off first – I don't want anyone listening in."

"Bloody hell! Is my phone being tapped?" Rego asked in disbelief and annoyance.

"Of course not," Vikram said with a cynical laugh. "Because that has to be authorised by the Chief Constable and Home Secretary. And anything you or Godber found would be non-evidential and hasn't been through the RIPA process: that would be breaching human rights by conducting surveillance."

"Your halo is slipping, mate," Godber said drily.

"Security services are a law unto themselves," Vikram replied. "Let's just say it's been eye-opening." His voice became serious. "I'm just being careful. I don't know if anyone is listening in, but I can't take that risk."

Rego and Godber exchanged a look. Neither of them was happy about this turn of events.

"Godber," Vikram said, "set up the decoder – I want to know everything that drone can tell us."

Rego watched while Godber used the small square

device to digitally unlock the drone and start streaming data to Vikram.

"Be careful, Godber!" Vikram said testily. "This is sensitive equipment!"

"Then I'll try not to hurt its feelings," Godber said easily.

Vikram didn't laugh.

"I don't know how long it'll take me to decrypt this," he said. "But first thing in the morning, I want you to hand over the drone and GoPro to an officer they're sending from Vauxhall Cross. Make sure your paperwork is squeaky clean."

"Okay," Rego said. "And I'll do it with witnesses. One question..."

"Go ahead."

"Why did your lot break into Tamsyn's garden shed when you knew that she'd given me the drone and GoPro?"

"I'm sorry about that, but it was a test," Vikram said, his voice hardening.

"What sort of test? Don't tell me you suspect her?"

"Not her, no," said Vikram cryptically.

"Then who?"

"I can't tell you that, Rob, I really can't. I *can* tell you that it wasn't us that broke into PC Poldhu's shed."

"Is Tamsyn in danger?" Rego asked abruptly.

"I don't know," Vikram admitted.

His words chilled Rego to the core.

Because if it wasn't MI6 attempting to recover the drone from Tamsyn's shed, then it was someone who had intercepted the information.

Which meant that MI6 had a mole.

CHAPTER 17

Tamsyn had been looking forward to two days off but her grandmother woke her with a mug of tea at 11am, just two short hours after she'd fallen into bed after her nightshift.

"Gran! I'm off today and tomorrow," she mumbled, throwing her duvet over her head. "I've only just gone to bed."

"I know, angel, but your Mr Rego telephoned first thing. He wants you and Ozzie to take him and his kids out on the *Daniel Day*."

Reluctantly, Tamsyn rubbed her eyes and sat up.

"Today? He wants to do that today?"

Her gran placed the mug of tea on the small bedside table next to Tamsyn and turned the handle towards her.

"You meet them at Newlyn in an hour. Ozzie's already over there," she said cheerfully.

Tamsyn groaned and flopped backwards just as Mo scampered up the stairs and jumped on the bed next to her.

"Rise and shine!" Tamsyn's grandmother called over her shoulder.

Tamsyn swore softly, but Mo just gave a doggy grin. She would never share their secrets.

Twenty minutes later, Tamsyn was showered and dressed in shorts, wet hair dampening her t-shirt.

She was a little bit nervous, too. Meeting her DI's family was a blurring of the lines between work and home, and even though she and her grandfather had been the ones to suggest it, she wasn't quite sure how to feel about it now.

But she didn't have time to overthink it either, because after a quick breakfast, her grandmother was pushing her out the door with two enormous insulated cool boxes filled with sandwiches, Hevva cake, splits with golden syrup and a tub of Rodda's clotted cream to make thunder and lightning for dessert.

She loaded it all in the boot of her battered old Fiat, then refilled a gallon can with water from the outdoor tap.

Mo jumped into the passenger seat, watching her expectantly. Tamsyn didn't have the heart to leave her behind, but since Mo's unscheduled and death-defying mile-long swim in choppy seas earlier in the year, it made her anxious to let the little dog on board. So, Tamsyn had compromised by buying her a Jack Russell-sized life jacket with a loop on the top to make it easy to pull her out of the water.

Tamsyn's own life jacket was stored on the *Daniel Day*.

As she pulled away from the kerb, she saw Miss Nellie's curtain twitch and she raised her hand in a wave. It reminded her of the weird things that had been happening since the discovery of the body and the *thing*. But her grandmother and Miss Nellie weren't involved and didn't know anything. They'd be safe. She hoped.

Six months ago, she would have scoffed at the idea that they had anything to worry about, living peacefully in the centre of a small, unimportant village. She knew better now. She knew that bad things happened in beautiful places; she knew that bad people had no boundaries.

When she arrived at the harbour, she borrowed a small fish trolley and loaded the cool boxes and water onto it, listening to the familiar rumble as she pulled it along the pier towards where the punts, the smaller fishing boats, were moored, the rubber wheels clattering over the wooden boards.

Mo trotted ahead, which meant that Tamsyn was the last to arrive.

Rego was there, more casually dressed than she was used to, and looking a lot younger in trainers, shorts, and a t-shirt with a picture of Bob Marley. He had a long scar running across his left bicep that looked like a knife wound – not recent but not old either. Tamsyn wondered if he'd got it from working in the job.

His wife was tall and slim, her hair cropped close to her head and huge sunglasses hiding her expression. She wore a white cotton jumper and white shorts that showed off her flawless mahogany skin. Despite its simplicity, her look was put-together and effortlessly chic. Tamsyn felt like a country bumpkin next to her.

Rego's two children were talking to Tamsyn's grandfather, and Tamsyn heard the little girl giggle and the boy laugh out loud.

Tamsyn smiled to herself. Her grandfather was

famously grumpy, but something about children brought out the sunny side he preferred to hide.

"Hello, Tamsyn," said Rego, appearing relaxed. "Thanks for coming out with us on your day off. This is Cassie, my wife; Cassie, PC Tamsyn Poldhu."

"It's lovely to meet you, Tamsyn," said Cassie, extending her hand and smiling warmly. "It's very kind of you and your grandfather to take us out on your boat. We're all looking forward to it."

Tamsyn's eyes cut to Rego who was looking dubiously at the small fishing boat.

Cassie's grin widened. "Well, most of us."

The two women shared a conspiratorial smile.

"Max, Maisie, come and meet Mr Poldhu's granddaughter. She works with your dad."

The girl, who looked about seven or eight, came skipping over, her cloud of dark hair dancing in the breeze.

"You're pretty," she said shyly, then looked at Mo. "I like your dog."

"Thank you!" Tamsyn smiled. "Mo likes you, too. And I love your hair."

Thrilled, the girl tugged a ringlet self-consciously.

"Morwenna," Tamsyn called. "Come say hi. Her name is Morwenna, but she answers to Mo."

"She answers to jes' 'bout anything at supper time," said Ozzie gruffly.

They all laughed but it was true. And anyway, the gruffness was all an act – he loved the little dog almost as much as he loved Tamsyn.

"And this handsome young man is Max," said Rego's wife, tugging on her son's short dreadlocks.

"Mu-um!" he croaked, in the squeaky man-child voice of an adolescent.

"Hi, Max," Tamsyn said easily. "Could you help me bring the food and water aboard?"

Tamsyn was used to surly teens and pre-teens – she'd spent several summers teaching surfing and life-guarding beaches in West Cornwall; she knew how to get him engaged and interested in what they were doing. Giving him a job helped Max to relax with her, and they loaded up the small boat quickly, Tamsyn instructing him where to stow the picnic. Then she handed out life jackets to all the Rego family, slipping on her own as everyone took their places on the narrow bench seats.

Ozzie sat at the back with the outboard motor, one hand on the tiller. The children sat up front, their faded orange life jackets huge on their skinny bodies. Cassie and Rego sat in the middle, while Tamsyn untied the lines and jumped nimbly into the boat.

She smiled to herself as she saw Rego hanging onto the side, his knuckles white, his usually olive brown skin tinged with green.

"Rob, you can't be feeling sick already," his wife teased.

"I'm fine," he said, thin-lipped and severe.

"It helps to look at the horizon, sir," said Tamsyn.

Cassie gave her a warm smile. "It's your day off – I'm sure he won't mind if you call him Rob, will you?" she said, raising her eyebrows at her husband.

Rego was feeling too queasy to care what they called him, but he did need to speak to Tamsyn.

"Can we go out to the Lizard?" he asked.

She looked surprised. "The water's a bit choppier over

there – there's better fishing in the coves near here." Then she saw the serious expression on his face and correctly interpreted what he wasn't saying.

"You want to go near the *Mohegan*?"

He nodded, unable to speak without losing his breakfast.

She shook her head. "It's too far, sir— Rob. The *Daniel Day* has a top speed of 20 knots – more like 15 on a day like today."

"How fast is that in miles per hour?"

"About 17 mph."

"Can't we go any faster?" he grimaced, feeling his stomach lurch towards his throat.

Tamsyn shook her head. "Fifteen knots is a good cruise for us. We'll have three-foot seas going around the Point anyway, so any faster and you'll feel like you're on a rollercoaster." She paused. "It'll take us a couple of hours to get there. Probably more."

Rego didn't think he'd last two minutes, let alone two hours, but he gritted his teeth and tried to smile. He failed.

"Can we head in that direction?"

She crouched down next to her grandfather, lowering her voice so no one else would hear her over the outboard motor.

His thick, white eyebrows pulled together in a scowl, but he changed direction, heading further south and east towards the Lizard, mainland Britian's most southerly point.

As the little boat crossed the chop of Mount's Bay, Rego vomited over the side of the boat.

Maisie shrieked, and Max yelled, "Awesome!"

Cassie rubbed her husband's back, her expression one of weary tolerance.

Tamsyn tried not to smile and her grandfather shook his head in disgust at such a lightweight landlubber.

Deciding to try and entertain the kids instead of watching their dad lose his breakfast, she climbed over the bench seats to the front of the small boat, pointing out the local wildlife to the children, and Max was so interested that he forgot to be cool.

"See those birds? The ones that look like arrows? They're swifts – they're eating insects while they're flying. They spend most of their lives in the air and only land to nest."

She pointed out shoals of pilchards and a school of jellyfish drifting through the water.

"These can sting a bit," she said, "but it's just like a nettle sting, and they don't want to hurt you. They're gentle creatures. These ones are Barrel jellyfish, and they'll move away from you if they sense swimmers in the water."

But nothing could beat their excitement when they saw a small pod of dolphins heading west, leaping out of the sea, droplets of water catching the light as they performed their amazing acrobatic routine. Morwenna barked enthusiastically, certain she'd chased them away.

Even Rego managed to look slightly enthusiastic and Tamsyn gave him a bright smile, the kind of smile that caught his wife's attention.

As they passed Gunwalloe, Tamsyn told them all about the night the King of Portugal's ship *St Anthony* was wrecked at that very spot, some five hundred years ago, and the treasures of silver and gold that went down with many of the crew.

"That is so cool!" Max said, staring at Tamsyn with hero worship in his eyes. "I can't believe you've dived all these shipwrecks."

"Only one so far," said Tamsyn, "and that's on the other side of Lizard Point."

"Lizards!" Maisie squealed. "Yuk!"

"You're such a *girl*," Max said scathingly.

"There aren't any lizards," Tamsyn said before another fight broke out. "Well, there are sand lizards, but they're really rare. I meant, that's not why it's named 'the Lizard'."

"That's just dumb," Max scowled, earning a look from his mother.

"Actually, there are two really cool reasons how it might have got the name," Tamsyn continued, raising her eyebrows at Max. "The cliffs there are made out of a special kind of granite called Serpentine – it's been bent and folded so many times over millions of years, that it looks like a snake."

"Pretty cool, right, Max," said Rego, smiling around another urge to throw up.

Max just shrugged.

"What's the other reason?" Cassie asked.

"They think it might be a corruption of old Cornish words '*Lys Ardh*', meaning 'high court'. They think it might have been where a king lived once, someone like King Arthur."

This time, Max looked marginally more interested.

"It's also mainland Britain's most southerly point and is surrounded by razor-sharp rocks – you could say it protects us from everywhere else in the world. But it's also why there are so many wrecks around here."

"I'd dive every day if I could!" said Max.

"It's fun," Tamsyn said, nodding her agreement, "but it's really expensive, too. And I don't always have time because I have to work."

"Oh yeah," said Max, his face falling. "The police."

"You don't want to join the police when you're older?" she asked, wondering if she was straying into dangerous territory.

But it was Maisie who answered.

"No, because Dad never comes home anymore. Mum says that the police don't let him have a life and that she feels like a single mum."

The little girl's voice was matter-of-fact and Tamsyn was silent, glancing across at the Regos who both looked stricken.

She changed the subject and showed the kids a couple of so-called pirate caves.

Rego threw up twice more before they reached the site of the *Mohegan*, but after that, amazingly, he started to feel better. Not well enough to sample some of Mrs Poldhu's fabulous food, but enough to sip on the slightly plasticky-tasting cup of water that Tamsyn gave him.

Ozzie cut the engine and let Max throw the anchor overboard, then he chatted amiably to Max, explaining about the tides and the moon, neap tides and grounder seas, while Tamsyn told Maisie all about the Cornish delicacy of splits – buns that were a little like brioches – with thunder and lightning (clotted cream and golden syrup). Morwenna begged shamelessly from Maisie and Max, as if she already sensed that they'd be soft touches, then hoovered up the crumbs and lay curled up on a coil of ropes.

Then they all washed their sticky hands in the sea and turned their faces to the sun.

Max was keen to try fishing and Rego thought it was the kind of father—son bonding thing that he ought to do. Tamsyn baited two fishing rods for them and one for herself, as Ozzie puttered the *Daniel Day* slowly across the bay.

"There's mackerel in the millions come the summer," he said, blue eyes squinting against the bright sun sparkling on the water. "Bait balls the size of your 'ouse. Pollack like the rusted old ribs of shipwrecks."

"Are we near the *Mohegan?*" Rego asked.

"What's that?" Cassie said, opening her eyes.

"A steamship that went down in 1898," said Tamsyn, glancing at Rego. "My first wreck dive."

"An a big ole eel down there, so big he could swallow your leg without blinking," Ozzie said to Max.

Cassie laughed, but Tamsyn knew that her grandfather wasn't exaggerating by much.

She put her own rod aside to help Max who soon caught his first fish, a mackerel with a silvery belly and mottled green back.

Maisie wasn't keen to see the fish die, but Ozzie explained that's where her fish fingers came from, and that the oily fish was good for you.

She didn't look convinced, so after a short discussion, the hapless fish was tossed back into the sea.

Ozzie muttered into his beard about "the snowflake generation".

Then something caught Tamsyn's attention, a flash of light in the distance, and she straightened her back, shielding her eyes from the sun.

"Dunno who they are," said Ozzie quietly, "but they've been watching us almost since we got here."

Tamsyn realised that the flash of light had been from a pair of binoculars catching the sunlight.

"They don't look Navy," said Ozzie. "This summat to do with that dead diver you found?"

"I don't know, Grandad," Tamsyn said, unease slithering in her stomach, "but I think we should head back now."

Ozzie helped Max weigh anchor, and Tamsyn took the opportunity to tell Rego in a low voice of her suspicion that they were being watched. His eyes grew tight as he glanced at his children, but he didn't say anything more.

As they headed back, Tamsyn kept one eye on the small RIB that followed them until they were west of the Lizard, when it turned abruptly and disappeared into the distance.

Rego was only sick once on the way back, so they all took that as a win.

But he was furious at himself for taking his family to the wreck site and potentially putting them in danger. Whoever had been watching them, they'd followed them far enough to make sure that they left the area. Rego didn't believe it was a coincidence.

It had seemed like a good idea when he'd discussed it with Vikram and Godber: check the place out, keep it casual, but now he thought very differently. Whoever was watching now knew that he had his family with him. And that made him vulnerable.

Not only that, it had been a miserable experience, and his stomach was still protesting even though they were back on land.

Ozzie was showing Max and Maisie how to tie off the boat, and Tamsyn was unloading the empty cooler boxes.

"Thanks for today, Tamsyn," Rego said, surprising her with a quick hug.

A jolt of attraction made her stiff and awkward.

"You're welcome, sir." She gave a quick smile. "I can't get used to calling you 'Rob'."

"Well, I'll be in touch about work but we're not there now," he grinned. "Right, I'm going to go and lie to your grandfather about how much I enjoyed being on his boat."

Tamsyn laughed out loud as he walked over to speak to Ozzie who listened, nodded, accepted his thanks, and the two men shook hands.

Max and Maisie didn't need to be told to say their thanks, too, which was heartfelt.

"I really liked the dolphins," Maisie said.

"Yeah, they were awesome!" Max added. "But the best part was seeing Dad puke his guts up."

"Hey!" Rego yelped, as they all laughed. "I'm getting better. I only puked once on the way back."

The family waved goodbye to Tamsyn and Ozzie, leaving them to tidy the boat, clean and stow the equipment, as the family walked away along the pier.

Rego felt Cassie's warm hand on his back and caught the scent of her perfume as she leaned in closer to him.

"Have a good day, luv?" he asked.

"The kids loved it," she said with a smile. "Max definitely loved seeing his dad chuck up his breakfast for five hours nonstop."

Rego groaned.

"Ah, come on! I wasn't that bad." Then he glanced at Tamsyn who was still watching them. "I'm glad you got along with her – she's a nice girl; she'll make a good copper one day."

"A good copper? Really?"

"Yeah, sure," he said, confused by his wife's tone.

"For goodness' sake, Rob!" his wife said, her tone exasperated.

"What?"

Cassie shook her head. "For a smart man you can be really stupid."

"What are you talking about?"

"Can't you see that Tamsyn has a huge crush on you?"

Rego was appalled. And slightly flattered – he was only human.

"No, she doesn't," he said quickly.

"She really does. Even her grandfather sees it – that's why he doesn't like you." Cassie paused, considering. "Of course, I wouldn't blame you for fancying her; she's young and beautiful so I can see why you might be attracted to her, too

"I don't!" he yelped, sounding like he'd just been stung. "I'm not!"

"I'm glad to hear it, because I'd remove your balls with a rusty spoon."

"I thought you said you wouldn't blame me."

She gave him a look that said, *Don't push it if you want to keep both balls attached.*

"I'm serious, Rob. She has some real hero worship going on. Don't get me wrong, I like her, but you have to be careful."

His wife's comments left Rego uneasy. He hadn't picked up any vibes from Tamsyn, but he knew that victims latched onto their perceived saviours and could quickly get caught up in a spiral of attraction that wouldn't otherwise be there if not for the circumstances – and he had saved her life a few months back.

He glanced behind him and saw that Tamsyn was still watching him. She gave a bright smile which he returned cautiously, and vowed to be very, very careful. The wrong signals to an infatuated junior officer had ruined too many marriages and more than one career.

He turned his head to look at his wife and she raised her eyebrows, as if saying, *See? I told you so.*

"Rob," Cassie said quietly, "when you do say something to her, be kind."

Rego was glad his wife had pointed out to him the huge pit that he'd been marching towards completely oblivious, but the timing was shit. He knew that he needed to distance himself from Tamsyn to avoid any potential problems, but at the same time, he needed her help and expertise on the Kuzma case – and he was going to have to lie to her about it and put her career in jeopardy as well as his own.

First thing that morning, he'd gone to the station and signed over the device and GoPro to security service agents. They'd watched over him as the digital files had been locked and sent to a secure server before they left.

Officially, he was off the case; unofficially, he was running an off-the-books covert op that meant he had to behave as normally as possible. And what could be more normal than a man taking time off to be with his family on their summer holiday.

God, Cassie was going to kill him if she found out what he was doing. He hated not being able to tell her, but it was safer that she didn't know. He hoped that she never knew.

Rego had many faults – his wife reminded him of them daily – but his dedication to the job was never questioned.

That evening, he took his family to supper at *Mackerel Sky* in Newlyn, where Maisie refused to eat the mackerel or any other kind of fish – awkward, considering it was a seafood bar. At least she ate the chips.

Back at the cottage, with Maisie sleeping and Max playing a computer game on his laptop upstairs, Cassie opened a bottle of wine and handed him a glass.

"Are you going to tell me what's really going on?"

Rego looked up guiltily.

"What?"

"Come on, Rob," she sighed.

He grimaced.

"I can't," he said quietly.

"So," she said slowly, "this is about the job?"

"As always," he sighed.

"Anything you *can* tell me?"

Rego thought for a moment. "You might see Godber knocking about."

"Oh no!" she half-laughed, half-groaned. "I thought he'd left the police?"

"He's ... consulting," Rego said vaguely.

Cassie shook her head.

"Well, I'm going to bed and I'm taking the wine with me. Are you coming up?"

"In a minute," he said.

"Promise?"

"Promise."

Tamsyn was dragging by the time she and her grandfather arrived home at the cottage. Operating all day on just a couple of hours sleep, she was shattered.

Her grandfather didn't seem tired – he seemed as immutable as the granite walls of their cottage, and he'd clearly enjoyed being with Max and Maisie. It made Tamsyn wish for things that she had no business wishing for.

Too tired for self-reflection, she hit the shower then sat on her bed drying her hair, smiling as she heard her grandmother's strident disbelief that they'd returned home without any fish.

Jess FaceTimed her just as she was crawling into bed.

"Hey, you! You look rough. What are you up to? How did the date with hot DI go?"

Tamsyn rolled her eyes.

"It wasn't a date, you wench! His wife and kids were there."

"I know, but it's fun to wind you up. So, what were they like?"

"The kids are great, really nice. Max is twelve, and he was trying so hard to be cool – it was cute. I showed him how to bait a rod and he picked it up really quickly. And Maisie is eight going on eighteen – she promised to give me a makeup tutorial while she's down here."

Jess laughed.

"She's right – your makeup sucks. Mostly because you hardly ever wear it anymore since you started with the police."

"I don't have the time ... and I don't want to be mistaken for a stripper."

"What? What are you talking about?"

"Nothing, it's a joke."

"I wonder about you sometimes.".

"I wonder about me, too."

"Well, get to the good stuff: what's his wife like?"

"I really liked her," Tamsyn sighed. "She's gorgeous, like a model, great with the kids, great with Rob."

"'Rob', is it now?" Jess said, raising a pencilled eyebrow.

"He told me to call him that when we're off duty," Tamsyn said defensively.

"Hmm."

"What does that mean?" Tamsyn asked, then wished she hadn't.

"It means you're crushing on your boss big-time," Jess said accusingly.

"Oh God, no way! He's, like, *old*."

"Yeah, tell it to someone who believes you. He's *hot*."

"And married. And I really liked Cassie."

Jess sighed. "Sucks to be you."

"Anyway," Tamsyn grimaced, "he was seasick all day – I lost count of the number of times he threw up. He's a terrible sailor – it would never work."

"True dat," Jess laughed. "The guy you end up with would have to be half fish."

"That's gross! Look, I've got to get some sleep, I'm absolutely knackered."

"Yeah, okay. Tam?"

"Yeah?"

"I don't know how you do it, day in, day out, seeing people at their worst."

Tamsyn was surprised by Jess's serious tone.

"It's not really like that, not always. I *am* seeing people at their most vulnerable but most people are good; only 1% are bad."

"You really believe that?"

"Yes, I do."

Jess smiled crookedly. "Of course you do, ya big softie."

"Softie?"

"Better than ho-bag," Jess laughed.

"Yeah, yeah, whatever."

"Alright, talk soon. Love you!"

"Love you, too."

Tamsyn fell into a deep sleep with Morwenna curled up at her feet.

CHAPTER 18

On Tuesday morning, Rego left Cassie and the kids sleeping, and drove the 80 miles to Plymouth to talk to Nate Tregowan face to face. He needed to see the man when he asked for his help. He found him at Sutton Harbour running a training exercise for the next fleet of police divers, equipping them with the skills they'd need to combat maritime crime.

High-tech equipment was stacked on cobbled streets that lined the harbourside, framed by some 200 listed buildings, including the Plymouth Gin Distillery, housed in a former monastery which dated back to the 15th century, and the Mayflower Steps where the Pilgrim Fathers set sail for the New World in 1620.

Rego watched for a moment as pairs of divers practised finding small items such as mobile phones in the murky water.

Tregowan saw him from a distance, nodded, then within a few minutes had worked his way across to Rego.

His steps would look slow and casual to onlookers, but Rego could see the tension in the man's body.

"I'm surprised to see you here, sir," Tregowan began formally.

"Not as surprised as I am, Nate," Rego admitted. He looked around at the historic buildings, attracting tourists in numbers. "Seems like an unusual place for a training session."

"The harbour has protective double-lock gates that guarantee depth of water at all stages of the tide, as well as shelter from extreme weather." Tregowan met his eyes. "I take it you're not here to find out about my training methods, sir."

"Nate, I need your help – but I have no right to ask for it. All I can say, is please hear me out before you make a decision."

Tregowan raised his eyebrows. "I'm listening."

Rego explained as much as he could, leaving out Vikram's name and any reference to Godber, ending with their belief that the device was a drone used to listen to encrypted underwater cable intel.

"I'm aware that I'm asking you to ignore a direct order from ACC Gray to cease investigations, and I'm aware it's wrong on so many levels," Rego paused, "but I wouldn't ask if I didn't think it was a case of national security."

Tregowan had been watching Rego intently, but now he turned and stared out to sea.

"Your friend, the one who sent you to talk to me, do you trust him?"

"With my life," Rego said honestly.

"And this friend of yours, he doesn't want to trust the senior ranks of Devon & Cornwall Police?"

"As far as I'm aware, he doesn't trust anyone."

"Except you," Tregowan stated.

Rego shrugged. "He's told me as much as he can, but even I don't know everything. He says he needs my help, and I need *your* help. Nate, you can walk away, no hard feelings. I have no authority here: none. You don't know me and I'm asking you to trust me with your career, if it all goes to shit."

"No, you don't know me, but you're trusting me with all this secret squirrel stuff."

Rego acknowledged the truth of his words.

"I've got to start somewhere ... and I need someone with dive knowledge." He met Tregowan's gaze. "And I know you weren't happy with what happened at the *post-mortem*."

Tregowan sucked his teeth.

"I'll be honest with you, Inspector, it sounds so far-fetched, it pretty much has to be real, but I need to think about it."

"Okay. I'd like to say take as much time as you want, but I don't think time is on our side."

"What exactly do you want me to do?"

"You told me that you know some of the divers at Culdrose? And when we were at the PM, you offered to have an informal chat with them. That's all I'm asking you to do. Just talk to them, talk their language, find out what they heard, thought or guessed about the body you found. What did the rumour-mill come up with? I'd imagine that they'll already be gossiping about the body being found, so start there. Did anything seem strange about the Ukrainian dive team? Was their equipment different in ways that seemed incompatible with what they were doing? What was the general feeling about why the Ukrainians left so quickly."

"Ukrainians?" Tregowan interrupted, his eyebrows shooting up. "You think ... that's where you think the body comes from, isn't it? The combat dive team that visited two years ago."

Rego drew in a long breath.

"I'm just asking you to find out what the chat is, that's all."

Tregowan was silent, appearing to study the request from all angles. Finally, he nodded slowly.

"Okay, I'll do it. It's time I met up with some of my old dive buddies anyway."

Rego drove back down the A30 deep in thought. He was beyond relieved that Tregowan had agreed to help. But that was only one step in an increasingly complex dance.

He was loath to involve more people because every time he did that, the chance of a leak increased exponentially. The next step could make or break the case.

And he needed an update from Vikram.

But as he headed home, he was determined to be the other Rob Rego again – husband and father. And he managed for several hours while they visited Flambards amusement park, but that evening, as soon as the kids were upstairs, his mind was on the case.

"What the hell is going on with you?" Cassie asked in exasperation. "You're acting like you don't want us here."

"No, that's not it," he sighed. "This case is kicking my

arse and I can't, *can't* let it sit – I have to deal with it now. Godber is on his way over."

Cassie looked at him, sadness reflected in her beautiful eyes.

"There's always going to be a case," she said. "If not this one, then another. The kids are growing up so fast, I worry that you're going to miss it."

Rego wrapped his arms around her and pulled her in close.

"I'm sorry. I have to do this."

"I know," she said, pushing away and giving him a small smile as she walked up the cottage's tapering staircase. "Tell Godber I said hi."

Less than a minute later, Rego heard a soft tap on the back door.

"Am I interrupting?" Godber asked, peering inside.

"Yes, but it's not your fault," Rego sighed.

"Missus giving you an earful?"

Rego nodded. "Not that I blame her."

Godber patted him on the shoulder awkwardly.

"Cassie's a good girl. She'll be alright."

Rego hoped he was right.

Then his burner phone lit up with a video call from Vikram. Rego didn't bother to say hello.

"Have you retrieved any useful data so far?"

Vikram was in a darkened room and he looked exhausted, his manner furtive.

"I've run a few decryption software packages but … well, I think I'll have to write some new coding and…"

"Vik, cut to the chase, mate," Godber said shortly.

"I think the drone is a Russian copy of a Ukrainian

UUV," said Vikram. "It uses technology very similar to what the Ukrainians have been developing, although it's not a 100% match. This *could* mean they recovered Ukrainian technology from the Black Sea or found some other way to steal it. I'm hoping decryption will tell me more."

"How do you know it isn't a Ukrainian device and they're the ones trying to listen in?" Rego asked.

Vikram hesitated before answering.

"It's a fair question. All I can say right now is that I don't think so. And I suspect the drone was there to listen into more than Sea-Me-We-3. The US military has a submarine cable network for data transfer from conflict zones to command staff. And you don't need me to tell you that interruption of the cable network during intense operations could have direct consequences for the military on the ground."

"Yeah, but the drone wasn't *on* any cable," said Godber. "It was inside a flamin' century-old wreck."

"Yes, and that's part of what worries me," said Vikram. "During the Cold War, the NSA succeeded in placing wire taps on Soviet underwater communication lines, but these days, the use of end-to-end encryption minimises the threat of wire-tapping."

"Yeah, and?"

"I'm still working on it, but I think this drone has capability of accessing, even decrypting, underwater comms without even being near to the targeted cable. And I don't think this drone needs to surface to transmit intel. That would be a huge leap forward in the technology."

"Bloody hell!" said Godber.

Vikram hummed his agreement.

"It's beyond anything I've seen but at this point, I can't risk sharing what I know and what I suspect. It's frustrating, but I'm hoping I'll know more when I get my hands on it."

"Your courier picked it up just before I left work at lunchtime. It should be with you any moment."

"Good." Vikram hesitated, then spoke. "Look, I know we wanted to keep this a closed loop ... I just don't think that's possible anymore."

"What do you mean?" Rego asked unhappily.

"Do you have any contacts at Culdrose, Rob?" Vikram asked. "Someone who can covertly investigate Paul Jameson? Someone who can talk to who was working with the Ukrainians?"

"I spoke to Nate Tregowan today. He's going to have a casual chat with some of his old dive buddies, see what chatter he can pick up."

"Good, that's good," Vikram said thoughtfully. It'll be useful, but I think we're going to need something at a higher level."

Rego frowned. "It sounds like you think Jameson could be involved in more ways than he's saying."

"It's possible," Vikram agreed. "I'm just trying to think over every angle."

Rego's eyes darkened. "So, he comes to me with a plausible story, gets me to re-open the case in an off-the-books op, then ... what? Uses what I've found?"

"It's a possible explanation," Vikram said carefully, "but just one of several. It concerns me that Jameson is a communications expert."

It bothered Rego more than a little.

"Has his name come up on any of your searches?"

"No, he wasn't on our radar at all."

"Is that good or bad?"

"At this point, I couldn't say. But I can't investigate him without putting a giant target on his back," said Vikram.

"Have you at least been able to find the exact dates that the Ukrainians were at Culdrose?"

"Yes, and I'll email those over to you."

"I'm more interested in knowing if there was any chatter about them leaving in a hurry," said Rego.

"Not that I know of," Vikram said carefully. "But I don't have the highest security clearance."

"That doesn't usually stop you," Godber said blithely.

"This isn't a game," Vikram said sharply.

"No, it fuckin' isn't!" Godber shot back. "And you aren't the one putting your neck on the line!" He pointed at Rego. "He's got his wife and kids sleeping upstairs and you've got him messing around with the fuckin' Russians!"

"Okay, guys, this isn't helping," Rego interrupted before his two friends got into a slanging match. "However we set about investigating Jameson, it's going to start alarm bells ringing."

"But you do have a contact there," Vikram pushed, deliberately ignoring Godber's uncharacteristic outburst. "I know this is all getting a little too close to home, Rob," said Vikram at last, "but you've got to keep an open mind."

"My mind is so damn open, my brain is in danger of falling out," Rego said wearily as Godber snorted in amusement. "I met Culdrose's Bronze Commander, Sergeant Ed Bladen, on the Hellbanianz case earlier this year," he said. "And he did send me Jameson's service record. Nothing stood out. But I don't know the man, and I've never worked with him. I've had no reason to have anything to do with Culdrose's MoD plod. I could ask my DS, Tom Stevens. They'd have worked together on the G7 back in 2021 – assuming Bladen was at Culdrose then."

Vikram was silent for several seconds.

"No, it has to be you – we can't risk bringing anyone else in."

"Stevens is a good man," Rego said defensively.

"Do you trust him with your life?" Vikram asked and Rego didn't answer.

He liked Stevens and he respected him, he'd even started to think of him as a friend after working with him for the last four months, but trust him with his life?

"Look," Rego said at last, "I've thought about setting up a meeting with Sergeant Bladen. I've already asked him to expedite information on Jameson from the MPs." He hesitated. "I suppose I could tell him that I want to meet up, discuss fostering closer links between us and them."

"But he's MoD plod you're CID," said Godber, frowning. "If you were setting up any familiarisation meetings at Culdrose, you'd be talking to the Special Investigation Branch of the Royal Naval Police, the guys 'n' gals who do the detective work there, not the boots on the ground."

"The SIBs of the Royal Naval Police, Royal Military Police and Royal Air Force Police amalgamated a couple of years back – they're called Defence Serious Crime Unit now."

"Blimey," Godber said, shaking his head. "I haven't

been out that long and they've gone and changed their bloomin' names already. But that's not the problem, mate. The kind of liaison you're talking about would be uniform; it should be your station's inspector making a connection with Ministry of Defence Police, not you talking to Bladen. He'll immediately wonder what you're up to."

"I know," Rego said shortly.

"But if you see Bladen face-to-face, there'd be a chance of keeping this off the record," Vikram said quietly.

They were all silent for several seconds. Finally, Rego spoke.

"Do we have any options before we take that step?"

"Okay," Vikram sighed, "we'll do some more digging on Jameson and keep it discreet. Being gay in the military is viewed as a risk of compromise. I'll look into him from my end, as well – maybe get access to what his service records don't say. I'll let you know if I need you to contact Bladen – I'll need to run some checks on him, too."

"Fine," Rego said tersely. "And I've requested CDR information on Jameson's phone."

"Priority One?"

"Yes."

"Good."

"What's the latest on Adam Ellis?" Rego asked, remembering Tamsyn's friend.

"His debrief will be complete by now," Vikram said. "We'll cut him loose. He won't say anything to anyone. He's been instructed to say he was treated at a specialist medical unit and the hospital screwed up the paperwork. You can take him out of the equation."

"That's it?"

"That's it," Vikram agreed.

"So, what do I do now?" Rego asked.

"Enjoy your holiday with the kids," Vikram said drily. "Carry on as normal."

Rego was struggling to remember what 'normal' was like. When he'd first told his friends and colleagues that he'd be working in the south west, they'd all suggested it would be a snooze-fest of epic proportions and that he'd spend his time eating pasties and expanding his waistline with cream teas. So far, not so much, although maybe he could put that right while his family were visiting.

He decided to take Vikram's advice.

CHAPTER 19

Tamsyn slept until lunchtime after another busy late shift.

When she finally woke up, she felt groggy as she lay in bed, letting her mind wander. What was special about the *Mohegan* wreck site? Had someone been watching them on that trip? She had so many questions about the dead diver and the strange device, most of which would probably never be answered.

It had to be connected, it had to be. And it made her angry that no one was trusting her with what was going on, even though she'd been the one to first report it to DI Rego.

Her breathing accelerated and she suddenly felt furious at being left out of the loop. Mo raised her head, yawning at the sudden movement. She threw Tamsyn a baleful look and hopped off the bed, scampering down the stairs.

Tamsyn sighed, the angry energy draining out of her. The last time she'd acted without knowing the full story, she nearly got herself and her grandfather killed.

She let out a long, slow breath. *This is what I signed up for. I might not know the whole story, or how or even why, but I'm still a part of it.*

The thought was soothing, and she let her muscles loosen under the duvet, stretching like a cat.

As a child growing up in the cottage, she'd never been allowed the luxury of a lie-in. It had been drummed into her that the Poldhu's were hard workers. Her grandparents' attitude had necessarily softened since she'd started shift work.

Anyway, apart from catching up with chores, she had nothing to do. Jess would be working, and having checked her trusty surf app, Magic Seaweed, there weren't any workable waves within an hour's drive.

She decided to put some laundry on, break out the textbooks, take Morwenna for a walk, then peg out her washing. Her fun-filled day would include watching it dry.

The cottage was empty except for the little dog, and Mo was overjoyed that Tamsyn was finally up and about.

They shared a bacon sandwich, and Tamsyn was just about to head for the shower when there was a knock at the front door.

Friends and neighbours tended to come in through the back garden and knock at the kitchen door, so Tamsyn wondered who it could be. Mindful that strange things were happening and strange people were hanging around, she looked through the door's peephole first.

"Adam!"

She flung the door open.

"Oh my God, Adam! Are you okay?" she asked,

gesturing at his arm in a sling. "Come in, come in. Do you want a coffee?"

He shook his head, staring at her coolly, and her hand fluttered to her unwashed and uncombed hair, mortified that he'd caught her in an old t-shirt and the leggings she'd slept in.

"I'm not coming in."

"Okay, then...?"

"I've come to get my dive equipment. Mum thinks you've got my cylinders and harness. I've been over to the *Lowenna* and my car, and they're not there."

Tamsyn raised her eyebrows at his aggressive tone.

"Well, I'm really sorry, but I can't give you your cylinders or harness because they were stolen. We had a break in."

His lip curled. "A break in ... sure. Of course you did. Fuck's sake."

"It wasn't my fault," Tamsyn said, feeling annoyed. "We were burgled."

"Well, what about my GoPro?"

"That was retained as evidence."

Adam shook his head.

"Fucking great. This just gets better and better. Look, I'm sorry, Tam, but I don't want to see you again. All the shit I've had to deal with..." he shook his head again. "My mum was frantic and you did fuck all."

"That's not true!" she said defensively. "I..."

But he wouldn't let her finish.

"I don't know what the fuck you've dragged me into, but I've had enough. It ends here. Someone even complained to the dive club for taking you on your first wreck dive without having a coxswain or diver recall system."

"It wasn't me!"

But he was in full spate and not stopping.

Morwenna growled at him, baring her teeth, and Tamsyn had to pick her up to stop the little dog taking a chunk out of his remaining good hand.

"You're toxic," Adam said bitterly. "Do us both a favour and find another dive club – and lose my number while you're at it."

He turned on his heel and headed to his car.

"Hey!" she yelled, following him in her bare feet. "Adam! What the fuck?"

He stopped so abruptly, she almost crashed into him.

"Do you know what it's like?" he snarled. "I was detained for nearly 72 hours – three fucking days! I didn't know what the hell was going on and nobody would let me call my mum. She was going crazy with worry. *All because of you!*"

"You are such a dickhead!" Tamsyn fumed. "That was nothing to do with me! I didn't know what had happened either! And I tried to help your mum – I called the custody officer and Control, and I told my boss, too. He was probably the one who got you out! I'm just a probationer – they don't tell me important stuff. I did everything I could to help!"

He crossed his arms over his chest, his eyes filled with anger.

"Whatever, Tam," he said, coldly. "Go and fuck up someone else. I'm done."

" I saved your life!" she shouted after him as he walked away. "You're welcome, asshole!"

Adam didn't look at her as his car screeched from the kerb, leaving her furious and confused, with nothing but the smell of burning rubber.

She hated the arguments that turned words into razors, she always had.

CHAPTER 20

"Earth to Rob!" Cassie muttered, prodding him in the side so Rego yelped.

They were sitting on the beach at Sennen while the kids played with their new bodyboards, jumping through the water and riding the small waves back to the shore.

Rego's eyes had been on the kids, but his mind was elsewhere – and Cassie knew it.

"What?"

"I've been talking to you for the last two minutes and you haven't heard a word."

"Sorry, luv. Got a lot on my mind."

"I can see that," she said drily, "and I'm sure it's about this case you're working on, but seeing as for the last four months, we've only had the pleasure of your company once a fortnight, I think it would be nice if you at least pretended you're pleased to have us down here."

Rego hadn't made DI so early in his career without realising when he'd made an error of judgement. And he wouldn't risk compromising Cassie by telling her what was really going on. Retreat was inevitable.

"I'm sorry, luv," he said immediately, as part of his 'acknowledge and grovel' tactics that worked 75% of the time. "You're right."

"I know I am."

"But actually, I was thinking how great it is to have you and the kids down here," he improvised. "What would you think about making it permanent?"

"Move down to Cornwall?"

"Why not? There's all this space and the beach, and we'd get the kids away from the city before Max gets sucked in."

"We live in Prestwich, not downtown Compton, Rob."

"The kids would love it," he pressed, warming to his theme. "Max could learn to fish and surf, and Maisie could go bodyboarding. You said yourself that she's a natural in the swimming pool. She's a real water baby."

"And what about *my* job," she asked, her voice rising.

"You've been talking about going freelance. Maybe now is the time to do it. You said yourself that a graphic designer can work anywhere."

She slid her sunglasses down her nose and gave him an appraising look.

"Where's this coming from, Rob? You said this was just going to be for a couple of years before going for your DCI exams and coming back to Manchester."

"I know," he said, feeling his way. "But take a look around you, Cassie. Look at this beach – look at all this space. We could have this all year around ... and we'd be together."

"I've only just got to Cornwall and now you're asking me to make a decision about moving here?" she asked incredulously.

"Just think about it," Rego said. "It could be good for us."

Cassie didn't look even slightly convinced.

"It's very white here. I don't want to take the kids somewhere they'll feel judged for the colour of their skin. There's enough of that in the world already."

Rego sighed. "The first time I was called a 'fucking black gorilla in a uniform' wasn't down here, it was up in Manchester."

"You know what I'm talking about, Rob. School kids are feral. They'll pick on anyone who's different – we've been here two days and I've only seen one other person of colour."

Rego shrugged.

"At least there isn't anyone around to call me a 'coconut' for being a police officer."

It was one of the criticisms that had stung the most when he'd first joined the Force. A coconut: brown on the outside, white on the inside. And the slur came from a man Rego had considered a friend. He shook away the memory.

Cassie continued to frown at him.

"And anyway, you said you'd be transferring back in a couple of years. Why mess up the kids' education twice?"

"I like it down here, Cassie," he said, more truthfully than he'd known until he said it out loud. "In Manchester, I'm one of a hundred DI's – here, I feel like I can really make a difference."

She chewed on her lip. "You've only been down here

for four months. I think we should wait a bit longer before we make any life-changing decisions."

He thought about reminding her that a minute earlier she'd been complaining about how little she and the kids had seen him in the last few months, but he was a smart guy, so he kept his thoughts to himself.

"Anyway," Cassie continued, "Mum isn't getting any younger and I wouldn't want to be that far away from her." Then she gave him a sly smile. "And you still haven't told me what Patricia said when you told her that the kids would be down here with you all summer."

Rego held up his hands, cringing at the memory. "Fine! You win – discussion shelved. For now."

Cassie smirked at him and kissed his cheek.

Then Rego's burner phone pinged with an incoming message and his hand twitched, wanting to read it but knowing he'd promised his family this day, this perfect beach day, in the sunshine, in Cornwall, together.

Cassie watched his struggle, amused and touched that he hadn't immediately looked at his phone.

"Go on then," she sighed with an understanding smile. "I know it's half-killing you not to look."

He gave her a sheepish grin. "I'm sorry, luv. It could be important."

"I know."

He stood up and walked a short distance away to read the message. It was Vikram, reporting that he'd safely received the GoPro and drone in London.

Rego breathed a sigh of relief. Getting rid of those was a weight off him – and it should mean that Tamsyn and her family were now safe.

He tucked the phone away with satisfaction then checked to see that Cassie wasn't watching and pulled out his work phone, catching up on the news. There was one message from Tamsyn saying that Adam Ellis had appeared on her doorstep, and that he appeared to be well enough, and another from DC John Frith asking to speak to Rego.

He was pleased that Ellis had finally resurfaced – Vikram said the official story was that the hospital's paperwork had gone missing and caused the problem. Rego called DC John Frith who was eager to update him, too.

"Boss, I've been through the CCTV from Treliske and I've got Ellis leaving the hospital with two men, but there isn't enough for a good ID – they're both wearing baseball caps in the car park and keep their heads down as they enter and exit the hospital. I ran the car's number plate and it came up as a rental from a company in London, but the guy renting it used fake ID. So, my last chance was to track the credit card they used to pay for the car park, but it looks like they paid cash. There's not much else to go on. What should I tell the mother?"

Rego withheld a sigh.

"You've done good work, John," Rego said. "And I'm happy to inform you that Ellis has been found."

"Sorry, boss? What?"

"I know. The hospital lost the transfer paperwork."

"But ... why did they say the police had taken him?"

"No idea," Rego lied. "It was probably a misunderstanding. I'm just glad he's been found."

He paused, wanting to tell his colleague more but not being able to.

"You did good work, John. We had to treat it like a misper, possible abduction scenario. I'm sorry it turned out to be a wild goose chase. Write up your notes and forget about it."

He ended the call, feeling like ten kinds of shit. Then just to add to the joy, his burner phone buzzed with a text from Vikram.

> Set up the meeting with Bronze

Vikram must be getting desperate.

He shoved both phones away and plastered a smile on his face as he turned to his family.

"Right, who fancies an ice cream?"

He was clearly on edge but trying to act normal for the rest of the day. He wasn't sure he'd managed it. In the end, Rego excused himself to go and make the call. He heartily wished that this case had never dropped in his lap, then before he could talk himself out of it, he called Sergeant Ed Bladen, the Bronze Commander at Culdrose, a member of the MoD Police.

Bladen was surprised to hear from Rego so soon after having submitted the information about Jameson's service record, but remained polite, and agreed when proposed that a meeting of minds between D&C Police, the Culdrose RNPs and MoD plods would help to foster a useful working relationship.

In other words, Rego was lying through his teeth.

Bladen was even more surprised when Rego suggested that they meet up as soon as possible.

"Actually, Sergeant Bladen, I was wondering if we could meet for an informal chat first so when we have our tri-party meeting, we know that we'll be moving in the same direction."

Bladen hesitated for a moment and then agreed to meet Rego at the *Blue Anchor* in Helston that evening.

Rego hoped that Cassie would forgive him.

She wasn't happy; in fact, she didn't say much at all, so Rego kept his head down and promised he wouldn't be long.

But when they arrived back at the cottage, forgiving was the last emotion he was going to get from her.

He dropped Cassie and the kids off at the cottage with all their towels, bags and empty coolers, then went to park the car. He walked back slowly, mentally planning how he was going to handle the meeting with Bladen, when he was confronted with a furious Cassie channelling her inner Amazon as she scowled at him.

"Your! Mother! Is! Here!" she hissed at him, the moment he opened the kitchen door.

He stared at her, bemused, until he heard his mother's voice shattering the silence for a mile around.

"Robert! Robert, is that you? Is that my bwoy?"

His eyes widened. "What is she doing here?" he whispered to Cassie.

"Don't ask me, ask *her!*" she replied angrily. "I thought you'd sorted this out, Rob! You told me that she understood we needed this time for us."

"I did!"

"Clearly," she snarled.

"I'll talk to her."

"You'll do more than that, Rob. You'll put her on the next train home."

"Cassie..."

"The next train, I mean it." She paused dramatically. "That's if you want to stay married to *me*. I'm going for a walk."

And she slammed out of the door.

Patricia Rego was a formidable woman, and no one underestimated her twice, so Rego knew that he couldn't give in to the tears and tantrums that were sure to follow.

"Hello, Mum. This is a surprise."

The end of his sentence was muffled as she wrapped her arms around him and yanked his head down, almost smothering him against her substantial bosom.

Maisie giggled and even Max cracked a smile.

"It's so good to see you! I missed my family so much," Patricia grinned, letting Rego up for air.

"Mum, we have to talk," Rego said firmly.

"Nonsense! I just come on the train and in a taxi to see my grandbabies. Is no time for talking!" and she turned her back on him.

But Rego was all too familiar with her tactics and knew that she was using the children as a human shield.

"No, Mum," he repeated. "We have to talk now."

"What nonsense this, Robert? Me parched, gasping for tea. And I'm an old lady! You treat me with some respect! You're not too old to get a smack!"

"Kids, give us some space, please," he said.

Max was happy to leave the drama behind, but Maisie looked disappointed.

"Now, May Day," Rego said, using his pet-name for her.

Muttering to herself, she grabbed her phone and slowly

climbed the stairs to the third of the cottage's tiny bedrooms.

Patricia was busying herself with making tea, keeping her back to Rego.

"I know what you're doing, Mum," he said quietly.

"What am I doing, clever clogs? Making tea, it looks like to me."

"You can't stay here," he said, feeling like a shit as her shoulders tightened.

"When I was a girl, ten of us slept in a house this size," she said, "and you say I can't see my own family! My own grandbabies! You want me to make an appointment to see them? Unwelcome in my own family!" and she began to cry, blotting her wet cheeks with a tissue she plucked from her handbag.

"You can't stay," he said again, gritting his teeth.

"Turn me out, would you?" she cried, her bosom heaving.

"Stop it, Mum!" he said sharply, his temper wearing thin. "I told you that Cassie and I needed this time, just the four of us. I explained it to you."

"I can help!" she said, changing tack. "I'll take me precious grand-babies out while you and Cassie spend time together," and she smiled so hopefully, his resistance began to crack.

She honed in on the weakness immediately.

"Yes, yes! You know they miss their gran. You can't take them away for the whole summer. They *love* me."

"Mum, just stop. Please."

"But..."

He cut her off.

"No, Mum. This isn't fair."

"You think it fair to leave me behind? You think it fair me be so lonely?" and she began to wail.

He ignored the caterwauling and went to stand at the sink, pouring himself a glass of water and one for her. Then he waited until the volume lessened.

"Mum, I asked you not to come..."

"No!" she said sharply. "You tole me. Is different t'ing. I am your *mother*."

"And Cassie is my wife. I told you that I need this time with her. I am *not* going to end up divorced and be another police statistic. 'Join the force and get a divorce' – I know you've heard that."

Her voice moderated.

"I know, Robert. Cassie is difficult, she always has been..."

He pointed his finger at her and she huffed quietly.

"I'll tell you what I'm going to do and you're going to listen..."

"Don't you take that high and mighty tone with me, Robert!"

He spoke over her. "I'm going to book a room at the Premier Inn in Penzance for two weeks," Patricia started to complain but he kept going. "The first week is for you, and the second week is for Cassie's mum – and we've already promised Kenise, because that way, the kids get to see both their grandparents. Then Cassie and I will have the rest of the summer *by ourselves.*"

"But..."

"No, that's it, Mum. If you don't like it, I swear to God, I'll take you back to Penzance train station right now."

She gasped. "What wicked t'ing to say!"

"I mean it. Take it or leave it."

"You are an ungrateful bwoy."

"Take it or leave it."

She gave a curt nod, and Rego pulled his phone out of his pocket praying that the Premier Inn would come through for him.

Luckily for him and his marriage, they'd had a cancellation, and Rego booked the room for a fortnight.

Patricia negotiated to have supper with the family and Cassie had agreed, somewhat mollified now that she knew her mother-in-law wouldn't be sharing the cottage with them.

The uneasy entente lasted until Rego had to leave for his meeting in Helston, and eventually he persuaded his mother to let him drop her off at the hotel on the way.

The double room was small and neat with a view of Penzance harbour. He watched his mother as she silently inspected the travel-size kettle, sachets of coffee, tea and sugar, and a packet of shortbread.

Then she turned to stand by the window, looking out toward the sunset, her back to him.

"I'm not trying to make your life difficult, Robert," she said, her voice so much quieter than usual that it jolted him.

"I know, Mum. It's just been a tough time for us, what with me coming down here. Cassie has had a lot to put up with. I know you miss the kids, but I do, too." He paused, giving her a chance to respond, but she didn't. "And we have to invite Kenise, as well. Cassie misses her mum as much as I miss you."

She nodded, not answering immediately, and Rego let out a frustrated sigh.

"Mum, what's really going on?"

She sighed loudly and changed the subject.

"Nothing! Now how about a cup of tea before you go?"

But Rego hadn't reached the rank of Detective Inspector by the age of 34 without knowing how to question a suspect – or persuade his mother to talk to him.

"Mum, enough. Give me a good reason why I should let you do this?"

"And what is it I'm doing, Robert?" she shot back, her temper igniting immediately.

Rego stared at her steadily.

"Ignoring the fact that you've seen more of my kids than I have, and that I wanted, *needed* to spend some time alone with them; ignoring the fact that I have to be fair to Kenise, too – and she already sees a lot less of the kids or Cassie than you do." He took a breath, "which is why I suggested that each of you stay a week, and then the rest of the time I have with Cassie and the kids."

She blustered a little more while Rego sat their patiently, waiting for her to get to the real reason that she was being unreasonably reluctant to share.

Finally, she sat down heavily and tears began to trickle down her cheeks.

"I had to go to the doctor for one of them women's checkups," she said quietly. "They found a lump. They want to operate."

Rego drew in a sharp breath, shock and concern rippling through him.

"Where? When?"

"Where is none of your business," she said firmly. "It women's t'ings. And I was told the day before I caught the train down. I wanted to see my grandbabies," she said her lip trembling. "Is that a crime?"

Rego wrapped his hands around hers.

"No, Mum. Of course not. But ... what did he say about treatment? You can't hide your head in the sand about this."

"It was a lady doctor and she says I can start treatment when I go back at the start of September."

She stared at him defiantly.

"Mum, is that ... safe," he asked quietly. "Delaying treatment?"

"I told them I didn't want to be chopped about."

"Mum, for God's sake!"

"Let me finish, Robert! I told them no operations, but they say I have to. So, I say it have to wait until the summer holidays is over so I can spend time with my son and my precious grandbabies. They say a few weeks make no never-mind. So, here I am. I want to see my family. I want one, perfect summer of memories that will see me through what comes next, God willing."

Rego went to her and wrapped his arms around her, breathing in the familiar scent of vanilla and something spicy.

"Why didn't you tell me?" he whispered.

She waved a hand dismissively.

"It's not your business. I only told you because you'd have put me on a train otherwise."

"Mum..."

"And I don't want you telling anyone. Just say you've changed your mind about me staying."

"Mum, no. I'm not lying to Cassie."

She pursed her lips.

"Fine, tell her. But not my grandbabies. Promise you won't tell them."

"For how long? They should know, Mum."

"No! They chil'en. Let them have their perfect summer, too." She gazed up at him, her eyes wet. "That's all I ask. One perfect summer."

Rego felt his chest get tight. His mother had always been there.

She saw the expression on his face and squeezed his hands.

"Robert, I'm going to see my grandbabies grow up."

He nodded, trying to smile.

"So, I can stay?" she asked hopefully.

Rego let out a long sigh.

"Yeah, Mum, you can stay. But not at the cottage. I'll find you somewhere close that will do a summer rental, I promise."

She didn't look entirely happy about that but accepted it. Then she gave a small smile.

"Now, get home to those precious babies and kiss them goodnight from their grandmother."

"Okay," Rego said, reluctant to leave now he knew why she behaved the way she did.

"On you go," she said, all but pushing him out the door.

Then he drove to Helston, worrying about his mother the whole way and trying to decide what he'd say to his wife when he got back.

The small market town was the nearest place for men and women from Culdrose to come and have a drink and do their shopping. There were three supermarkets, no bank, and half a dozen pubs.

The *Blue Anchor* had been a pub for more than 600 years, brewing its famous Spingo ales. Its thatched roof dipped below the roofline of the its neighbouring Georgian buildings, and inside was just as quirky, a warren of small, cosy rooms with stone fireplaces and thick granite walls.

Bladen was sitting at the back of the room with a view of the door. He stood up as Rego walked towards him, and the two men shook hands.

"Can I buy you a drink?" Rego offered, but Bladen shook his head, lifting a bottle of Cornish Gold Cyder and raising it in a friendly salute.

"Already got one in. I wasn't sure if you'd be drinking as you've driven here."

"No worries, just give me a sec."

Rego ordered himself a J2O fruit juice and sat at the small table.

"Cheers!"

Rego lifted his bottle and took a small sip.

"Thanks for meeting me so quickly," he began, then hesitated.

Bladen raised an eyebrow.

"Is this really about liaison between Penzance station and my staff?" he asked astutely.

"In a way," Rego hedged, then plunged straight in. "I asked to meet you unofficially because something of a concerning nature has come up during the course of routine enquiries."

"To do with the body of the diver you found?" Bladen asked, leaning forward and lowering his voice.

"Partly," Rego said.

"And something I should be concerned about?"

"Yes," Rego said. "Very concerned."

"You have my attention, Inspector," Bladen said.

"It's Rob."

"And we're meeting here because...?"

Rego explained what he'd learned about the dead diver's identity and Jameson's relationship with him. He didn't mention the drone, Vikram, or the fact that ACC Gray had ordered the case closed.

Bladen's face was stony as he listened, and when Rego had finished speaking, he folded his arms across his chest.

"Why didn't you tell me immediately?" he asked, clearly aggravated.

"My bosses thought a less formal approach would be better," Rego said evasively.

Bladen gave a wry smile.

"I see. Well, I guess thank you for that. But I can't leave this, Rob. I'll have to talk to Jameson as soon as possible. Sooner."

"I know and I'd like to be there."

Bladen was already shaking his head.

"Just as an observer," Rego said. "Jameson knows me, he's comfortable with me ... and I'm the one he came to. You've got more chance of him talking if I'm there."

"Oh, he'll talk alright," said Bladen stiffly.

Rego tried not to let his annoyance show.

"As a gesture of goodwill," he said.

Bladen picked up his cider and took a long drink.
"I can't promise anything," he said at last.
Rego nodded.
"Thank you."

CHAPTER 21

Rego wasn't looking forward to telling Cassie, but when he finally arrived back at the cottage, she was already in bed.

He sat on the bed next to her, and she listened silently as he explained what was going on with his mother and why she'd been so insistent about visiting.

His wife surprised him again.

"Of course, Rob. Of course she can stay. Two of my friends have had breast cancer – and I'm assuming this is what she means – and having things to look forward to, staying positive, it's really important." She smiled. "Anyway, it'll give her time to spend with my mum, too."

Rego didn't think he could love his wife more than he already did, but he was wrong.

"Thank you," he said, his voice hoarse.

She wrapped her arms around him, burying her head in his neck.

"It's the right thing to do. It's going to be okay."

"I'm worried that she's not starting treatment straightaway," Rego admitted

"If the doctors are okay with it, then it's Patricia's choice."

"Yeah, well, that's the problem. I wonder if they did tell her that."

"I'll make some calls, talk to some friends who've been through the same thing, see what I can find out." She laid her hand on his chest, "Either way, Robert, it's her choice. We'll just have to help her have a great summer."

Rego rolled onto his side to look at her.

"You're really okay with her staying all summer?"

Cassie smiled and raised her eyebrows.

"We'll work it out. But I'm still having my mum down, too. We'll have to find a place for Patricia to stay for the whole summer. Better get on the case, Inspector."

Bladen had worked fast.

By the time Rego had woken up the next day, there was a message on his phone from Bladen saying that the interview with Paul Jameson had been set up – and was starting in an hour.

Rego swore softly and scalded his mouth trying to drink his coffee, then hurried out of the door before Cassie killed him.

He arrived at Culdrose with a cosy minute-and-a-half to spare and was directed to a shabby reception area.

Bladen shook his hand and introduced Rego to his

opposite number in the Defence Serious Crime Unit, the tri-service unit that replaced the MPs across the Army, Navy and Air Force. Rego wasn't happy that another person was involved but there was nothing he could do about it.

Corporal Clyde Campbell was a short, dour Scot with zero sense of humour, but Bladen assured Rego that he was an experienced investigator.

The decor of the interview room was minimal to say the least, furnished with an old metal table that had seen better days, and five weary folding chairs.

Rego was there only as an observer and had no official role in the interview – Bladen had made that crystal clear. Of course, he'd tried to discuss the interview strategy with Bladen and Campbell, although the latter hadn't had much to say, but it was clear that his input wasn't required and he was there as a courtesy only.

Jameson was wearing his uniform when he walked into the room. His confidence seemed to waver when he saw Rego, but he nodded in greeting and sat at the single chair positioned behind the metal desk.

Rego expected the interview to begin when a woman with short brown hair wearing a black business suit entered the room carrying a file, nodded at Bladen and Campbell, but ignored Rego and Jameson.

Who the hell are you? Rego thought to himself.

"Mr Jameson, thank you for seeing us at such short notice. I'm Sergeant Bladen from Ministry of Defence Police; my colleague is Corporal Campbell from Defence Serious Crime Unit. You will note that we have an observer from Devon & Cornwall Police, Detective Inspector Rego, as well as Ms Jones, another observer."

DEAD MAN'S DIVE

Rego still had no idea who 'Ms Jones' really was. If she was military, she'd be wearing a uniform – and Bladen hadn't mentioned that she'd be present at the interview but had clearly been expecting her. That pissed him off, but there was nothing he could do about it now.

Jameson glanced at Rego again, then seemed to resign himself to the questions that would be coming his way.

"If it's okay with you," said Bladen, "I'll switch on a voice recorder. This is to ensure that there is no ambiguity about the matters we discuss. We hope not to keep you too long."

"Fine," said Jameson. "Let's get this over with."

"I'll come straight to the point," said Bladen. "We want to ask you a few questions about your knowledge of, or involvement with, the Ukrainian military team who were undergoing joint training at *RNAS Culdrose* two years ago, between 15th September and 31st March. Before we start, I want to make it perfectly clear you are not under arrest and you can go whenever you want."

At the mention of the word 'arrest', Jameson looked visibly rattled.

"Do I need a solicitor?"

They'd discussed Jameson's likely response beforehand. Rego had asked Bladen to downplay the seriousness of the issue, because he really didn't want to involve solicitors. It might not be fair on Jameson, but there was more at stake here than Jameson's best interests. Harsh, but true.

It helped that the laws differed when it came to a military installation.

"Well, it's up to you but we haven't got much to ask

you, and it would be really helpful if we could clear up the matters today. I don't want to influence your decision, but as a suggestion, do you want to assess our questions and if you feel that you need legal advice, we can arrange this for you. The matters also potentially involve national security so we can be a bit more candid with you if it's just us here. I think you understand as your specialised role and training will give you a better understanding of where we are coming from."

Corporal Campbell nodded in agreement.

"Also," Bladen continued, "this conversation – we won't call it an interview – it's being recorded, which is a safeguard for us all."

Jameson was looking increasingly anxious, clearing his throat several times.

"Okay. Yeah, okay. I'm happy to continue ... but can I have a cup of tea and a glass of water, please?

Rego suspected that this was a delaying tactic, a way for Jameson to regain some control of the situation, giving him a little breathing space and allowing him to gather his thoughts.

Bladen looked at the corporal expectantly. Campbell rolled his eyes and left the room, clearly annoyed.

The woman didn't speak or even seem to be particularly interested, but kept her head down reading from her file. Bladen didn't chat to Jameson or Rego while they were waiting either, but bent his head over the notes in front of him until Campbell returned a short time later carrying a battered tray with five cups of tea and a glass of water.

"Thanks," said Jameson. "Can I have some sugar, please?"

The corporal's face was a picture, a very pissed off picture, and Rego had to stop himself from smiling. Campbell went out again returning a minute later with ten sachets of sugar and a dirty plastic spoon.

Jameson sipped his tea, pulling a face that didn't go unnoticed by Campbell.

Bladen gave a swift, meaningless smile.

"Okay, Paul, there's just a few background questions about you to start with. You'll be aware that I've read your service record, which is very detailed. I know that you haven't come to the attention of DSCU previously. I can also see that you have extensive communications training," he looked up and smiled. "A model student on all of your courses, in fact."

Jameson didn't return the smile.

"Could you fill some of the gaps about your personal life?"

Rego watched the woman's face. She might pretend disinterest, but he was sure she was listening keenly. He'd been around the intelligence community enough times to guess that she was from one of the services. It was possible that she was a colleague of Vikram's, but if his friend knew about her involvement, Rego felt fairly certain that Vik would have told him.

Although working for MI6 had definitely changed him – and not necessarily for the better.

"My personal life?" Jameson said, his gaze flicking to Rego then back to Bladen. "What's that got to do with anything?"

"Well, if I can guide you," said Bladen, "let's start with some brief background about your homelife before joining the military; you know mum, dad, school life, interests at school, interests and hobbies now?"

Jameson looked both annoyed and puzzled. Rego knew that Sergeant Bladen would use this technique of asking personal questions as way of building up a rapport and to get the suspect talking about matters that they were comfortable discussing, in their own words. Giving a number of topics to cover allowed the suspect to speak without Bladen having to ask a series of closed questions.

Then Jameson seemed to decide that getting the interview over and done with was better than prolonging it, because he started talking.

"I grew up in Bootle. My dad worked at the docks and my mum was a dinner lady at the local primary school. Dad still works at the docks but in the offices now; mum is retired. I went to the local comp, played football, got 6 GCSEs and 2 A Levels in Maths and Physics. I thought about joining the Royal Navy, but then I heard about the Accelerated Apprentice Scheme in the Royal Fleet Auxiliary in Communications Information Systems, and that seemed like a good fit for me. I joined when I was 21."

"What did you do between A Levels and joining the RFA?" Bladen asked.

Jameson shrugged. "Worked in a bar in the evenings and a sports clothing store in the day until I was accepted onto the scheme."

"So, you're a hard worker?"

Jameson half-shrugged, half-nodded.

"And you joined the RFA when?"

"Thirteen years ago. I did my ten weeks basic training at *HMS Raleigh*, before passing out as a Provisional Leading Engineering Technician. I was then deployed to sea for six months to consolidate and learn key at-sea skills before returning for Leading Rates courses. I qualified as a Leading Engineering Technician Communications and Information Systems Specialist, and I manage a team of network engineers."

"And what specifically does that role entail?"

Jameson licked his lips.

"My role is to enable the secure exchange of mission-critical and sometimes top-secret information. I'm responsible for delivering and administering specialist communications and IT equipment, including classified information and cryptographic material."

Rego leaned forwards. It sounded like Jameson's work had a direct bearing on what he'd learned about the drone, possibly the Ukrainian's mission, too. If he could find out exactly what the Ukrainian's 'training' had been...

Either way, Jameson definitely hadn't told him that before. It made him wonder what else the man had withheld.

"And you're a Leading Hand?"

Jameson nodded.

"From Apprentice, you were promoted to Seaman Grade 1 and Seaman Grade 2 quite rapidly."

Jameson folded his arms defensively.

"But you've been a Leading Hand for eight years now. How do you explain that?"

"You'd have to ask my Chief Officer," Jameson said tightly.

"I'm asking you."

Jameson remained silent, and Bladen exchanged a look with Corporal Campbell. The woman was still staring at her file. Rego didn't think she'd turned over a single page yet.

"You're Head of Section, yet you haven't been promoted to Petty Officer."

Jameson continued to stare straight ahead.

Rego wondered at what point they were going to bring up Jameson's sexuality. They seemed to be tiptoeing around it for reasons he didn't fully understand.

"Do you still play football?" Bladen asked.

"No."

Bladen leaned back in his chair, his eyes dipping to glance at his file on the desk.

"Your Chief Officer says you're not a team player."

Jameson gave a bitter smile.

"Some people on my team," and he enunciated the word clearly, "some of them don't like the team I play for."

"Meaning?"

Jameson drew in a long breath.

"They don't like working with a gay man."

"That seems surprising in this day and age," Bladen said blandly. "My understanding is that the RFA is fully inclusive."

"Yeah, right," Jameson snorted.

"Well, Paul," said Bladen. "Thank you for that. Now, I'd like to get on with the crux of this matter and ask you about the Ukrainians who were based at RNAS Culdrose 22 months ago. Again, just briefly: what you knew about them, did you have any dealings with them on- or off-duty, that sort of thing."

Jameson stared straight at Bladen.

"That sort of thing?"

"Yes," said Bladen, not deterred by the patent hostility that had crept into Jameson's voice. "Did you have any formal dealings with the Ukrainians as part of your current role?"

"Yes, I did," Jameson said after a short pause. "My team was responsible for the data-processing network systems, utilising the latest satellite technology to deliver complex warfighting communications, tactical and strategic communications. I liaised directly with two of the Ukrainians who were in a similar role to me."

"And what were their names?"

"This should all be on record," Jameson replied.

"It will save time if you tell us," Corporal Campbell said impatiently, earning him a sharp look from Braden.

"Lieutenant Andriy Kovalenko and Senior Lieutenant Melnyk Danylo."

"How did you like working with them?"

"They were okay."

"Professional?"

"I'd say so. But I don't speak Russian."

"They spoke Russian, not Ukrainian?"

Jameson frowned. "I think so? I don't really know. I was told that there's a shared core vocabulary – like 60% or something."

"And you don't speak Russian?"

Jameson sighed heavily. "I went to school in Bootle – we were Scousers. We barely spoke English."

Rego saw Bladen hide a smile.

"Would you say it was stressful, working with the Ukrainians?"

Jameson paused.

"They were pretty intense."

"In what ways?" Bladen asked.

"Worked hard, played hard – determined to fight the Russians to the death. They all worried about their families back home."

"It sounds like working with them could become quite stressful."

Jameson didn't comment. If Rego had been leading the interview, he would have pressed that point, wanting to know exactly what that liaison meant and who they reported to.

Bladen leaned forwards.

"Did you have any informal dealings with the Ukrainians outside of work?"

Jameson's face reddened, and he glanced at Rego again.

Both Sergeant Bladen and Corporal Campbell picked up on the unconscious gesture.

"Mr Jameson? Did you meet any of them socially?"

"Yes."

"Was that at social meetings as a group or individually?"

"Both."

"Was there anyone in particular that you socialised with on a one-to-one basis?"

"Yes."

"And who was that?"

"Fedir Kuzma: he was a combat diver with the 73rd Naval Centre of Special Operations."

"So, he was special forces?"

"I didn't know that at the time but yes, I heard that later."

"What was the nature of your relationship with Fedir Kuzma?"

"We were friends."

"Close friends?"

Jameson's lips tightened. "Yes."

"Did you communicate with Fedir Kuzma or any of the other Ukrainians either by phone, text message, email, or via social media?"

"Yes: email communications with the Ukrainians was through my work email. Freddie ... Fedir, he had my personal phone number and email address, but he was the only one."

"Could you give me your personal email account username and password, as well as your mobile number and work phone number, please."

Jameson hesitated and Bladen tapped his pen against the desk.

"Do I have to?"

"It would be helpful if you did."

Bladen's voice was unemotional, but Jameson's shoulders slumped, accepting the notepad that Campbell slid across to him.

Bladen glanced down at the notes.

"Are those the only two numbers you have?"

"Yes."

"How long have you had that mobile number?"

"About three years."

"What about social media, what platforms do you use?"

"The usual: WhatsApp, Snapchat, Insta, TikTok."

"Facebook?"

"No."

"Twitter?"

"I look at it sometimes but I don't have an account."

"Anything else?"

Jameson lifted his chin. "Grindr."

Bladen looked up, clearly having no idea what that was. Rego was trying hard not to smile at the Sergeant's bemused expression.

"It's a dating app," Jameson said. "A gay dating app."

"Ah," said Bladen and looked down at his notes. "Please list your user names for all platforms."

Jameson was clearly unhappy but complied.

"I'm prepared to answer these questions," he said, "but I'm not sure where this is leading or what you think I've done. If you've got something specific to ask, just ask it."

Campbell looked annoyed, the expression on his face seeming to say, *cheeky fucker! We're the ones asking the questions!* But Sergeant Bladen didn't seem fazed, and 'Ms Jones' was apparently ignoring them all. Rego felt an immature urge to poke her to see if she'd react.

Bladen met Jameson's gaze.

"Were you in a relationship with any of the Ukrainians? Were you in a relationship with Fedir Kuzma?"

Jameson sat upright in his chair.

"Yes," he said clearly. "I'm not going to sit here and lie

to you, Sergeant Bladen. I suspect that you already know that I was in a relationship with Fedir Kuzma for almost all of the six months that he was based in Cornwall. I'm told that the RFA is a diverse workforce where being gay is no big deal these days."

His voice was laced with sarcasm, and he dropped his gaze to his lap, his hands clenched into fists.

Then he took a deep breath before slapping both palms flat on the desk in front of him. The noise made everyone in the room look at him, even the mysterious Ms Jones.

"But," said Jameson, "we all know that isn't true. I'm also aware that by admitting my sexuality, I'm risking my career."

Bladen nodded minutely. "Thank you for your honesty, Paul. I know this may have been difficult for you. When was the last time you spoke with Freddie?"

Rego was impressed by the lack of censure in Bladen's voice. The sergeant had been in the service long enough to have been part of a less tolerant crowd.

"Okay," said Jameson tiredly. "I'm not sure what's going on, but the last time I spoke to him was two days before the Ukrainians left Culdrose. And then ... nothing. I had a letter from Freddie's sister, Kateryna, last October. She said that she hadn't seen him or heard from him for nearly a year. She said that the Ukrainian Navy were denying all knowledge of him. The thing is, I thought he was just ghosting me. I was ... upset, but it happens. I mean, it's not like we could have had a future together." Jameson's voice became quieter. "He was fighting for his country, and that meant more to him than anything. At least, that's what

I thought. It was so weird that his sister couldn't find him. I wrote back to her, but I never heard anything. She was in Mariupol, so I don't even know if she got the letter. I don't even know if she's alive."

"Do you have the letter?"

"Yes. Not with me, but I can email you a copy."

Rego could have told Bladen that he had a copy on his phone, but kept his mouth shut.

"Thank you," said Bladen, leaning forwards again. "Paul, your role allows you access to some very sensitive equipment and intelligence. I need to ask these questions ... I need to ascertain whether or not, because of your sexuality, you were being pressured, coerced, or in any way blackmailed by anyone to pass over any information – any information, however small or insignificant you think it may be."

Jameson opened his mouth to reply, but Bladen hadn't finished.

"Before you answer, think very carefully. We're not here to judge you or hang you out to dry, but we need to be 100% sure that no one is trying to get at you, because there are measures we can put in place to stop this."

For the first time, the woman's eyes turned to Jameson, her gaze chilly and calculating.

"No," said Jameson. "There's nothing like that. Nothing."

Rego was intrigued, especially by the woman's reaction to this question. Not only that, he was studying Jameson, looking for the tell-tale indications of whether or not Jameson was lying. But he wasn't wringing his hands, rubbing his face or refusing to make eye contact, but still, Rego couldn't help feeling that the man was hiding something.

"No," Jameson said again. "I didn't divulge any information and I am not being blackmailed."

"Did Freddie ask you to give him any classified information?" Bladen asked.

This time Jameson did look away, unable to meet Bladen's gaze.

"No," he said again. "Nothing."

This time, Rego was sure he was lying.

Bladen glanced at Campbell then continued.

"Final couple of questions, Paul. Have you spoken to anyone about your relationship with Freddie?"

Jameson immediately looked at Rego.

"Yes," he said. "I told Detective Inspector Rego last week. I assume this little interview is thanks to you, Inspector?"

Jameson was clearly furious and Rego fully understood that anger, the loss of control, the humiliation the man felt. And most likely, concern for his career, too.

"Yes," he said candidly. "What you told me was too important not to take further. I told you that I'd look into Freddie's death, and that's what I'm doing."

"Thank you, Inspector Rego," Bladen said sharply, not happy that Rego had spoken. He turned back to Jameson. "Has anyone asked you to look after any equipment that is non-UK military?"

"Equipment? No," said Jameson.

Rego wondered about his stress of the word

'equipment'. Again, if he'd been leading the interview, he'd have asked if Jameson was holding anything belonging to Kuzma or any of the other Ukrainians. 'Equipment' meant different things to different people.

He made a note to ask Jameson about that later, in private.

Bladen was still talking.

"Has anyone asked you to install any hardware or software into any of the communication systems on this base?"

"No!" Jameson said hotly. "And if they had, I would've reported it immediately! I'm not a fucking traitor!"

Bladen closed his file. "That's all I intend to ask you today, Paul."

The woman stood up to leave the room, then paused at the door and spoke without looking at any of them.

"Mr Jameson, any disclosure to anyone outside of this room pertaining to any part of this conversation, and you will be well and truly fucked. No pun intended." Then she glanced at Rego for the first time. "And that includes you, Detective Inspector. This is a sensitive inquiry on a need-to-know basis. Information in the wrong hands could jeopardise the investigation." She gave him a disdainful smile. "Your role in this is now ended."

And she walked from the room, closing the door behind her.

Rego wondered who the hell she thought she was. He could guess, of course he could; but the only person he was going to listen to on this was Vikram, although he had his doubts about how smart he was being doing that.

Jameson looked like he was going to be sick.

All Rego wanted was to go home, kiss his wife and have a bloody big drink.

What the hell have you got me into, Vik?

There was nothing more he could do.

For now.

CHAPTER 22

Tamsyn was having a shitty time working her first ever shift at Camborne's custody suite, and it was Friday, which meant that it was going to be party central for anyone off their faces with drink and drugs. Yes, it was a necessary part of her portfolio, and yes, she was pleased to be ticking it off the list, but it was shit.

She was not thrilled to have been sent to the custody block for a night shift just because they were short of female staff. She definitely preferred to be out and about at the sharp end, not sent to be a glorified waiter, which is how several of her more experienced colleagues had described it.

She'd just started the shift when another officer brought in a man who clearly hadn't washed himself or his clothes in months. The body odour was appalling.

"Welcome to the mad house, Tamsyn," said the custody sergeant. "I'm Alan Richards. Is this your first time working the custody suite?"

"Yes, sir. I've been here before but not on this side of it."

"Okay, well, we're pretty busy tonight, so you'll be right in the deep end, but I'll give you a quick rundown first." He smiled reassuringly, sensing her nervousness. "I'm in charge of this circus, so I'm the only one who can authorise detention. All the information about a detainee gets input here," and he pointed to a woman in her thirties with a bleach-blonde pixie cut seated in front of a computer screen who looked up and smiled at Tamsyn. "We're lucky that we've got Kelly tonight but when we don't have admin staff, that could well be part of your job."

"If we get a free moment, I'll give you a tour of the software," Kelly offered.

The look that Sergeant Richards gave Kelly made Tamsyn doubt that there would be any free moments.

"Even if an officer inputs the details, they still have to repeat all the circumstances to the Sergeant – to me – to authorise detention. The big custody blocks like at Plymouth or Exeter also have an Inspector posted to them for the purposes of PACE, but we're not big enough here for that." He glanced at her to see if she was taking it all in, then continued. "Throughout the time a person is in police custody they're subject to reviews at certain time periods. The first review is no later than six hours after detention was first authorised; the second review is nine hours after that, which takes us to 15 hours; and the third review is nine hours after that, which takes us to 24 hours. At that point, it's a custody review, and that can only be conducted by an Inspector. After that, a Superintendent gets involved who can authorise a time period extension up to a further 12 hours. After that 36-hour period, a prisoner can be brought before a Magistrates' Court where a magistrate can authorise a time in police custody up to a maximum of 96 hours ... but that's only in really exceptional circumstances. Got it?"

"Yes, sir," Tamsyn nodded.

She'd revised the section in her textbooks about the protocols of custody suites, but she really appreciated Sergeant Richards reviewing it with her.

"Of course, the exception to *all* of that is terrorism offences where a prisoner can be held in police custody for 14 days before a charging decision is made." He smiled. "But I don't think we'll have to worry about that tonight. Right, let's crack on. Follow me."

Tamsyn walked into utter chaos. It definitely wasn't the calm, controlled scenario that she'd watched in training videos. The custody suite block was like the wild west and the din made it hard to think straight.

"Yeah, it's a bit noisy," said Sergeant Richards with gross understatement. "We've got a group of golfers who clashed with a bunch of lads on a pub crawl. Nobody seems to know what triggered the fight, and I don't think they care either, but it had kicked off bigtime. Several of them from both sides have been arrested for assault and/or criminal damage. They're cooling off a bit now, and it looks like the damage will be paid for, so if no one complains about being assaulted, they'll all be released. Eventually."

He led her down a long corridor to the back of the custody block and pointed to a door.

"That leads to the car park. As you know, officers bring in someone they've arrested to the custody holding cells, a sort of holding tank where they have to wait until there's space at the charge desk – and that could take anything up to 40 minutes."

In Tamsyn's brief experience, it could often be longer than that. Sometimes it seemed that the queue never ended, and officers could spend hours kicking their heels while waiting to book in the person they'd brought in.

"Kelly – or you – logs in the arrest time and arrival time, along with location of the arrest. They'll be photographed, fingerprinted and a DNA swab taken. The medical room is that door there, so if anyone appears to have healthcare needs, we have a nurse on call."

Tamsyn had arrested enough people during her four months in the job to know that she could assess some healthcare needs such as obvious injuries, but she'd had to wonder at the mental health of some of the people who'd been arrested, especially when nearly every single one of them was either drunk, high, or stoned. How could you tell which ones might try to hurt themselves?

"Right, 4Rs protocol on this, Tamsyn," said Sergeant Richards. "Just run me through what you understand by that."

He smiled at her encouragingly.

"The 4Rs is applied to a person under the influence of drink or drugs whose mental or physical faculties are so impaired that it reduces their ability to think and act with ordinary care."

"Good. Go on."

"All detainees under the influence of alcohol and/or drugs, or who are believed to have inserted drugs inside them, must be placed on 4R checks where they are visited and roused at least every 30 minutes to have their condition assessed in accordance with PACE Codes of Practice."

"Any why do we do this?"

"To check that they don't have an injury or condition that's being masked by or mistaken for the drink or drugs."

Sergeant Richards nodded.

"You missed out anyone who is suspected of having a head injury, but otherwise, that was pretty good." His face became serious. "As you're our only female officer on tonight, it'll be up to you to search any women who have been brought in – and we've got two waiting for you. 'Fraid it's not going to be much fun."

The women were in their forties and had been arrested on suspicion of selling class A drugs. They looked like housewives but swore like squaddies, although with every other sentence being, "Fuck you!" they weren't going to win any points for originality.

"Right, Tamsyn. They need to be searched, so you'll have to get them to open their legs and have a good look."

Which was why, within her first hour of working in the custody suite, she found herself looking up a woman's vagina with a torch.

Her nose wrinkled when she found that the first woman had a Kinder egg shoved inside, protecting a powder that she suspected was crack cocaine.

The woman shrugged. "You have your hobbies, I have mine."

Tamsyn knew that she'd never eat another Kinder Surprise.

The second woman took a dump in her cell's toilet, then proceeded to smear her own shit all over the cell.

Tamsyn gagged at the smell, wishing she was wearing a full barrier suit, not just a face mask, and wondering if it was worse than the unwashed man who'd been brought in earlier.

Sighing, she closed the cell down, placed the woman in a different one, and phoned the contract cleaner who did the jobs with hazardous waste. She didn't envy him that.

The custody block was almost full. There were two mental health prisoners waiting for their social workers to arrive, and a drink driver who'd managed to crash his car right on top of a roundabout, taking out two palm trees and a lighted bollard.

Then there was a man arrested in warrant who continually banged on his cell doors and shouted at everyone who went past, threatening to fight them. Several of the other prisoners yelled, screamed and swore back.

Next was a 19 year-old girl, a complete zombie, off her face on spice.

The cell block was airless and windowless, with an unending stream of detained persons in various states of intoxication.

As custody officer, Tamsyn worked with Kelly to book in the prisoners, then escorted them to their cells, taking items of clothing from them with which they could harm themselves, especially items like hoodies or tracksuits with cords.

Some of the prisoners were regulars and opted for legal representation, so everyone had to wait for their brief to arrive.

Sergeant Richards gave her a hurried explanation.

"When the solicitor turns up, the interviewing officer

gives them disclosure which is the offence for which they have been arrested and topics that they'll be interviewed about. Legally, that's all a rep is entitled to – just a copy of the custody record." He gave her a tired smile, "but if that's all you give them, then you'll just get a 'no comment' interview, so it's best to give disclosure. With more serious offences, the disclosure will be phased, so if you plan to do several interviews, you only disclose the topics you plan to speak about in that part of the interview. For example, we would normally not disclose CCTV or DNA evidence until the last interview. So, if we get a pack of lies initially, as the evidence builds up, they start to sweat and hopefully they'll start to talk."

Tamsyn nodded. She'd studied the PEACE interview model as part of her course work: Preparation and Planning; Engage and Explain; Account; Clarification, Challenge, Closure; Evaluation.

Against the background of chaos and despair, a woman's shrill wail pierced the noise like a siren. But after five hours of that, Tamsyn felt nothing. Had the blinkers been taken off or was she just becoming hardened to the world?

"Take another look, Tamsyn," said Sergeant Richards. "See if she needs anything or if she's just kicking off."

The woman wanted more toilet paper. Tamsyn gave her a few sheets – she didn't want anyone deliberately blocking the toilet and causing a flood. Been there, done that, and felt sorry for the cleaner who was called to mop it up once already less than an hour ago.

It wasn't long after that when Tamsyn heard Jamie Smith's voice as he brought in another drunk detainee.

"Hi, Tam," he said cheerfully. "I heard you were on here – must be your lucky day."

"Yeah, I'm going to go home and buy a Lotto ticket after this," she said, deadpan.

He laughed. "You gotta be in it to win it."

"So, what have you won with this one?" Sergeant Richards asked, nodding his head at the man slouched on the bench in a holding cell. He had blood on his face and crisps stuck to his cheek.

"He's not giving his name and he doesn't have any ID on him, but he was picked up at Rumours on Market Jew Street. Landlord got it all on CCTV. Fella, here, came in about 11.15pm, ordered a pint of Doombar and a bag of plain crisps. He necked that and was six deep when he started drinking whiskey chasers and ordered more crisps, presumably to soak up the alcohol," Jamie said, rolling his eyes. "He didn't talk to anyone, and spent all his time staring at his phone and folding his empty crisp packets into neat little triangles."

Tamsyn noticed that the man even had bits of crisp in his hair.

"Matey fell asleep in his last packet of Cheese & Onion, then face planted on the bar. The landlord tried to shake him awake, and I suppose it worked, because Sleeping Beauty, here, realised that a couple of locals were filming him on their phones, laughing their asses off, filming his drunken mess. Well, matey didn't like that and decided to grab their phones and give them a smack. But he was still drunk, so he just fell off his bar stool and hit his head on the way down."

Jamie sighed.

"Anyway, the landlord called it in and lucky me, I was the closest. So, I nicked him for a Section 5 public order offence. You'll probably see it all on TikTok by now, 'cos those two scrotes got the whole shitshow on their phones. They were howling with laughter, said it was sick, and the best evening they'd had in months." He met Tamsyn's gaze. "Perhaps they don't get out much. Anyway, I cuffed Prince Charming and he spent the twenty-minute ride banging on the panel of the police van."

"He seems quiet enough now," said Tamsyn.

"Probably getting ready to hurl," Jamie grinned at her.

"Right, book him," said Sergeant Richards, glancing at the drunk. "And get the nurse to assess his head injury."

Tamsyn hoped that Jamie was wrong about the man being sick. He staggered to his feet and propped himself up against the custody desk.

"He looks completely bladdered. Right, Tamsyn, follow 4R again."

"Yes, sir."

Tamsyn was tired and fed up that another drunk had been brought into custody because he would have to be roused every 30 minutes, which meant they'd be even more rushed.

Tamsyn took the man straight to a cell that was covered by CCTV. He was either so drunk he couldn't remember his name, or was just being a dickhead and refusing to give details. So, after searching him for valuables, she removed his shoes, and checked for anything else that he might use to harm himself.

But instead, he lay on the hard bunk bed, and began to

cry, tears running down his face as his chest heaved. He turned away from Tamsyn, refusing to look at her.

She watched him for a moment, wondering what had gone so wrong in his life that he'd been brought to this state, then remembered that it wasn't her job to fix everyone, and went back to the custody sergeant.

"I'm worried about that one, sarge. He's still not giving us his name and he seems pretty vulnerable."

"Alright, I'll make a note," said Sergeant Richards. "Give him twenty minutes, then go and take him some water. See if you can get him to give you his ID when he's calmed down a bit."

Tamsyn nodded but didn't say anything. She told herself that she didn't care about another drunk. But she did.

She'd just finished the booking in of another detainee when the buzzer went off in the cell of the nameless drunk. Tamsyn opened the hatch and looked through, jumping back as a face stared at her from a few inches away.

"Everything okay?"

"Nothing is okay," he slurred, swaying slightly.

"Do you want some water?"

He nodded slowly, and Tamsyn brought him a paper cup of water from the small kitchen. They didn't give out bottles of water because they could be a choking hazard. But it was more work for the custody officers, to-ing and fro-ing with cups of water.

"There you go," she said, entering the cell and handing him the paper cup. "Do you want to tell me your name now?"

Perhaps her soft voice put the man at ease, because he heaved a sigh, then glanced up at her.

"I live on the base at Culdrose."

"You're with the Royal Navy?"

He shook his head. "No, Royal Fleet Auxiliary. My name is Paul Jameson."

"Thank you, Paul," Tamsyn said with a small smile. "I'll tell the custody sergeant."

He hunched his shoulders.

"Do you know me?"

Tamsyn frowned. "No, we've never met."

The man shook his head. "I mean, have you heard of me?"

Tamsyn didn't know what to think.

"Are you famous?"

He gave a hoarse laugh.

"If you have to ask, I guess I'm not." He accepted the paper cup and took a long drink, almost draining it. "I thought Inspector Rego might have ... I don't know, told people about me."

Tamsyn's eyebrows shot up.

"No, I haven't heard anything." She was really curious now. "What would he have said?"

The man stuck out his lower lip, considering her question.

"About me and Freddie."

"Who's Freddie?"

"He's my ... he *was* my friend." He looked up. "My boyfriend."

The man's words made no sense. *Why would the DI care about someone's boyfriend?*

"Did ... did you break up?" Tamsyn asked, wondering if that's what had brought on the binge-drinking.

The man sighed and looked up at her, tears still streaking his bloodied face.

"He died. Drowned."

"I'm sorry to hear that."

"He was a diver – and divers found him by the wreck of the SS *Mohegan*. That's funny, isn't it? Divers found a diver. You must have heard about that?"

Tamsyn's skin prickled with awareness and she felt hot all over.

"Yes," she croaked. "I heard about that. So, DI Rego found out who it was?"

"Fedir Kuzma," he said softly, giving a crooked smile and putting his forefinger to his lips. "It's all top secret, mustn't tell. Freddie..." his mouth turned down.

"But DI Rego knows?"

Jameson scowled. "I thought he'd help me but he's just made it worse."

As far as Tamsyn knew, they hadn't even found the diver's name, only that Adam was back and not talking to her. *What on earth was going on?*

"Do you want to tell me what happened?" Tamsyn asked, feeling very confused as her mind churned through the possibilities.

Jameson looked up at her, his eyelashes wet with tears.

"Can't," he said sadly, then turned his back to her, lying down on the mattress again. "It's all over."

Tamsyn didn't know what to say. *It can't be that bad* was too trite, and anyway, for all she knew, maybe things *were* really bad for Jameson.

She left the cell reluctantly, but the custody suite was still busy and she had work to do. She wasn't even sure how much of the conversation she could or should report to Sergeant Richards. She glanced at the clock on the wall, disappointed to see that she still had nearly two hours left till the end of her shift.

She made a decision, pulling out her phone and sending a quick text to DI Rego, letting him know that Jameson was in custody and was claiming that the dead diver was his boyfriend.

If it woke him up, tough.

She didn't hear back from DI Rego, so she just carried on working through to the end of the shift. She checked on Jameson every thirty minutes, but each time he opened bleary eyes then rolled over and went back to sleep.

CHAPTER 23

As morning approached, the natives began to get restless, and the noise in the cells increased with people banging on doors and shouting.

Tamsyn decided to check on Jameson once more before she went off shift.

She opened the hatch, expecting to see him lying on his bed, but he wasn't there. In fact, she couldn't see him at all – which was impossible.

Her skin turned ice cold and she hit the panic button, fumbling with numb fingers to use the cell keys to get inside. She pushed against the cell door with all her strength, her boots slipping on the corridor's polished floor, forcing the door open a crack.

The weight of Jameson's body made it difficult, but she finally widened the gap enough to slip through, hearing the sound of people running up the corridor behind her.

Jameson had knotted his shirt and tied it around his neck, attaching the other end to the latch on the cell door. Then he'd let his body slump, his backside not reaching the floor as hung suspended. And even though he had a small frame and weighed no more than 70kg, the makeshift noose was tight around his neck and doing the job Jameson had intended it to do.

Where Tamsyn got her strength to lift the man, she would never know. Holding him under his arms, half-leaning him against her body, she managed to dislodge his shirt, unhooking it from the hatch.

Her muscles screamed as she laid him flat on his back on the floor. Her hands shaking, she checked his pulse: nothing. She checked again, willing herself to find it: nothing.

"He's not breathing!" she shouted. "He's not breathing! Get the nurse!"

Sergeant Richards skidded into the cell and started removing the ligature from around Jamesons's neck.

"The nurse is coming but don't wait for him – start CPR *now!*"

Tamsyn's mind cleared the panic that had threatened to overwhelm her, narrowing down to this second, this moment.

Put the subject on their back.

Done.

Check the airway is clear.

She put her cheek against Jameson's mouth and looked along the line of his chest. She couldn't feel any breath on her face or see his chest rising.

She'd never done CPR on a real person.

She placed the palm of one hand over the back of the other hand, interlocking her fingers and locking her elbows, before slamming the heel of her hand about two inches below his sternum, then started chest compressions.

Thirty chest compressions at a rate close to the beat of the Bee Gee's *Staying Alive*.

They'd laughed during training. *Staying Alive?* How cheesy was that?

She wasn't laughing now.

Where's the nurse?

Two rescue breaths: head back, pinch the nose, tilt the chin – two good breaths watching Jameson's chest rise minutely as she inflated his lungs.

Breathe! Breathe!

Nothing.

Where's the nurse?

Tamsyn started chest compressions again, *Ah, ha, ha, ha, staying alive, staying alive; ah, ha, ha, ha, staying alive.*

Sweat dripped into her eyes but she didn't have time to wipe it away. She felt a rib crack under her hand.

Oh God!

Better a broken rib than dying.

Don't die!

She'd only done three cycles and was sweating hard, ready to hand over to Sergeant Richards who was poised to take over, when the on-duty nurse brought in the defibrillator.

Jamesons's bare chest made the process a little quicker as the de fib box was opened and it sprang to life, the protective coverings were ripped off the pads which were placed diagonally across Jameson's heart.

The machine was talking, issuing instructions to guide the user through the process.

"Stand back – shocking!" yelled the nurse.

Tamsyn scooted back, sitting on her heels as Jameson's body jerked in a grotesque, inhuman jolt.

Then, his chest began to rise and fall by itself, and Tamsyn let out the breath that she didn't know she'd been holding.

Sergeant Richards glanced up, meeting her wide-eyed stare. He nodded and gave a thin smile, then looked back at the defibrillator which remained attached, monitoring Jameson's cardiac rhythm.

The adrenaline that had surged through Tamsyn's body began to ebb, leaving her weak and shaky. She'd been so focused during the CPR that she hadn't even had time to look up, but now, as she glanced around the cell, there must have been 15 members of staff staring at them, not doing anything, but just rubber-necking.

Sergeant Richards realized that they had an audience and cleared them out using some very ripe Cornish vocabulary.

"Bleddy agerever. Let's see some louster!"

Which translated as, *Bloody useless lot, get back to work*.

Tamsyn sat with the nurse on the cell floor next to Jameson, watching his chest rise and fall, watching the faint flutter of his eyelids. He was alive. He'd died, she knew that, but he was alive now.

It didn't seem possible.

She stared at him, her eyes burning with tiredness. She hardly dared blink, just in case, in that brief instant, Jameson's life would be snuffed out. So, she watched and she waited.

DEAD MAN'S DIVE

Every minute felt like a thousand as they listened for the ambulance's sirens. It had only been twelve minutes, but in that moment, death had visited – and been denied.

The noise in the cells hadn't abated and detainees were calling out questions and suggestions, some sincere, some angry, some cynical, some even yelling that the police had tried to kill Jameson, that he'd been beaten up, that he'd been tasered, that *we know the truth!*

Finally, two paramedics arrived with their kit bags and went to work straight away, taking details from the nurse, disconnecting the defib and attaching their own, more sophisticated kit. They worked smoothly in tandem, communicating clearly with each other, the routine of a long-established partnership.

One of them covered Jameson with a foil blanket to keep him warm, then the other asked Tamsyn how long it had been between checks of Jameson's cell. She knew that she'd done more than was required, looking in at least every 30 minutes, but still, it hadn't been enough.

They weren't judging her; they didn't need to – Tamsyn judged herself.

"Who started CPR?" asked one of the paramedics.

"Me. I did," said Tamsyn.

Was she going to be criticised for breaking Jameson's rib?

"Top work, officer," said the paramedic. "We'll be speaking to your boss. You saved this man's life. It's not often we get one back, but your swift actions saved him. Well done."

Tamsyn's cheeks went red, she felt like such a fraud. But then Jameson's hand crept out from under the blanket and tightened on hers, as if he, too, was thanking her.

Twenty minutes passed, both paramedics were still on their knees as Jameson appeared to regain consciousness. He was confused, but able to answer some basic questions. Eventually, the paramedics placed him on a trolley and wheeled him towards the ambulance.

Jameson looked up at Tamsyn, his expression pleading, and he wouldn't let go of her hand. Tamsyn squeezed it gently.

"You'll be alright now, Paul. The paramedics are taking you to hospital – they'll take care of you."

"Stay, please?" he whispered, his voice weak.

Surprised, Tamsyn looked at Sergeant Richards, who just nodded. So, she walked alongside the trolley, only letting go where the corridor narrowed.

Tamsyn had no clue what time it was; all she knew was that she was very thirsty and utterly exhausted. Outside the station, dawn was breaking, the sky still grey but with a hint of pink behind the clouds. It was going to be another beautiful summer's day.

He nearly died. He wanted to die.

She felt numb, her well of emotions empty.

It had been so intense – the fear had nearly overwhelmed her. Nearly, not completely.

She leaned against the side of the ambulance and closed her eyes as Jameson was loaded into the back. When the paramedics had made sure he was comfortable, Tamsyn climbed in behind him, holding his hand when he reached out for her again.

It was still so early in the morning, the roads were

almost empty, and with a blue-light run to the hospital, they covered the twelve miles from Camborne to Truro within ten minutes – less than half the time an ordinary journey with daytime traffic took.

Jameson hadn't let go of Tamsyn's hand throughout the journey, his skin pale and slightly clammy. Gently, she brushed the embedded crisps from his hair, and the paramedic riding in the back handed her a wet wipe which she used to freshen him up Jameson's face. His eyes followed the movement of her hand, but he didn't speak.

The ambulance drew up directly outside the entrance to A&E where Jameson was rushed inside. A doctor who didn't look much older than Tamsyn was waiting for them, along with two more experienced nurses. Again, the paramedics recounted Jameson's stats to the team, as well as Tamsyn's actions.

The doctor turned to her and winked.

She blinked, surprised. Did that wink mean, *well done for saving his life* or *let me give you my phone number?*

But her brain was muddled and her body numb. She really didn't care what the wink meant. A man had tried to kill himself. *Stupid winking doctor*.

Tamsyn sat in A&E, her thoughts drifting. The waiting area only had two other people in it, but she could feel them staring at her. Was it the uniform?

She looked down at herself and smiled wryly. The doctor's wink definitely wasn't about wanting to give her his phone number because she looked like a bag of shit. Grey dust coated her knees, sweat and blood had dried on her shirt, and her hair had come out of its tidy bun.

Standing up slowly, she made a half-hearted attempt to

brush the dirt and dust from her trousers, and blew some stray hair from her face, patting it into place, but none of that really helped.

Moving as if each of her police boots weighed ten kilos, she stumbled over to the women's toilets, catching an unfortunate glimpse of her reflection in the mirror as she opened the door. She looked like she had been dragged through a hedge backwards and then dived back in to have another go. She had no brush, no comb, not even a lip balm for her dry lips. She pulled her fingers through her hair futilely, grabbing handfuls to shove into a scrunchie, trying to tame the rats' tails. What little makeup she'd been wearing was long gone, so she simply splashed cold water on her face, then dried it with a paper towel. Best she could do.

At least she had Apple Pay on her phone to buy a cup of tea. Her stomach rumbled, a reminder that her sandwich was back at Camborne in her go-bag. It could wait.

Tamsyn took her tea, sipping it gratefully. The couple in the waiting area seemed to find this fascinating and followed her every movement.

Forty minutes later, one of the nurses who'd been with Jameson on arrival walked across to her.

"We're moving Mr Jameson to the Acute Medical Unit – it's on the first floor of the Trelawney Wing."

"Are you admitting him?" Tamsyn asked.

"No decision has been made on that yet. We'll let you know." She glanced at Tamsyn's dishevelled state. "Long night?"

"The longest," Tamsyn sighed.

"Yup, been there," the nurse said sympathetically.

Tamsyn trudged through the largely silent hospital, her footsteps echoing down the long corridor, but her mind was elsewhere. Paul Jameson was still a prisoner, but as he was in hospital, his 'custody clock' had stopped. She would have to stay with him until he was either returned to the cell block or she was relieved by another officer.

Her next thought jumped to Rego. Her message to him had been delivered, but she had no way of knowing if he'd read it. She sent a second message saying that Jameson had tried to kill himself.

"Oh, crap!"

Although her phone still had some life in it, she was down to the last 10%. She should have charged it before her night shift: coulda, shoulda, woulda.

She considered turning it off to save the battery, but thought that her boss might try to contact her.

Maybe she should ring him now while she still had some juice in the battery? If she waited until a reasonable hour, he would probably be annoyed if she didn't call ... or he'd be annoyed that she'd woken him up. Pretty much a lose-lose situation. Tamsyn went for option one; she rang him, but his mobile went straight to voicemail. She knew he would call back as soon as he picked up the message.

She repeated what she'd said in her text message, adding that her phone battery was low, but that she was in the waiting area of the Acute Medical Unit.

Next, she updated the custody sergeant about Jameson's status.

"Okay, Tamsyn. I'll try to get someone to relieve you sooner rather than later, but it'll probably be a couple of hours yet."

Tamsyn thanked him. She knew how it went – even sergeants couldn't always keep promises like that.

The custody sergeant wasn't aware of all the facts surrounding Paul Jameson, but Tamsyn wasn't about to breach any confidences or tell him anything that she knew about the dead diver case. But as he was her CO, she did offer her opinion that Jameson wasn't a criminal or a violent person.

"He told me he'd been going through a hard time," she paused. "Perhaps when he's back in custody and has sobered up, maybe just a caution would be appropriate."

Tamsyn hoped she hadn't overstepped with the sergeant, but she guessed that DI Rego would back her up. Her gut told her that Jameson was telling the truth, in which case, he didn't need to be charged, he needed help – and she would try to to get it for him.

The sergeant was silent for several seconds, neither agreeing nor disagreeing with her.

"Use the time to write up your notes," he said, then rang off.

After another half an hour, Tamsyn was allowed to sit with Jameson. He was still in her custody, and she was responsible for him and responsible for making sure he didn't escape. Even though he wasn't exactly a career criminal and didn't have 'Great Train Robber' stamped on his forehead, the shit would hit the fan if he escaped from custody, no matter how trivial the offence.

She didn't have any handcuffs, although she knew that she could have asked for some to be brought to her, but she also knew that Paul Jameson wasn't going to make a run for it. She sat by his bed, watching his shallow breaths. Even in sleep, she could tell he was in pain, and she felt another twinge of guilt about his broken rib – or ribs – no one had told her how many she'd broken.

She continued watching him until he began to wake, opening his eyes slowly and looking up at her.

He swallowed several times, licking his dry lips.

"Thank you for staying," he said at last, his voice ragged, the ugly lividity around his neck telling its own story.

"That's okay," Tamsyn said quietly. "Look, Paul, I know what you've been through recently. I'm going to get you some help."

She wasn't sure he was taking in what she was saying.

"What's your name?"

"PC Poldhu, Tamsyn."

"Good Cornish name," he said, his eyes closing and his mouth twisting with the semblance of a smile. He opened his eyes again. "The doctor says you saved my life."

Tamsyn nodded. "That's what they told me, too."

Jameson closed his eyes again.

"I haven't decided if I want to thank you yet." He let out a long sigh. "Everything has gone to shit. I thought it was bad when Freddie left ... I thought that was bad enough. I loved him, and I thought he loved me." His eyes opened tiredly. "Have you ever been in love, Tamsyn?"

"No," she said honestly.

"I loved Freddie. And then I find out he didn't leave me, he died. He was murdered, wasn't he?"

"What makes you think that?"

"If it had been an accident, everyone would have been talking about it when it happened, and they wouldn't have left him ... they wouldn't have left him down there, but it was all hushed up."

He tried to shrug but winced instead.

"Do they know who killed him?"

"I don't know. I'm just a student PC – no one tells me anything."

"I know how that feels," he said quietly.

Tamsyn was being slightly disingenuous, but she really didn't know what was happening with this case ... or even that there *was* a case.

Jameson thought for a moment and sighed.

"Do you know Detective Inspector Rego?"

"Yes."

"Can you get him for me? Just him, no one else." He looked up and met her gaze. "There's something I need to tell him."

CHAPTER 24

When Rego woke up and saw Tamsyn's messages, he didn't even wait long enough to make himself a cup of coffee.

"Sorry, luv," he whispered to Cassie, who was watching him dress. "I've got to get going – it's important."

"Seriously? You mean you're leaving me with your mother? For how long? It had better not be all day!"

Rego nodded and gave her a quick smile.

"It won't be all day. Scout's honour."

Cassie rolled onto her back and closed her eyes.

"You owe me, Robert."

"I know," he said, leaning down and kissing her. "I'll make it up to you."

She pulled him down to deepen the kiss.

"I'll be waiting," she smiled at him, running her hand over his thigh.

Rego squeezed his eyes shut. There were times when he *really* hated being a copper.

As soon as he was in the car, he tried calling Tamsyn,

but the call when straight to voicemail and he guessed that her phone had died. He decided that he'd wait to speak to her in person rather than going through Treliske's switchboard where anyone could be listening.

He wanted to speak to Jameson as soon as possible, and definitely before he was taken back to Camborne.

He didn't know what had precipitated Jameson's attempt to kill himself, it could be any one of several different things: finding out that his boyfriend was dead; the interview at Culdrose; admitting to senior officers that he was gay – any of those things could have triggered him. It was also possible that there was something else going on – maybe Jameson knew more than he'd been prepared to say during the formal interview.

He felt a small pinch of guilt but then immediately dismissed it: it was a legitimate line of enquiry and Jameson had come to him. There was nothing in their previous conversations that could have led him to believe Jameson would try to end his life. Were there any signs that he'd missed? Rego didn't think so, and from what he'd read in the report he'd accessed on his phone, it wasn't a planned attempt, more like drunken desperation to end the pain and confusion.

It was shit, but shit happened. And Rego knew that the custody sergeant would be swimming through the stuff now, having a detained person very nearly successfully commit suicide.

Rego was so deep in thought that he almost missed a weary-looking Tamsyn standing at the bus-stop.

He pulled up and rolled down his window.

"Get in."

She opened the door and slid into the passenger seat with a soft groan.

"Long night?"

"The longest," she yawned.

"I tried calling you back," Rego said.

"My phone died," she said sheepishly.

"Don't go on duty with anything less than a full charge."

"I know. Sorry, sir."

"Tell me about Jameson."

Tamsyn recounted everything she could remember as they drove to the hospital car park, up to and including Jameson's request to speak to Rego.

"And who's with him now?"

"PC Chris Rowe from Camborne."

"What's he like?"

"She. She seems nice. Paul ... Mr Jameson ... he's been crying a lot."

"Okay. Thank you, Tamsyn. You did well last night."

"Thank you, sir."

"Do you want to wait for the bus or I can give you a lift back to the station in about half an hour or so."

She hesitated, then said tiredly.

"I'd love a lift back but my car's at Camborne."

"No problem."

"In that case, yes please. Um, is it okay if I just take a nap in your car?"

Rego smiled at her as he parked and opened the driver's door.

"Of course. See you in a bit."

When Rego arrived at the Acute Medical Unit,

Jameson was asleep and an older woman officer was sitting next to him, reading something on her phone.

She stood up when she saw him.

"Good morning, sir."

"Chris, isn't it?" he said pleasantly.

"Yes, sir," she smiled, clearly pleased that he knew her name.

"How is he?" Rego asked, gesturing to Jameson. "Has he said anything."

She glanced down at her tablet.

"He's been sleeping since PC Poldhu left at 8.25am. The only thing he said was to ask if you were coming."

"Okay, go and get yourself a cup of coffee and wait outside while I talk to him."

"Yes, sir."

Rego studied Jameson's unhealthy pallor, the dark circles under his eyes, and the ugly purple ligature marks around his neck, the heart monitor still attached to him and the man's shallow breathing. Gently, he shook his shoulder, hoping that none of the doctors or nurses would have a go at him for waking a patient, but they were all too busy to notice.

Jameson's eyes opened slowly and he blinked up at Rego.

"Thank you for coming."

"I hear there's something you want to tell me."

"Can you help me sit up a bit, please?"

Rego fumbled with the bed's remote control until Jameson was half-lying, half-sitting.

"Thanks. Can I have some water?"

Rego smiled to himself, remembering similar stalling

tactics during Jameson's formal interview. His smile faded as he thought about the man's subsequent decision to kill himself.

He helped Jameson take a few sips of water, then set the plastic cup back down.

"Freddie *did* ask me to share classified intelligence," Jameson began. "He said it would help the Ukrainian cause. All he cared about was a free Ukraine – he was passionate about it – really hated Putin, really hated the Russians." He licked his lips. "I wanted to help him but I was scared. I thought I'd be found out. He kept asking me but I kept saying that I needed to think about it. He started getting angry with me. A couple of times, he hit me." He closed his eyes. "I didn't tell anyone because I was embarrassed. I just said I'd fallen down a flight of stairs."

"Did you give Freddie any sort of intelligence at all, classified or non-classified?"

"No, nothing. I promise."

Rego sat back, wondering what this information added to the case.

"Do you think Freddie asked anyone else to share intelligence?"

Jameson pulled a face.

"I thought he might have been seeing someone else. There were quite a few times when no one seemed to know where he was. I thought it was just because we had to be careful about our relationship, but one time..."

"Go on."

"Well, one time I found an earring on the floor in his room." He hesitated, then looked up at Rego. "A woman's earring – a long, dangly one. Not something a guy would wear ... unless he was a drag queen."

Jameson laughed hoarsely at his own joke, then winced in pain.

"Do you have any idea who that was?"

"None. I was afraid that he'd dump me if I asked him about it."

"Okay, thank you for your time, Mr Jameson and..."

"Wait, Inspector!" Jameson said urgently. "I haven't told you the most important part!"

Rego hid his impatience well.

"And what's that?"

"During the interview, they wanted to know if I'd been asked to look after any equipment that was non-UK military. I didn't think it counted," and his cheeks coloured at the lie, "but I had Freddie's laptop. We were watching a film on it in my room the night before the training mission. And then ... the next thing I knew, the Ukrainians had gone."

Rego's heartrate sped up but he made sure his expression remained neutral.

"That could be useful," he said. "When can I pick it up?"

Jameson pulled a face. "I don't have it anymore."

This time, Rego showed his irritation.

"I know, I'm s-sorry," Jameson stammered. "It was stolen about three weeks after Freddie disappeared. Well, it could have happened sooner. I'd put it away because I thought ... I don't know what I thought, but I hoped..." Jameson sighed. "Anyway, it was stolen. I didn't report it – obviously – and I was sort of glad it was gone. I was so angry with Freddie by then. I'd have enjoyed telling him that his precious laptop was gone. He never used to let me touch it." Jameson's face fell. "I don't know who took it."

Rego's mind was racing.

"Could it have been the woman he was seeing?"

Jameson pulled a face.

"I don't know."

"Who knew you had it? Did you tell any friends? Any colleagues?"

Jameson threw him an incredulous look.

"No one even knew that I was seeing him! Let alone that he'd left his laptop in my room."

Rego shook his head. "Someone knew."

"Maybe ... maybe it was just coincidence?" Jameson suggested.

Rego really didn't think so. He waited for more but it seemed that Jameson had nothing left to say.

"I'm sorry I didn't tell you before," Jameson said weakly. "It doesn't seem to matter now."

Rego didn't tell him that it bloody well did matter. He also didn't tell him that he believed Kuzma had been grooming him. It wasn't something that was only done by paedophiles to children: grooming was about getting someone to trust you, and once you did, they would persuade you to do something that you wouldn't normally, because, hey, you trusted them, right? No one was immune to that; grooming could happen at any age.

"Do you remember the make of the laptop?" Rego asked, focusing on the here and now, focusing on where he *could* make a difference. "Was there anything distinctive about it?"

Jameson closed his eyes in frustration.

"A military laptop, you know, a seriously tough piece of kit designed to withstand the knocks of a military environment – police use the Panasonic Toughbook, right? Freddie's was similar and he was proud of it; he said it exceeded the strictest MIL-STD requirements and IP ratings for shock, drop, and resistance to dust and water. It even had a full magnesium alloy case to protect the LCD screen."

His gaze brightened.

"Did you know that the Danish Army strap the tablets in front of their armour so they can receive commands and see where both friends and enemies are located."

"Paul, focus."

"Okay, I'm sorry ... it looked a bit like the Toughbook CF 54, black and silver, but it was a Russian brand name."

He squeezed his eyes shut, trying to remember.

"It could have been Asus? But I'm not sure. It had its own handle but he kept it in a black messenger bag – just like every laptop everywhere."

His voice dropped again.

"You don't know what it's like for me. I left that interview room feeling totally humiliated. It felt like you were all laughing at me for being so fucking naïve. And that woman, the one with the face like a smacked arse, I'm sure she was pissing herself laughing at me."

"No one was laughing at you," Rego said.

Jameson looked up, his expression bleak.

"I'd never felt so lonely in my entire life. I mean, yeah, some of the people I work with know I'm gay, but it was kind of an open secret, you know? After being interviewed about Freddie, it was like school all over again," and he gave a bitter laugh. "It felt like I'd been 'outed'. And I kept thinking that the whole of the shore establishment would know about me. And I know that it isn't supposed to matter and you say that no one would judge me, but I just couldn't shake it from my mind that my career was over. So, I went to my room, changed out of my uniform and decided I had to get off the base. I really bloody needed a drink. I ditched my wallet, only taking some cash. I didn't want to run into anyone I knew, so I headed for Penzance. I left my RFA ID in my glove box – I knew it would cause a shit storm if I lost that. And then..." he met Rego's gaze. "Well, you know the rest."

Rego stood up to leave the cubicle.

"Thank you for your time, Mr Jameson. I may need to ask you some more questions, but I'll let you know."

"Inspector?" Jameson called weakly.

"Yes?"

"When you find out what happened to Freddie, will you let me know?"

Rego nodded slowly. "I'll tell you what I can."

It was only when Rego got back to his car that he remembered Tamsyn was there.

She'd lowered the backrest as far as it would go, and her head was pressed against the passenger window at an awkward angle. Her blonde hair fanned across the seat, and her mouth was slightly open.

Rego paced away from his car and pulled out his burner phone to call Vikram.

"Vik, I've just spoken to Jameson again. He said that Kuzma had a laptop which was left with him when the

Ukrainians left, but that it was stolen from his room approximately three weeks later."

"Interesting," said Vikram. "Very interesting. Did he have any idea what was on it?"

"I don't think so. He mentioned watching a film on it with Kuzma, but he used the term 'his precious laptop' which made me think Kuzma viewed it as something important, and he was never allowed to touch it. The other thing Jameson told me was that Kuzma *had* solicited intelligence from him, but that he'd refused. He gave me the impression that if Kuzma had stayed around – or alive – he would have given in eventually. I'd say he was in love with Kuzma, but that Kuzma was grooming him. He also thought that Kuzma was seeing someone else – a woman. He found a dangly earring in Kuzma's room."

Vikram whistled through his teeth.

"Do you believe him?"

"Yeah, Vik. I do. The man tried to kill himself."

"Could be a guilty conscience."

"I guess it could be but that's not the vibe I was getting from him."

"Do you believe the story about the laptop? That it was stolen? That it even existed?"

Rego nodded even though Vikram couldn't see him.

"If you'd seen him, you'd have believed him, too. And at this point, what's he got to lose?"

"His career?"

"Mate, I think that's already shot. He tried to kill himself – he won't be allowed to work on anything classified again."

Vikram was silent for several seconds.

"You're right. I think he might actually have been telling the truth. It ties in with a few other things." He paused. "I'm still working on the drone's encryption, but there were some interesting data spikes. If someone was downloading to a laptop ... yeah, yeah, that could..."

He broke off his monologue.

"I've got to go, Rob. I've had an idea."

Rego could almost hear Vikram's ginormous brain at work.

"Okay, call me when you know—" but Vikram had already hung up. "Cheers to you, too," Rego said sarcastically.

CHAPTER 25

Tamsyn had slept for a few hours, but now she was at the harbour stocking the *Daniel Day* with her grandmother's wonderful picnic, wishing like hell that she hadn't been volunteered by her grandmother to take the Rego family out on her grandfather's boat again. And her grandfather couldn't come with them because he had a meeting at the bank.

She was tired, depressed, and definitely not up for socialising with her boss's family after a 13-hour shift. But she'd promised.

And anyway, her grandmother had woken her up.

She looked up when Morwenna started wagging her tail madly, and Tamsyn saw the Rego family strolling along the pier to the punt.

Except DI Rego wasn't there. Instead, there was an older black woman with a regal bearing who didn't look happy as she stared around the harbour.

Cassie saw Tamsyn looking past them all for her boss.

"Sorry, Rob had to go into work so it's just us," she smiled. "I hope that's okay."

"Sure, no problem," said Tamsyn, feeling a little awkward. "Was it something ... serious?"

"I've no idea," Cassie said breezily. "We came to an agreement long ago that I don't ask. If he wants to talk, and assuming that he's allowed to, he will."

"Oh, okay."

"Although it could be that he didn't want to be seasick in front of the kids again," she said, her eyes sparkling with amusement.

Tamsyn laughed and the two women smiled at each other.

"Let me introduce you to my mother-in-law, Patricia Rego."

Tamsyn was very curious to meet the DI's mother. She smiled and held out her hand.

"Hello, Mrs Rego. It's very nice to meet you."

"It's Ms Rego," the woman said. "*She* is Mrs Rego," and she jerked her chin at Cassie, ignoring Tamsyn's outstretched hand.

"Oh, sorry," Tamsyn said faintly, her eyes widening at Cassie who just looked pained.

Mo didn't try to approach the newcomer, eyeing her warily. The feeling was obviously mutual.

"Is that dog coming, as well?" Patrica Rego asked.

"Yes," said Tamsyn. "She goes everywhere with me."

The woman muttered something under her breath and theatrically stepped around Morwenna.

"Sorry about her," Cassie sighed. "She wasn't invited but..." and whatever she was going to say trailed off.

Tamsyn wondered why the DI's mother had come at all if she was going to find fault with everything. She seemed so unlike her son. It puzzled Tamsyn. Luckily, she liked puzzles – she liked searching for the hidden patterns.

She lifted Mo aboard and the kids scrambled after her, bombarding Tamsyn with a million questions.

"Can fish smell?" asked Max.

"That's silly!" said Maisie. "They don't have noses."

"They don't have noses but they do have nostrils," Tamsyn explained, quelling the fight that was about to break out. "It's really important for them. Next time you catch one, look for the little holes just above its mouth. They need their sense of smell to help them find food or to warn them if there's a predator in the area, or where their families are, and it helps them to find their way home, too."

"Why don't they get cold?" Maisie asked.

"Fish are cold blooded, so they don't feel the cold the way we do."

"What are you going to do, Maze?" Max teased. "Knit them a scarf?"

"Is this your boat?" Patricia Rego asked, interrupting the flow of questions.

"It's my grandfather's," Tamsyn answered.

"It's very small," huffed the DI's mother.

Tamsyn's smile turned steely. "It may be small but it's kept our family fed for three generations."

Patrica Rego gave her a look that Tamsyn couldn't interpret, but accepted her help to climb aboard the *Daniel Day*.

As soon as everyone had taken a seat and Mo was curled up on a coil of rope, Tamsyn started the engine and steered them out of the harbour, waving at the fishermen she knew, which was most of them.

The children bickered on and off for the whole 40-minute ride out to Piskies Cove, a small, secluded beach just around the headland from Cudden Point.

"They're not normally this annoying," Cassie said conversationally to Tamsyn.

"*Muuuum!*" both children wailed at the same time.

"They're being obnoxious because they miss their dad," Cassie continued as if the children hadn't just yelled at full volume.

"My bwoy works too hard," Patricia Rego added. "You'd think he'd want to be at home more," and she shot a quelling look at Cassie who simply looked the other way.

Tamsyn wished the day were over. She was still tired and didn't feel much like spending another of her days off with the Rego family. Right now, she was craving her own company, little Mo being the honourable exception.

The children eventually fell into a sullen silence while Cassie basked in the sunshine, looking put-together and elegant as usual, gazing serenely through her designer sunglasses at the passing coastline.

Tamsyn didn't bother to start up a conversation, and continued to steer the little boat heading east.

"Have you lived here your whole life?" Cassie asked after several more minutes had passed.

"Yes, I was born just a few miles from here."

"No dreams of going to the bright lights and big city?"

Tamsyn scoffed. "No, no way. I like the space here, and it's peaceful. Mostly."

"Mostly," Cassie echoed with a smile, looking fondly

at Max and Maisie who had made up and were leaning over the side, trailing their hands in the water, looking for fish.

"Are you from Manchester?" Tamsyn asked.

"No, I'm from a small town in Cheshire. My mum still lives there. I went to Manchester for art college."

"You're an artist?"

"A graphic designer. I work for the Council at the moment, but I'm thinking of going freelance."

"Robert didn't tell me that," Patricia interrupted. "Why would you give up a good, steady job. It sounds like nonsense to me."

Cassie took a deep breath. "I haven't made any decision yet, but when I do, you'll be the third to know."

Swing and a hit, Tamsyn smiled to herself.

She cut the engine as they approached Piskie's Cove and dropped the anchor over the side.

The water was a perfect aquamarine and the sand was pale gold – and completely empty.

"Looks like we've got it to ourselves," Tamsyn smiled at the kids.

"It reminds me of home," Patricia said wistfully.

"Manchester?" Maisie asked with a puzzled expression.

"No, chile!" Patricia laughed. "Bermuda! My home. Except it's hot there in summer, not like an English summer," and she pulled her cardigan around her shoulders more tightly.

Tamsyn wondered why she'd bothered coming to Cornwall at all.

"Okay," she said to the kids, "let's get the picnic

ashore," and she pulled off her shorts and t-shirt and jumped into the water.

The children followed her, shrieking as the cold water hit their bodies.

Tamsyn reached for Mo who was standing on the bow, and the little dog swam confidently towards the beach.

Next came the coolers and waterproof containers which Tamsyn floated ashore and then Cassie jumped into the water, wearing a killer white bikini.

For a moment, Tamsyn wondered if Patricia was going to sit in the boat by herself, but eventually she disrobed, displaying a bright, floral one-piece and a sour expression.

She had some difficulty levering herself into the water, and eventually belly-flopped over the side, spluttering as she surfaced. But the sour look had gone and she was smiling brightly.

"I haven't swum in the sea for years!" she laughed. "I swam every day when I was your age," she said to Maisie.

They waded ashore and laid out towels, slathered themselves in suncream, and dug into the coolers for sandwiches, crisps and cold drinks.

The harmony didn't last for long.

"Do you have a boyfriend?" Maisie asked with the direct innocence of the very young.

"No," Tamsyn replied shortly, thinking of her fledgling relationship with Adam that had crashed and burned.

"Maisie, that's a very personal question," Cassie chided.

"But she's so pretty, Mum! Why don't you have a boyfriend?" Maisie asked.

"Maisie!" Cassie said sharply.

"I'm not allowed to say anything! It's not fair!"

Maisie stormed off to the other side of the beach in a huff.

"I'll go after her," Patricia said, throwing an aggrieved look at Tamsyn.

Max was at the other side of the beach with Mo investigating the rock pools.

"Sorry about that," Cassie grimaced.

"Is she always like that?" Tamsyn asked.

"Maisie or Patricia?" Cassie answered with a tired laugh.

"Uh, well, I meant Patricia. I don't think she likes me."

"Don't take it personally, she doesn't like anyone. Certainly not me. Well, she loves the kids and thinks the sun shines out of Rob's arse, but anyone else, not so much."

"That sounds fun," Tamsyn commiserated.

Cassie groaned. "Honestly, we didn't even invite her here, she just showed up – said she missed the kids. It was just supposed to be a holiday for the four of us. But ... well, she's not so bad once you get to know her. She has her reasons." She forced a smile. "Oh well, I'll get my own back next week when my mum comes to visit." She glanced at Tamsyn. "I'm sorry about Maisie, too. She's eight going on eighteen, and completely boy-obsessed. Rob doesn't know the half of it. He threatened to stake her first boyfriend on the front lawn as a warning to the others."

Tamsyn laughed out loud, intrigued by this paternal side of her DI that she'd never seen.

"My grandad can be a bit like that," Tamsyn admitted. "He doesn't think anyone is good enough," and she rolled her eyes. "Anyway, I don't mind Maisie asking me, but I don't have anything interesting to tell her. I had a boyfriend but..." Cassie looked at her curiously so Tamsyn shrugged and continued. "He dumped me because of the job, pretty much."

Cassie didn't look as surprised as Tamsyn thought she would.

"The job is hard on relationships," Cassie said. "Maybe you've heard 'join the Force and get a divorce'?"

Tamsyn shook her head.

"Well, you're young, but you'll hear it. Maybe not as much now as it used to be because understaffing means that you're single-crewing for most of the time so relationships don't develop in quite the same way. I think the Met is different though when it comes to double-crewing. And shift patterns can be hard on family life – there were times I felt like a single mother, especially when he'd only get one weekend off in seven or eight weeks. It was a bit better when he joined CID – at least there are more weekends off, but the days are longer. It used to be just when there was a big case on, but it's all the time really." She shrugged her slim shoulders. "And now he's down here, we see him for maybe four or five days a month."

"How do you do it?" Tamsyn asked quietly. "How can you make a good relationship if you're a police officer?"

Cassie gave her a bleak smile. "Find someone with a lot of patience." Then she smiled more naturally. "Rob is one of the good guys in a job surrounded by bastards. I trust him – I know he'd never cheat on me ... or risk losing the kids."

Tamsyn couldn't help feeling those last words were aimed in her direction, and her cheeks grew hot.

CHAPTER 26

Tregowan walked into the *Blue* Anchor's pub garden and found Rego sitting under a sun umbrella and drinking a fruit juice.

The men shook hands and Rego pushed a bottle of Spingo towards him.

"Cheers!"

Tregowan glanced around him to see who was close enough to hear them, but Rego had chosen their table carefully, selecting an area well away from everyone else.

"Thanks for coming, Nate."

Tregowan nodded, looking uncomfortable.

"What did you find out?"

Tregowan took a long drink from the bottle then picked at the label absently.

"Nothing solid, lots of chat."

"Go on."

"The Ukrainians were a team of combat divers and support techs with the 73rd Naval Centre of Special

Operations: Spetsnaz, the SEAL teams of the Ukraine." Tregowan looked up. "That's special forces, boss."

Rego already knew that but didn't give anything away.

"Special intelligence," Tregowan said quietly, pressing the point home. "From what my buddy told me, they trained hard, worked hard, played hard. Friendly enough and pretty heavy drinkers, but completely dedicated to freeing Ukraine from the Russians."

So far, Rego had learned nothing new, but he had a feeling that Tregowan was building up to something.

"But it was strange – they were here for six months and you'd think they'd work with our boys the whole time, but they didn't. They spent a month with each of the specialist Fleet Diving Units ... and then stopped. No one knows what they were doing for the next three months. All sorts of rumours were circulating, but whatever they were doing and whoever knew about it, no one was talking."

"I'm a bit out of my depth here," said Rego, and Tregowan attempted a brief smile at the unintentional pun. "What do the three specialist units do?"

"Fleet Diving Unit 1 provides support to our Special Forces. They train with the SAS and SBS to neutralise any explosive threats during Maritime Counter Terrorism operations – basically, clearing IEDs from the path of any assault force, whether devices are attached to hostages or structures like oil rigs, ships – both underway and in port – as well as on land. They're trained in various insertion techniques such as by small boat, via submarine and by parachute."

Rego made a few notes and Tregowan continued.

"FDU2 specialises in shallow water mine clearance operations in support of UK and NATO deployments. That would include carrying out beach reconnaissance ahead of amphibious landings. Now, this is where it gets interesting," Tregowan said, leaning forwards and lowering his voice still further. "FDU2 divers use unmanned underwater vehicles to check the boat lanes and beaches leading to the proposed landing site for mines. Their work with UUVs is cutting edge, boss." He raised his eyebrows. "Sound familiar?"

Rego knew that Tregowan was referring to the drone, but from what Vikram had said, the drone was a listening device.

"And the third Fleet Diving Group?"

Tregowan raised his hand in a seesawing motion.

"Possibly less relevant. FDU3 operate mainly in the mine investigation. They check for mines in ports, under ship's hulls and in deep waters. They also worked in Afghanistan, embedding with Royal Engineer Field Squadrons to clear out IEDs and mines. They're the patch, make and mend guys, carrying out battle damage assessment and repair operations across the fleet."

"So, the Ukrainians trained with each group ... and then what?"

Tregowan leaned back.

"Good question. No one knows. Except my buddy said they seemed to be pretty tight with the RFA's comms team – lots of high-level technical discussions." He shrugged. "The only other intel is that the Ukrainians were equipped with top of the range dive sets – the full range of Stealth CDLSE."

He saw Rego's confused expression.

"That stands for Clearance Divers Life Support Equipment. These are closed circuit, electronically-controlled mixed-gas rebreathers which can use oxygen for dives down to 200 feet and a heliox/trimix mix for dives down to 390 feet. In the UK, they're made by Divex, but these were different. Remember when I saw the dry bag at the PM, I said there were modifications I didn't recognise. My buddy said the same thing. All CDLSE sets are made from non-magnetic materials – neoprene with non-magnetic zips and inflation valves. You definitely don't want anything magnetic when you're de-mining."

"So, what were the Ukrainians doing?"

"No clue. But they left in a hurry. There were plans for some joint socialising, a pool tournament – and then they were just gone. My buddy assumed it was because of something that had happened back home." His eyes flickered. "There was no suggestion whatsoever that one of the divers hadn't made it back from a training mission ... or whatever they were doing out there."

Rego drank from his bottle of J2O, myriad questions running through his brain. A pattern was beginning to emerge, but he still had more questions than answers.

"Thanks, Nate," he said.

Tregowan nodded. "Okay, but now what?"

Rego drew in a deep breath.

"I have a couple of ideas."

That night, after he'd finally driven his mother back to the Premier Inn, seen the kids off to bed and promised Cassie on pain of death or his spare kidney that he wouldn't leave her alone with his mother the following day, only then could Rego speak to Godber and Vikram.

Godber tiptoed stealthily into the kitchen, tripping over Max's shoes and waking dogs in the next street.

Rego pushed a mug of tea across to him.

"Good thing you didn't take up a career as a cat burglar."

"Who leaves their trainers in the middle of the room?" Godber complained.

"A teenage boy," Rego replied.

"Bloody hell! Since when did Max become a teenager? I thought he was a kid."

"He's twelve going on twenty: too kool for skool, and giving his dad grey hairs."

"Nah, he's a good kid."

Rego nodded. "Most of the time."

"If Max is twelve, how old is Maisie?" Godber frowned.

"Eight, going on twenty-eight."

Godber shook his head.

"Mate, we must be getting old."

Rego didn't disagree – this case was aging him by the hour.

The burner phone lit up and Vikram's face appeared on the screen.

"What did you learn from your diver friend?" Vikram asked, launching straight in.

Rego laid out the conversation for Godber's benefit, too.

"Long story short, the Ukrainians had undergone training with the elite Navy Clearance Divers and then were working on something top secret with the RFA communications team." Rego glanced between Godber and the burner phone. "I won't be able to get any further intel without making it official. Vik, I've gone as far as I can go. I'm really hoping I won't get burned."

"We're all hoping that," Vikram said sharply.

Rego and Godber shared a look: their friend wasn't usually so testy.

"I'm sorry," Vikram said wearily. "I know you've both gone above and beyond on my say-so. But we're getting close now, I can feel it."

"Close to what?" Rego challenged. "Close to finding out who killed Kuzma, or close to finding out who planted the drone, what's on it, or what the hell is going on over there?"

Vikram gave a faint smile.

"Maybe all of that. Look, after you told me about the laptop that Jameson *says* was stolen, I was able to identify an email and IP address of a device which I think is associated with the drone."

"You think or you know?" Godber asked.

"Don't ask questions you don't want the answers to," Vikram snapped.

"Fuck off, Vik!" said Godber. "We're doing you a favour so just..."

"The favour is to our country!" Vikram said hotly.

"Alright, girls," Rego said calmly. "Let's play nicely. Vik, what are you thinking about this IP address?"

Vikram shot Godber a scathing look, then continued.

"The device with that IP address, I'm going to send it a trojan so the next time it's opened, it'll be infected with a virus that covertly explores its data, opens the camera on it, and I'll even be able to see the keystrokes used."

"Niiiice," said Godber, their spat forgotten.

"Have you decrypted any of the data on the device so far?" Rego asked.

"Some of it, yes."

"And?"

"It's not good," Vikram said quietly. "I'll need to download and identify the full network behind the use of the drone, but what I'm seeing so far are secret conversations between the US and UK. I'm talking seriously top secret, classified intel – so highly classified, it never existed."

"The kind of data someone would kill for," Rego said.

"Definitely," Vikram agreed.

They were all silent for several seconds.

"So, what's next?" Rego asked at last.

Vikram cleared his throat.

"Firstly, I need to send the trojan and find out where the laptop is located and who's using it. But that depends on someone logging onto the laptop, which may or may not happen in the next day, week or month. I really don't want to wait that long. So, I've got another idea," and he glanced at Rego and Godber.

"I have a feeling that we're not going to like this," Godber grinned.

"Probably not," Vikram agreed. "But I need you to bring Tregowan on board."

"He *is* on board," Rego said. "I just told you he was sounding out his diver buddy at Culdrose."

"I know. But I need him to go back to the shipwreck

and find the rest of the drone," said Vikram, "without anyone knowing."

Rego stared at his phone in disbelief, his eyebrows lost somewhere in his hairline, but it was Godber who said it for both of them.

"You've got to be bloody kidding me!"

"I'm deadly serious," Vikram replied.

Rego scrubbed his hands over his face.

"Vik, you're talking about a night dive in a highly militarised area, where at least one man has lost his life, with unknowns keeping their eyes on the wreck site – there's no way that's a one-man operation or even a two-man operation. And without Nate Tregowan, we'd be dead in the water."

"Funny," said Godber.

"I'm not laughing," Rego said, his frustration showing. "What you're asking is suicide!"

"Calm down," said Vikram, making Rego want to reach through the phone and strangle his former best friend. "Calm down, Rob! You'll have a stroke before you're forty. You're right, I don't think it's a two-man job, but three of you could do it: Tregowan to dive, someone to drive the boat, and a lookout."

"Neither of us know how to drive a boat!" Rego all but yelled. "All those shipwrecks around the coast, they're not just to entertain tourists – it's because it's bloody dangerous out there. It would take years to learn to navigate it safely, especially at night."

"Your PC Poldhu could do it," Vikram said quietly.

"No," Rego said immediately. "She's a probationer and she's only 21!"

Vikram shrugged. "She's a sworn officer and she knows these waters better than anyone, except her grandfather." He pretended to look thoughtful. "You could ask him."

"He's in his seventies and got shot in the head at Easter if you remember, Vik! I'm not putting him in danger again."

"Well, we'll need one or other of them," Vikram said, his voice hardening.

"He's right, Rob," said Godber. "Because, mate, when it comes to boats, you're as useful as a sundeck on a submarine."

CHAPTER 27

Tamsyn's phone woke her shortly after midnight, and she rolled over to grab the annoying device, tempted to throw it across the room. Her mouth was dry, her head ached, and she had the sluggish brain of someone who'd been yanked from a deep sleep.

Seeing it was an unknown number, she swore and started to block it, then stopped. Just before Rego had left the previous day, he'd told her that he'd be in touch soon.

She took the call.

"Tamsyn, this is DI Rego. Sorry to call so late ... or early, but I need your help."

"That's okay, sir," she lied, suppressing a yawn. "Is it about ... what's been happening?"

"Yes, but this is a covert operation and you can't speak to anyone about this, ever. Do you understand?"

Her pulse quickened as a shot of adrenaline brought her fully awake.

"Yes, sir."

"Okay, I'm sending a friend of mine to pick you up. You

should be back for breakfast, but just in case, leave a note for your grandparents. Be vague but make sure they're not worried."

"Okay. Where am I going?"

"I don't want to discuss it over the phone. Look, he'll be with you in ten minutes. Get yourself ready and wait at the end of your road. Code word: Rising Damp. Got it?"

"Yes, sir."

"Thank you for this, Tamsyn," he said, his voice low.

Tamsyn dressed quickly as Mo watched her, almost quivering with excitement at the prospect of a nighttime jaunt.

She tip-toed down the narrow stairs and Mo scampered after her, but as soon as the little dog realised that she was being left behind, her tail drooped.

"Sorry, scruffalicious," Tamsyn whispered. "I'll make it up to you."

Mo's hazel eyes watched her sorrowfully as Tamsyn sneaked out, closing the back door quietly, cringing as the lock clicked loudly in the night.

The street was silent and all the cottages were in darkness as Tamsyn walked quickly to the end of the road. A black Range Rover was waiting at the kerb with the headlights off and the engine running. As she approached, the driver's window slid open.

"Rob Rego sent me," came a man's voice. "Hop in."

"What's the code word?" Tamsyn asked, her nerves jangling.

"Oh, bollocks," came the voice. "Rising Damp. Alright, luv?"

Tamsyn hesitated. She trusted her DI. She had to. If

you didn't trust the team at your back, what was the point? She climbed in, glancing dubiously at the hulking, unshaven man who was sitting in the driver's seat.

"Alright, Tamsyn," he said cheerfully. "I'm Godber – a mate of your DI's. Pleased to meet you."

And he held out a large paw, shaking her hand heartily with a firm grip.

"Right," he said, giving her a sharp, appraising glance. "Rob says you're good in a crisis and will keep your mouth shut."

Tamsyn raised her eyebrows, uncertain if that was a compliment *and* a criticism.

Godber waited until they'd left her street before he flicked the headlights on.

"Where are we going?" she asked, wondering how much it would hurt if she jumped out of the car while it was moving – just in case.

"Porthoustock."

He pronounced it, *Port-house-tock*, which made her smile.

"Porth-oo-stock," she couldn't help correcting.

"Blinkin' Cornish words," he grunted without seeming to be offended.

"Are we going back to the *Mohegan?*" she asked. "At night?"

"You're a quick study," he said, nodding. "Rob said you saw some suspicious types watching you when you went near the wreck site earlier in the week. He wants to search the area where you found the drone."

"That thing was a drone?"

He glanced at her then nodded.

"Yeah, the big brains at MI6 think so. What we don't know is who put it there."

"MI6? That's... wow!" Tamsyn's excitement quadrupled, along with her anxiety. "The DI said it was a covert op, but he didn't say ... I mean, MI6?"

She was having a hard time getting her head around the move from student PC sorting out traffic jams and helping people with mental health problems, to the secret intelligence services and national security.

"What we need from you, Tamsyn," said Godber, cutting through her surprise, "is to drive the dive boat from Porthoooostock out to the wreck site so we can send a diver down."

Her throat closed up. "I've never done a night dive! I don't think I can..."

"Keep yer hair on," Godber chuckled. "We've got someone for that job. We just need you to drive the boat, that's all."

"Oh, okay," she said weakly.

Godber drove quickly and efficiently, reminding her of the way her sergeant navigated the narrow streets and narrower lanes of West Cornwall.

"This is all top secret, isn't it?" she said after several miles of silence.

"How'd you guess?" Godber laughed.

"Well, Porthkerris dive school is more convenient but Porthoustock is a lot quieter – not so many people."

"Yep, we're trying not to get spotted."

Tamsyn bit her lip.

"Um, so I kind of forgot to tell DI Rego that I took a photo of the drone on my phone."

"Shit," Godber said softly. "Do you still have it?"

"Yes."

"Delete it, scrub it from your phone, and if your photos back up to the cloud, delete it from that, too. Do it now."

"Okay," Tamsyn said softly, following his orders.

"Do you have other photographic or written evidence? A text message? An email? Did you tell a friend? Share it on bloody social media?"

"No!"

"Good."

She finished clearing all and any digital remains of the drone photo, or hoped she had. And then glanced at Godber to see if he was still annoyed with her.

"What?" he asked, but seemed calmer now.

"I was wondering how you know DI Rego?"

"We were in the job together," he said, flashing her a smile.

She waited for more but then realised that was all she was getting. She wondered if he was MI6. But if so, why the hell were they taking a student PC on their midnight mission? Didn't MI6 have any of their own agents or something?

Maybe they'd tell her more about what was going on when they got to the wreck site.

Although, maybe not.

"It's going to be a difficult dive," she said as they passed through Helston's darkened streets. "We're coming out of the neap tides."

"You'll have to explain that," said Godber with a frown. "The only 'neeps' I know go with 'tatties'."

Tamsyn smiled in the darkened cab.

"It's when the tides are at their most moderate: high tides are lower than average, and low tides are higher, so there's less water moving about – makes fishing easier and it's better for diving – safer." She paused, her voice becoming serious. "We're coming into spring tides now."

"It's summer," Godber objected.

"Yeah, I know – it's kind of confusing, but basically it just means the tides are 'springing forth', so, you know, bigger."

Godber shook his head but didn't say anything. Tamsyn licked her lips, wishing she'd brought a bottle of water, and continued.

"You'll need a really experienced diver."

"Yeah, I told you – we've got that sorted," he said, confidently. "You worry too much, a lass your age."

After that, Tamsyn kept quiet.

They sped through the night, seeing only a few other cars on the roads and none at all once they turned off the main road and onto the Lizard peninsula. Occasionally a house or farm building would loom out of the darkness, but it felt like they were alone, the only people awake on the planet, and she started to drift.

The hiss and crackle of a radio woke Tamsyn abruptly, reminding her that they were on a secret operation. She wished she wasn't so tired.

Godber picked up the radio and answered it.

"Go ahead, Nemo."

"We've got a problem," came a man's voice. "Two old codgers fishing off the harbour wall. I've been watching them and they're set in for the night. Got thermoses and sandwich boxes. Advise? Over."

Godber swore, and Tamsyn understood his frustration. You couldn't have a covert operation when two members of the public were doing a spot of night fishing. Then she had a brainwave.

"Can I use the radio?" she asked Godber. "I think I might know the men."

He frowned. "Okay, but no names. The man you're talking to is 'Nemo'; I'm 'Tank', and you can be..."

"I'll be Cribbar," she said.

"You what?"

"Does it matter?"

"S'pose not, but ... cribber?"

"The Cribbar is the name of a reef off Newquay and a few times each year, you get really big-wave surf, over 30 feet." She paused. "I'm going to ride it one day."

He glanced across at her, eyebrows raised in disbelief, then flicked the radio switch.

"Nemo, this is Tank. Handing you over to Cribbar now."

"Um ... hi, Nemo. Can you describe the two men fishing off the harbour? I think I might know them. Over."

"Hello, Cribbar. I see two IC1 males, late seventies or early eighties. Can't tell their height as they're sitting on stools but both are wearing yellow bib overalls. One has a short beard and white hair, wearing a red jacket; the other is wearing a beanie and is clean shaven, wearing a blue or black jacket. Over."

They sounded like the two men Tamsyn had met at Porthoustock, but she couldn't be sure.

"Has one of them got a large, black and orange bait box? Or maybe a pair of bait boxes? Over."

"Affirmative, Cribbar. Advise? Over."

"They sound like the two fishermen who helped me and Ad— who helped me at the incident: Jack and Clemo. Friends of ... the family. Over."

Godber pulled a face. "Tell him to wait till we get there. Having a native on site," and he glanced at Tamsyn, "that could be useful. Tell him eta nine minutes."

Tamsyn relayed the message and the radio fell silent.

"What are you going to do with them?" she asked quietly.

"Nothing!" he grinned at her. "Bloody hell! Did you think we were going to off them and chuck them in the sea or do something else to them?"

"No, I just wondered..."

"You're going to talk nicely to them," he said, still laughing at her. "You're going to use all your charm to keep their mouths shut, and if that doesn't work, Nemo will call on their sense of civic duty. And if *that* doesn't work, I'll put the frighteners on them. Okay?"

"Not really," Tamsyn said sharply. "They're two nice old men."

Godber sighed. "Look, this is serious shit, and I'll do whatever it takes to achieve a successful outcome. If you can't handle that, you're in the wrong job."

Tamsyn didn't reply, and thankfully, Godber didn't appear to feel the need to talk either.

He turned off the headlights and put the car into neutral as they approached the harbour, but there was no disguising the sound of their tyres crunching on shingle as they pulled onto the beach above the highwater mark.

One of the old fishermen turned to look, and Tamsyn was relieved when she recognised him.

"Yes, that's definitely Clemo," she said.

Godber relayed the messaged to Nemo, who maintained his position out of sight.

"Right, Tamsyn. You're on. Go and sweet talk those two into keeping shut about seeing us."

She nodded and opened the car door.

"Hello, Clemo, Jack," she said, as she walked towards them.

"Who's that?" called Jack.

"It's the Poldhu girl," said Clemo. "What you doing here at the time o' night, bird? Thought you'd have had enough of fishing, what with being Ozzie's granddaughter an' all."

"Actually, I'm a police officer, and I'm here to investigate..."

"'Bout that body that was found, is it?" Clemo asked.

"Yes, but we need to keep this secret," said Tamsyn. "It's important that no one knows we were here tonight."

"Who's 'we', lovely? Thought you was by yourself."

"No, I'm with two colleagues. I thought I'd better come over and say 'hi' first. I didn't want to..."

"Scare us?" Jack laughed. "It'd take more than a pretty maid to scare us. Anyway, Clemo here, has hearing like a hawk."

Tamsyn smiled. "I was going to say I didn't want to scare the fish. What are you looking for?"

"Rockling, maybe a bit of bream," said Clemo. "Jack likes a bit o' wrasse, but I reckon theys taste like soap."

Tamsyn laughed. "Well, I'm afraid we're going to

disturb you a bit first, but perhaps if anyone asks tomorrow, you can just say we were some upcountry fishermen. But only if someone asks – otherwise, don't say anything."

They both agreed not to talk about what they were about to see and hear.

She signalled to Godber and he clambered out of the car, then strode towards them, surprisingly noiseless for such a big man.

"This is my ... colleague," Tamsyn said, introducing Godber to Jack and Clemo.

The two men observed him quietly, wariness in their old eyes.

Another man appeared out of the darkness and when Godber didn't react, Tamsyn assumed this must be 'Nemo'.

He greeted the two men and asked about their fishing, showing a knowledge of the likely catch, what bait and tackle they were using, which made them both relax a little, although they still threw watchful glances at Godber.

"That your boat over there, is it?" Clemo asked, pointing to a new-looking dive boat that was tied up at the far side of the beach by an old stone silo.

"Good guess," Nemo said.

"Nah, only boat here we don't know," Jack said. "You a Janner? You sound like one," he added, his voice rising with suspicion.

Godber looked confused, but Tamsyn just smiled. "Clemo is saying that our friend sounds like he's from Devon."

"Bugger me," Godber sighed. "I didn't know I'd need a Cornish dictionary on this op."

They left the men to their fishing and promises that

they wouldn't breathe a word about what they'd seen, or as Clemo put it, "A wink is as good as a nod to a blind hoss."

As soon as they were on the boat, Nemo introduced himself.

"Sergeant Nate Tregowan, Dive Supervisor from D&C's Dive and Marine Unit in Plymouth. Good to meet you, PC Poldhu."

Tamsyn was relieved to have another police officer there – it made her feel a little less out of her depth.

"I'm told you can get us out to the *Mohegan* without foundering on the Manacles, Tamsyn," Tregowan continued. "I hope you're up to it, because we'll be going in dark."

Tamsyn blinked. "No lights?"

"Nope, none. And I know that's illegal."

Tamsyn swallowed. This was going to be very dangerous.

He stared at her intently. "Can you do it?"

Do I have a choice?

"Yes, sergeant," she said, her gaze on the silky black sea behind them. "But it'll be slow going. I wouldn't go south past Veryan Rocks in the dark; I think we should head west past Maen Chynoweth, west-sou'-west past Gwinges, then follow the channel north of Maen Voes."

"That'll take longer," he mused.

"But we'll get there in one piece."

He gave her a quick smile. "You'll do."

Tregowan showed her where he'd stowed overalls, boots and a sou'wester for her and Godber, although the big man had trouble squeezing his frame into his bib overalls.

"Bloody hell," he grumbled, "it feels like my nuts are in a vice."

Tregowan shrugged. "Didn't know you'd be such a big bugger."

"I don't like the sound of them Manacles rocks," Godber grumbled. "Don't like manacles at the best of times, not even pink fluffy ones."

Tamsyn wondered if he'd feel better if she told him that 'manacles' was a corruption of the Cornish *maen eglos*, which meant 'church stones' because you could see the spire of St Keverne from them. But in the end, she kept her mouth shut and concentrated on the job.

It felt strange, wrong, to head out of the harbour without any lights, just chugging through the inky darkness, hearing only the waves against the hull, concentrating on the radar and GPS to guide her. Unlike most private small-craft which didn't have installed navigation instruments beyond a simple magnetic compass, the dive boat had both radar and GPS.

Her hands gripped the wheel as she concentrated hard.

"Don't fuck up," she whispered to herself.

CHAPTER 28

It took nearly an hour for Tamsyn to navigate them safely through the cluster of sharp-toothed reefs named 'the Manacles', four times as long as in daylight, but she was taking no chances. This part of the Channel was a graveyard for ships that strayed too close to the Cornish coast and foundered there; the wreck of the SS *Mohegan* was just one of many from across the centuries.

Her knuckles were white as she gripped the wheel, steering carefully around the unforgiving rocks.

When the GPS told her she'd arrived at the exact coordinates where she'd dived with Adam just a few days earlier, she breathed a deep sigh of relief. So much had happened in the short time since she'd dived the *Mohegan*, it seemed impossible. Her first wreck dive had been memorable ... and the way she was feeling about the pitch-black ocean right now, it might well be her last.

Being here after the sun had long since set felt eerie, as if all the restless souls of those drowned sailors were awake and wondering who disturbed their watery grave.

Although truthfully, the living scared her more than the dead. Were they being watched? Had the mysterious RIB from earlier returned, suspended in the darkness like a nighttime predator? Would they even know if there were eyes on them?

And then her question was partially answered as she saw Godber strap on a pair of night vision goggles. She wondered if he'd brought a spare pair for her. It would be cool to try them out.

Tregowan called her attention, and she zipped up his dry-suit then helped him into his harness and cylinders.

"How long you gonna be, Nate?" asked Godber, looking like he belonged in a steam punk film with the heavy goggles on his head.

"As long as it takes," Tregowan said grimly, then glanced reassuringly at Tamsyn who was clearly worried. "I've got over a thousand dive hours, Tamsyn. But you're a diver so you know that procedure and safety checks are everything. I've got a maximum of four hours with this rebreather, which at 22 metres gives me 90 minutes on the seabed. I've got a soda lime scrubber to clean the air, and my dive computer will monitor oxygen levels. Set your watch for three hours and 55 minutes."

"Yes, sergeant," she said, doing as instructed while Godber did the same.

"Good, now tell me your movements last Friday with as much detail as you can remember," Tregowan instructed.

Tamsyn described the descent to the *Mohegan*, the approximate time it had taken to fin the length of the wreck to the boiler room where Adam had found the device. *No, not a device, it's a drone*, she reminded herself.

She described the eel attack and admitted that she'd panicked.

"It's understandable," said Tregowan, "but from what I've heard, you bashed it with a rock until it let go of your friend. That's not panicking, that's clear thinking."

Tamsyn was surprised and secretly pleased at his words. But she didn't have time to bask, Tregowan was already moving on.

"This is the comms unit I'll be using," he said, showing her a hard black plastic case containing what looked like a ship radio. "This is an Aquacom SSB-2010 transceiver – to all intents and purposes an underwater telephone. It operates with all single sideband acoustic underwater devices within range and on the same frequency, so I'm going to keep comms to a minimum, and I don't want to hear from you unless it's an emergency." He gave her a stern look. "We don't know who else is out there and might be listening to us."

"Yes, sergeant."

"I'm going to put the receiver here," he said, pointing to a caddy by the wheel. "Emergencies only, got it?"

"Yes, sergeant."

"Alright, alright," said Godber. "Can't you wind yourself on a bit? Emergencies only – we've got it!"

Tregowan frowned.

"I've got a PTT – push-to-talk control. I don't intend to use it."

He did a quick radio check to make sure the comms were working, then he pulled a glow light out of his kit, looping it over his fist. He did a few final checks, dropped the shot-line, before giving Tamsyn and Godber a thumb's up and flopping backwards over the side of the dive boat.

A few seconds later, Tamsyn saw the ghostly light of Tregowan's glow stick slowly disappearing into the depths.

She followed the faint beam until it had completely disappeared, then checked the time on her watch. Three hours and fifty minutes to go.

The time passed slowly, and Tamsyn felt herself nodding off. Godber saw her drooping.

"Rob said you went straight from a night shift to taking out Cassie and his kids, to this," Godber said, never shifting so much as a millimetre from his lookout position.

"Yeah, pretty much," she yawned. "And his mother."

"Blimey! You got the short straw there," Godber chortled.

Tamsyn didn't disagree.

"Anyway, talking helps you stay awake on a night sentry duty," he said, conversationally. "Especially when you're doing surveillance. Tell me about yourself. Why did you want to join the police?"

"It's a good job," she answered cautiously.

Godber waited for a second. "Nah, I don't buy that. You could have a nice, easy life selling ice creams down here," he said, showing a blindingly uninformed idea of how most people in Cornwall struggled to earn a living. "There must be more to it. Unless you're one of those who just wants to get a cheap degree on the force's budget, then bugger off. Not that I'd blame you if you did – it's a tough job. But you? Nah. So, come on, what's the reason?"

"Why did you join the police?" she countered.

"Fair enough," he said easily. "I used to be a bad lad getting into trouble and running with a rough crowd. I spent my 16th birthday puking in a cell at the local cop shop and thought there had to be more to life than that. And my old man said if he had to come and get me from the police station again, he'd kick me out. That was what you might say was a wakeup call – definitely a motivating factor to get my shit together. So, I cleaned myself up, got my head on straight, and when I was 19, I joined the boys and girls in blue." She saw his lips lift in a smirk. "Your turn."

"My dad died when I was ten," Tamsyn said into the darkness. "He drowned at sea – at least, that's what we thought. Grandad was crying, Grandma couldn't speak, and I was just there by myself at the harbour. A police officer took care of me."

Godber was silent for several seconds.

"Shit! Sorry, kid. That must have been rough."

Tamsyn didn't reply, because even though it was an old grief, sometimes it still had the power to steal the air from her lungs.

"You said, you *thought* he'd drowned at sea," Godber said after a few seconds had passed.

Tamsyn cleared her throat.

"Turns out that he was murdered by his best friend because Dad refused to be part of a drug smuggling racket with Albanian gangsters. They were using local fishermen to bring in their product."

Godber whistled through his teeth.

"Yeah, I remember Rob telling me about that – his first case down here, right? The bastard got away, didn't he?"

"The Albanian gang member did, yes. But not before he shot my dad's so-called friend. Murdered him." Tamsyn took a shaky breath. "Besnik Domi: there's an International Arrest Warrant out for him."

Godber sighed. "Good luck with that. The Albanians don't like giving up their own citizens, no matter how much of a murdering bastard they are."

"I know."

There was a short pause before Godber started talking again.

"So, how are you liking being a member of Devon & Cornwall's thin blue line?"

Tamsyn hesitated, wondering how much to say to DI Rego's friend.

"It's ... good. It's not what I thought it would be."

"I bet I can guess," he chuckled, "but in what way?"

"Paperwork," she sighed.

"Thought that might be it," he agreed. "Bureaucracy and drowning in paperwork. It pisses off every officer I've ever known. Too much writing, not enough policing."

Tamsyn nodded eagerly.

"Exactly! Last week, I attended a burglary in this small, quiet village, the kind of place where everyone knows everyone else, and everyone thinks that means they're untouchable. The victim was a man in his eighties, and called us because someone had come into his house while he was asleep and stolen money, his late mother's jewellery, a bottle of wine and even his coat. I mean, what the fuck? They took his coat! He was upset and embarrassed because he'd left his door unlocked. I don't know if he'd forgotten or he thought the village was safe."

"Poor bugger."

"I was with him for about 45 minutes, but forensics said there were no viable surfaces, and they won't do doorhandles because of all the people who touch them; the only other surfaces the burglar had touched were wooden, so nothing there either. I went to three houses that had doorbell cameras, but two didn't have any footage and his next-door neighbour's internet had gone down in the night, so she didn't have anything either. I went to five more houses in the village, which took me another hour. Turns out he's a friendly old guy and talks to everyone. He might have even spoken to the person who burgled him at the village shop or something. Then I go back to the station, and spend two hours typing up reports that aren't going to go anywhere because there's nothing to investigate, and all I can say to an 83 year-old man who's had a stranger burgle his house, is to phone the local jewellery shops and auction houses in case his mum's jewellery turns up." She blew out a long breath. "It's frustrating. I thought I'd be out on the streets helping people."

"Ah, luv, that *is* helping people. All those neighbours of that old boy, they'll all be double-checking they've locked their doors and windows now, and maybe some of them will care enough to help the old fella and keep an eye on him, too. It's not much of a silver lining, but it's something. And don't discount how he felt having you show up in the first place. I bet he was grateful, right?"

"Yes," Tamsyn said grudgingly, "he was."

"There you go then. He's been reassured, and sometimes that's enough."

"Is it though?"

"What you've got to realise," said Godber in a kind voice, "is that the job is never going to go back to the old-style bobby on the beat. We'd need to double the number of police in the country and people don't want to pay for it. The cocking government certainly don't. But when you think about it, crimes have changed even if criminals haven't. There's so much cybercrime going on, that's where resources go – more desk jobs. And all that information you typed into the NICHE database or the STORM crime log system, that might pull up a pattern of behaviour one day." He nodded slowly. "You've gotta pace yourself, Tam, or you'll burn out. You gotta learn to take the rough with the smooth. You can have your best day ever on the job, and the worst – it's a rollercoaster, and you've got to strap in for the ride."

He turned his night vision goggles in her direction.

"Stick with Rob Rego – he's a copper's copper. He'll see you right. For all you know, you could end up being Chief Constable one day." He paused. "That's if you can play the politics game."

Tamsyn thought that making it through three years of policing while she worked on her degree was only a slightly more achievable goal.

"You're not a police officer anymore, are you?" Tamsyn asked tentatively.

"No, I did 14 years then decided I wanted a change – something where someone else wasn't telling me what to do all the time." He grinned in the darkness. "I thought working for myself would be better, but it turns out I've ended up having a new boss with every new client."

"Oh, I thought you were, um..."

"A spy?" he laughed quietly. "Only on weekends."
Then his tone changed.
"How long since Nate went down?"
"Ninety-two minutes. Why?"
"Because we've got company."

CHAPTER 29

"Small boat coming towards us fast," Tregowan said, his voice tense. "Shit! There's two of them!"

"They're not appearing on the screen," Tamsyn said, her heart beating wildly. "I can't see them! They're not there!"

"We've got to get out of here," Godber hissed. "Tell Nate. Now!"

"We can't leave him!" Tamsyn gasped.

"We have to, and he'll be safer down there than up here," Godber said grimly. "Get us back to Porthoustock fast! And Tam, you're going to have to use the shortcut through the Manacles. Hurry! I'll tie a marker to the shot-line so at least Nate will know where he is when he comes up."

He spun around to pull up the anchor, and Tamsyn didn't waste time either.

"Nemo, this is Cribbar!" she said breathlessly into the radio. "Code Zero! Code Zero! We have company: two RIBs. We're making a run for it. Out."

She started the engine, praying to St Piran and the *mari-morgans* to get them safely back to the harbour.

Tregowan's dive boat was substantially faster than the *Daniel Day* which she was used to, but even with the unknown RIBs approaching fast, she didn't dare use the top speed. Navigating in the dark was foolhardy at best; around the Manacles, it was suicidal.

She set as fast a pace north as she dared, wincing as the hull scraped against rocks while the sea plunged and churned around them. She could tell by the sound it was just a surface wound, a small ding, and not one that had ripped the bottom out of the boat. But at least the RIBs would face the same problems – and they were both bigger than the dive boat, and from the sound of their engines, a lot more powerful. They'd win in a straight race. Tamsyn prayed she knew these seas better than they did, because that was all they had going for them.

She swept up the coast, hugging the 6m mark around Veryan Rocks, but the RIBs were gaining on them.

"Can you swim?" she yelled at Godber.

"Yes!" he shouted back. "Why?"

"Because I'm about to do something really stupid! Hold on!"

Whatever he screamed back, Tamsyn didn't hear him. She pushed the dive boat to full throttle, heading straight for the submerged reef north of Veryan Rocks. Here, the depth fell to just two metres – the dive boat *should* miss it; she hoped that at least one of the RIBs would lose its propeller, maybe part of the hull, but God, it was a risk.

There was a horrible screeching sound as the dive boat clipped part of the reef, but then they were past it and had a clear run to the harbour where their car was parked, and...

"Godber!" she yelled. "What about Jack and Clemo?"

But he didn't reply because the first RIB hit the reef and did a spectacular 180° backflip, then started to sink. The second RIB slowed immediately, spinning in a tight circle to avoid the wreck of its mate.

Tamsyn didn't wait to see what happened next. She raced for the harbour, her heart pounding, only slowing as she saw the familiar, welcoming lights from several small cottages.

She could see Jack and Clemo silhouetted on the quay, and they stood up as quickly as their aging bodies would allow, catching the lines she tossed up to them.

Her legs were shaking too much to jump ashore, and even Godber seemed less than his usual laidback self.

He turned to Tamsyn, his face pale.

"Fuck me! That was close. Nice driving there, Nigel Mansell."

Tamsyn didn't know who he meant, but it sounded like a compliment. She tested her legs to see if they'd take her weight, and then she realised that the dive boat had sprung a leak and was taking on water. She hoped that Sergeant Tregowan wasn't going to be too mad at her.

If he made it.

"Nemo?" she asked, breathlessly, staring at Godber, but still aware that Jack and Clemo were listening to every word.

"He's swimming in," said Godber. "It's Plan B. I might have forgotten to mention that. We'll wait for him at the extraction point. Bloody hell! Are we sinking?"

Still feeling shaky and light-headed, Tamsyn forced herself upright, giving herself a mental slap as she pulled herself together, then stumbled about the dive boat, starting the bilge pumps working and found an old towel to shove into the hole for now. That job done, she was very happy to scramble out of the dive boat, gladly taking Clemo's hand as he helped her onto the quay.

"What's going on, Tammy?" he said. "The truth this time, maid!"

She glanced at Godber.

"Sorry, mate, she can't tell you. Official Secrets Act and all that. But I think you two should go home. Can't be too safe, if you know what I'm saying."

The two elderly men looked at each other, then started packing up their bait boxes and equipment immediately, grumbling quietly but without asking anymore questions that wouldn't be answered.

Tamsyn thanked them again, and watched them disappear into the night.

"Should we call the Coastguard?" she said. "Anonymously, I mean?"

Godber looked thoughtful.

"No. If it had just been one boat out there, I'd say yes, but there were two of them. They stayed to pick up the crew rather than pursue us, so I think we can safely assume that all of their personnel would be accounted for."

Tamsyn thought that was a rather large assumption, and having had personal experience of suddenly being plunged into the sea at night, fully clothed and with a long swim to shore... well, she wouldn't wish that on anyone.

Her whole body shuddered as memories flooded through her. She'd made a swim like that and nearly died.

She shook her head, trying to clear her mind, trying to push back the darkness that slithered at the edges. She knew that she ought to go back onto the dive boat, wring out the towel that she'd stuffed in the hole, and replace it with something more substantial like a piece of tarpaulin as a temporary plug – ideally lashed underneath the boat – but she couldn't face it just yet. And her hands wouldn't stop shaking.

Godber picked up his radio handset.

"Alpha, this is Tank. Come in, Alpha."

"Roger, Tank. This is Alpha. What's the sitrep? Over."

Tamsyn recognised Rego's voice and relief flowed through her. Somehow, hearing the DI's voice calmed her. He sounded composed; he sounded in control.

Godber updated him briefly, half his words in code. The upshot being that they were to wait for Tregowan on the other side of the old stone quarry which was one nautical mile from the *Mohegan* and the shortest distance back to shore. It would take an experienced open-water swimmer between 40 and 45 minutes, but it was still a hard swim. At least it was an incoming tide and a sheltered cove, all of which would help Tregowan, but Tamsyn was very glad that she wasn't the one making that swim at night.

She noticed that Godber didn't ask about informing the Coastguard, and Rego didn't mention it either.

No, I'm not thinking about that.

Once Godber had finished the call, he pulled on his night vision goggles again, scanning the darkness.

Tamsyn's brain finally managed to clear enough to think practically.

"What about the dive boat?" she asked, forcing the dark memories away. "I can't leave the bilge pumps running, and it will sink without them."

"Huh," said Godber, sounding indifferent. "Can you drive it up onto the beach? We can tie it up and leave it there. Nate can get a trailer for it tomorrow."

Tamsyn pulled a face. "I guess, but it'll damage the hull even more and the propellor will be wrecked."

Godber shrugged, making it clear that the state of Tregowan's boat was of zero concern.

"Well..." said Tamsyn hesitantly when she realised that he wasn't going to answer, "it's an incoming spring tide, so even if I can take it as far as I can now, in a couple of hours the boat will be swamped."

"Can't be helped," Godber said cheerfully. "And frankly, I want to get the fuck out of here before whoever was in those RIBs decides to come for some payback."

Tamsyn shivered at the thought. "Who do you think they were?"

"Best you don't ask," said Godber.

Tamsyn's temper roared to the surface.

"You do know that we nearly died tonight, don't you?" she snapped. "And Sergeant Tregowan is ... do you have any idea how difficult that swim is? What if he doesn't make it? We should be calling out the Lifeboat to search for him! This is insane, I can't even..." She took a shaky breath.

Godber regarded her calmly.

"Nate is aware of the risks and he knows what's at stake. He wouldn't have volunteered if it wasn't serious shit. You already know that your buddy found an underwater drone which MI6 are *very* interested in, and you know that we've just been hazed by unfriendlies who'd turned off their transponders so that they were, for all intents and purposes, invisible at night. You're not stupid, Tamsyn. You already know everything you need to know. I'm sorry you've been caught up in all this, but you did well tonight. Rob Rego was right about you."

Tamsyn just stared at him, then her shoulders slumped.

"I'll go and beach the dive boat," she muttered.

"Good girl," said Godber.

Tamsyn turned off the bilge pumps and took the dive boat as far up the beach as she could, ignoring the ugly grating sound as the hull scraped over the pebbles and the propellor was shredded. The dive boat slowly tipped sideways as it came to rest.

Tamsyn slogged through the water with the lines to tie up the boat so it wouldn't float out to sea, then did her best to wrestle a tarpaulin over the hole and tie it in place, to keep it as watertight as possible. She didn't have a key to start the tractors to drag it up the beach, and she'd already sent Jack and Clemo home.

At least Tamsyn was wearing a good pair of overalls and sea boots. Being cold and wet on top of everything would have finished her off.

Godber helped her secure the boat as far up the beach as they could, then they headed back to the Range Rover.

"I'm still shaking," she admitted quietly.

"Yeah, me too," he said, surprising her. "It's the adrenaline. Here, eat this. It'll help."

And he handed her a protein bar and a can of Coke from the back seat.

Tamsyn didn't think she was hungry, but she tore into the bar, shoving it into her mouth as if she hadn't eaten in a week, then guzzled the Coke straight down.

Godber glanced sideways with a smile, but didn't say anything. He handed her a second protein bar.

Then he drove slowly through the quiet lanes to the other side of the quarry, tugged the night vision goggles into place again, and munched on a jumbo bar of Trenance chocolate.

After the adrenaline rush, Tamsyn crashed, and although she didn't think she'd ever dare close her eyes again, she fell into a deep sleep, waking only when Godber shook her shoulder gently.

"He's here," he said, and she heard the deep relief in his voice.

She realised then that he'd been just as worried as her about Sergeant Tregowan but hadn't wanted her to see it.

They climbed out of the Range Rover into the cool night air, and Godber grabbed a blanket from the back seat before hurrying towards the man trudging up the beach in his dry-suit, apparently having abandoned his cylinders.

He looked utterly exhausted, but when he saw them, his face lit up.

"Found it," he said.

CHAPTER 30

"Your young PC did well last night," said Godber, stretching out in Rego's kitchen, tiredness etched into his face as they examined photographs of the piece of broken drone that Tregowan had found. "She's got questions though."

"Haven't we all," said Rego darkly. "First of which, who the hell was chasing you and her out there?"

Rego was really concerned about the immediate threat to his patch of West Cornwall, and it was clear that Godber was on the same frequency.

"Yeah, what's the intel on who tried to intercept us tonight?" he asked, "Because some serious arse-kicking is in order!"

"I'm working on it," Vikram said.

Rego couldn't help thinking that his friend already knew, or at least suspected, who was responsible.

"Vik, I need to know what the threat level is for the team," he said. "Tamsyn is 21 years old and a probationer. She isn't trained for this, and I'm not happy that we've had to involve her, let alone put her life on the line like this. She's fresh out of the box and I'm only a bloody DI. This is all above my pay grade. I've got my wife, kids and mother here, Vik. I need something from you."

Vikram sighed.

"I don't know for certain, but intel had a Venezuelan cargo ship moving past the Lizard peninsula toward the Channel last night."

"So?"

"After Russia, Venezuela is the recipient of the largest amount of Chinese development funding in the past two decades – we're talking over $100 billion dollars. That buys a lot of good will if someone needs to have two unidentified RIBs in the water."

"Holy shit!" Godber whispered. "Are you telling us that we've got the Russians *and* the Chinese trying to get hold of this drone?"

Vikram's voice was sombre.

"There's a good probability of that, yes. But my sources indicate that it was opportunistic rather than planned. We'll know more when the RIB that sank is recovered."

Rego rubbed his forehead as Godber leaned back in his chair shaking his head.

"Vik, mate! Your department has more leaks than my old nan's knickers. I mean, what the fuck?"

"I know. It's just so ... look, if I'm right, and it isn't looking good, then there's a mole either at Culdrose or ... or in my office. I don't know how else they'd have known about you having the drone in the first place. I don't know who followed you to the *Mohegan*, but I'm going to find out. There's a leak somewhere, that's why I've only been able to trust you and Godber."

Rego met Godber's gaze: neither of them looked happy. Vikram continued.

"There is some good news, too: your diver has definitely found the propulsion system for the drone. From the photos and video you sent, I'd say it's probably using the free energy reaction of Lithium and water as an energy resource – which is what you guessed, Godber – but it has several significant differences to the ones the Ukrainians have been testing. The bad news is, I've never seen anything like it. I'll know more when I see it tomorrow."

"I think you'll find that's later today, mate," Godber yawned, blinking bleary-eyed at the wispy pink clouds that tinted Newlyn's grey harbour waters.

"Nate caught the 5.03 from Penzance, so have one of your people meet him at 9.56. I've given him the usual codeword, and he won't go with anyone who doesn't have it."

"Sure, sure," said Vikram, his mind clearly on other things.

"I'll get my head down on Rob's couch for a couple of hours," Godber yawned, "then I'll go and sort out Nate's boat. Can I get your Tamsyn to help me?" he said to Rego. "I don't know bugger all about boats."

"She's on a rest day so I'm sure she'll be able to help you. Just let her sleep in a bit first, okay? She's earned it."

"Well, I've already asked her, and anyway, what about *my* beauty sleep?"

"Too late," said Rego, the corner of his mouth tipping up.

He let Godber have the small sofa and tried to be as quiet as possible in the kitchen so as not to disturb him, but if the ground-shaking snores that came out of the living room were anything to go by, nothing short of a bomb going off would wake him.

Cassie padded down the stairs wrapped in an enormous fluffy dressing gown, her bare feet almost silent.

She peeped into the living room then tiptoed into the kitchen.

"I thought I recognised those snores."

Rego smiled. "Have you missed them?"

"As much as I miss the dentist's drill. He's not getting divorced again, is he?"

"Not as far as I know," Rego said with a lift of his eyebrows. "It'll only be for a few hours. He didn't get much sleep last night."

"Nor did you," she said, wrapping her arms around his neck. "I heard you coming down hours ago."

"I still got more kip than Godber."

She studied his face.

"Is it serious, what's going on here?"

Rego nodded. "Very."

"Is there anything I can do?"

Rego smiled and pulled her closer. "You already do it. But if you want to feed Godber when he wakes up, that would be great."

She laughed as Godber's snores rumbled through the kitchen.

"Fine, but you owe me a very expensive dinner."

"Noted."

She opened the backdoor and gazed out at Newlyn

harbour as pink and orange clouds were reflected in the still water. Rego hoped that she was falling for the place and would end up liking it as much as he did; maybe even loving it.

He turned back to his phone, reading the latest information from the Coastguard on a vessel hitting the Manacles reef near Porthoustock.

A few minutes later, Cassie came back inside and smiled at him suggestively.

"I'm going to take a shower – join me?"

Rego grinned. "I'll be right there; I just need to finish reading this. Two minutes!"

He'd just turned his phone off and had one foot on the stairs when his mother walked in through the cottage's backdoor, loaded with shopping bags.

"Robert! There's my son!"

Rego groaned.

"Mum, what are you doing here so early?"

"Is that any way for a son to greet his mother?" she said, embracing him in a firm hug.

He was about to say something sharp when he caught the expression of vulnerability on her face.

"I thought I'd make you a proper Bermudian breakfast," she said, turning her back on him.

"Sounds great, Mum. I'm just going to go and have a shower."

"Don't be long!" she called after him. "Now, where are my grandbabies?"

Rego shook his head, a wry smile on his face. Max and Maisie wouldn't be impressed by the early-morning wakeup call.

Then he heard his mother's shrill voice echoing through the cottage.

"Godber! What you doing on my son's sofa? Get up! Get up!"

Rego groaned and closed the door to his bedroom.

Cassie was lying on the bed with a pillow over her face.

"Oh God," she said, her voice muffled. "How are we going to survive this summer?"

"I have a few ideas," Rego grinned, lying down next to her. "She's making a Bermudian breakfast – it'll take a while."

When the whole Rego family finally made it downstairs, they found Godber in the kitchen, a reluctant kitchen assistant to Patricia. A feast was spread out across the table – or a small family breakfast, according to Patricia: salted cod with potatoes, boiled eggs, bananas and avocados.

Shortly after 11am, Rego got a call from Vikram.

"Rob, I'll keep it short, I know you're with your family. I've received the rest of the device from Nate and it's ... no one here has ever seen anything like it. This propulsion system, it's some sort of new class of autonomous submarine drone that can perform long duration critical missions. This could change everything when it comes to undersea maritime dominance in contested waters. The lab will be running more tests, but it appears to operate completely independently of a host vehicle."

Much of this was over Rego's head but he understood enough to know that it was a secret worth killing for.

CHAPTER 31

Despite the excitement and sheer terror of the night before, despite her deep exhaustion, sleep had eluded Tamsyn.

As the race to the harbour replayed in her mind, she tugged the duvet around her more tightly. If she'd miscalculated, she'd have ripped the bottom out of their dive boat. They'd have been tossed into the sea and by the time Rego had sent help...

And what if the people who'd been chasing them had been the ones to find them, what then?

It all came back to the drone that Adam had found and its location. At least she knew what the strange device was now. What it *did*, well that was another secret that no one was sharing with her. But Tamsyn knew the seas around this coastline almost as well as her grandfather, and she was well aware that underwater communications cables had littered the seabed around Cornwall for nearly two centuries. The first successful transatlantic cable had gone from the west of Ireland in 1858; the first from Cornwall twelve years later.

And Tamsyn was a child of the social media age – she knew that data was often the most valuable asset that individuals and companies had.

She knew how to put two and two together to make four.

Tamsyn was dozing, still only half awake when someone knocked at the front door, and she heard her grandmother open it.

Yawning, she rubbed her eyes and staggered out of bed when she heard Godber's voice in the hallway. She'd forgotten that he was coming early to pick her up for the drive back to Porthoustock and to collect Nate's trashed boat.

A moment later, she heard her grandmother's heavy steps on the stairs and she peered into Tamsyn's room.

"Someone at the door. He's a bit old for you, angel," her grandmother whispered loudly enough for Godber to hear.

"Gran!" Tamsyn groaned, blushing to the roots of her blonde hair. "He's a friend of my boss. They were in Greater Manchester Police together."

"Oh, he's a policeman, too?"

Tamsyn wasn't sure what Godber was.

"Yes, that's right," she said. "Sergeant Godber."

She had no idea whether or not he'd been or a sergeant or even if that was his real name because no one had told her. There were a lot of things about this case that no one had told her.

She pulled on an old sweatshirt and plodded down the stairs, her hair in knots and dark rings under her eyes.

"Been out partying?" he asked, grinning widely as she scowled at him.

"Give me a frickin' break," she mumbled.

"Tammy!" said her grandmother crossly. "Language!" Then she turned to Godber. "Would you like a cup of tea, Sergeant Godber? I've just put the kettle on. Maybe a bit of breakfast, too?"

"You are a queen among women."

Godber grinned at Tamsyn's grandmother and kissed her hand, making her laugh.

"Oh, you're a smooth one!" she smiled. "I'll have to keep my eye on you!"

"And beautiful eyes they are, too," said Godber. "As blue as a summer's day."

To Tamsyn's amazement, her grandmother's cheeks turned pink and she seemed quite flustered.

"Right, I'm going to take a shower," Tamsyn grunted.

"Take your time," Godber called after her. "I'll be having breakfast with your delightful sister."

"Oh, please!" Tamsyn muttered at the same time as her grandmother laughed and batted Godber's arm.

"Dear of 'im," her grandmother smiled.

Ten minutes later, Tamsyn clomped down the stairs dressed in cut-off jeans and a t-shirt, her wet hair hanging down her back.

Her grandmother pushed a mug of tea across the kitchen table.

"Thanks, Gran," she said, covering a yawn.

"So, where are you two headed today?" her grandmother asked.

"Taking a damaged dive boat from Porthoustock to

Coastside Engineering in Falmouth," said Tamsyn after a discreet nod from Godber.

"Well, it's a nice day for it. Are you taking little Mo with you?"

Hearing her name, the small, hairy dog pranced across the floor and sniffed at Godber's trouser leg, then decided that he'd be acceptable company.

"I thought you were taking her visiting at the nursing home?"

"Oh, my days, you're right!" said her grandmother, looking annoyed with herself. "What was I thinking? Thank you, angel."

"Sorry, scruffalicious," Tamsyn said to the dog. "You've got to go with Gran." Then she looked at her grandmother. "Don't let her eat too many biscuits – she was sick last time."

Morwenna was a master at extracting biscuits and treats from the elderly folk in the nursing home where she volunteered as a therapy dog, and she got all the cuddles and pats and playtime that she could possibly want.

Still, Morwenna's tail drooped when Tamsyn and Godber left the cottage, closing the door behind them.

As they reached the Range Rover, Tamsyn rounded on Godber accusingly.

"You were flirting with my gran!"

"Nah, I'm just charming. All the ladies love me."

Tamsyn shook her head in disbelief.

"Yeah, right."

When they reached Porthoustock, Nate Tregowan's dive boat was in a sorry state, listing heavily to one side. She was resting half on and half off the beach, the stern in three feet of water, her keel touching the pebbles below.

Tamsyn could see part of the jagged scar across the fibreglass hull and part of the hole where the tarpaulin she'd tied over it had come loose as the tide had dragged the boat around.

"That doesn't look too clever, does it," Godber said with considerable understatement.

"It's probably not as bad as it looks," Tamsyn said doubtfully. "But you don't usually junk a sinker, and it's been less than 24 hours. I don't know about the motor – it's probably scrap, although that depends – and almost anything that isn't made of fibreglass or aluminium will probably need to be replaced, but she's not that bad. And if we pickle the motor, it might be okay."

Godber stared at her. "I know you just said something clever but at the risk of sounding like a complete pillock, I have no idea what."

Tamsyn laughed.

"Okay, well we need to refloat her as soon as we can, then get a tow to Falmouth where she can be washed with fresh water."

"Why not Newlyn?"

"Falmouth is a lot closer and I don't know how well the patch will hold. I'll drain the carbs, pull out the spark plugs and if we soak the engine inside and out with WD40..." she shrugged. "We might save it."

They both tensed when they heard the sound of another boat's engine just out of sight beyond the headland, but then Tamsyn recognised the silhouette of the

DEAD MAN'S DIVE

Coastguard's coastal patrol vessel. As the boat came nearer, she felt like cheering.

"We just got all our problems solved," she grinned at Godber, waving at someone on the deck.

The patrol vessel began to slow, and Tamsyn ran up to the stone harbour to catch the lines as they were thrown ashore, securing the boat to the giant rings in the harbour wall.

"Tammy! Where you to?"

The grey-haired skipper jumped ashore with the agility of a much younger man.

"Got the day off," she said with a smile but not really answering the question. "This is my, um, friend, Godber. Godber, this is Bernie Ryder, Maritime Operations Manager."

The two men shook hands, each eyeing the other.

"Did you hear about the accident last night, Tammy?" Bernie Ryder asked, turning his attention to her.

"You mean my friend's dive boat?" Tamsyn asked disingenuously. "I dinged it going past Veryan."

"You never!" Ryder exclaimed glancing across to the unhappy dive boat. "And you've ripped that propellor to shreds!"

"I know! I'm so embarrassed! It's been holed below the waterline. I stuffed it with a towel and tied a bit of tarpaulin over it, but we need to get it back to Falmouth and pickle the engine. Any chance of a tow?"

Ryder shook his head.

"Well, I wouldn't tell Ozzie if I was you, Tammy – he'll never let you on the *Daniel Day* again."

"I know," Tamsyn grinned, pretending to fan herself.

"Well ... but that's not what I meant. A call came in last night just after midnight. Some fella called in saying he'd seen two RIBs racing each other and one of them turned turtle. Lifeboat came out but couldn't find either of 'em. Very strange." He gave her an appraising look. "Know anything 'bout it?"

"Midnight? No, we were here much earlier in the evening. Was anyone hurt?" she asked off-handedly, as if she didn't really care one way or another.

"Not that we know of," Ryder said, then lowered his voice. "Who's the emmet?" he asked, glancing sideways at Godber.

"He's from the police in Manchester," Tamsyn answered.

"Ah, Manchester!" said Ryder, as if that was enough to explain Godber.

"So, could you give us a tow back to Falmouth," Tamsyn asked, knowing that Ryder wouldn't say no to her, even though he should.

"Ah, Tammy," he sighed. "Might as well. Tie her on then. That patch going to hold, is it?"

Tamsyn nodded. "If you'll let me borrow your Waterbuster and a couple of portable bilge pumps, we'll be good to go in twenty minutes. That and the patch should get us back to Falmouth."

They set to, emptying the seawater from the dive boat, then floated her back out to sea, tying her to the Coastguard's boat.

It was a slow journey back to Falmouth because they couldn't risk going too fast and sinking the boat again.

Tamsyn and Godber stayed on the little dive boat,

DEAD MAN'S DIVE

using the portable bilge pumps to keep it as buoyant as possible.

"You're a handy person to have about," Godber said as they slowly made their way north, past Helford River towards Falmouth. "You ever think about joining the private sector, give me a call."

Tamsyn stared at him in surprise.

"Are you offering me a job?"

"Yeah, think about it."

She smiled, but shook her head.

"Thanks, that's really nice of you, but I've wanted to join the police since I was a kid. I can't imagine doing anything else. I mean, I won't always want to do Response or Neighbourhood, and I haven't experienced Investigations or Public Protection yet, but in a few years, I'd like to become a detective," and she grinned at him.

"Ah well, you're a good copper and you'll make a good detective," he said. "Shame though – you can earn ten times the money in the private sector."

She shrugged.

"It's not about the money. Anyway, I wouldn't want to leave Cornwall."

"If you change your mind..."

"I won't, but thanks."

They were towed into Falmouth and Ryder took them to Coastside Engineering, a company Tamsyn knew.

"Thanks, Bernie!" she said, throwing her arms around the older man's neck.

"You say hello to your grandfather for me," he said, waving her off with a weathered grin.

One of the engineers came out to help her tie off the

dive boat, and she discussed with him what needed doing and getting Godber's okay for the repair costs.

She knew Tregowan would be insured, but his premiums would skyrocket after this adventure.

"Shall we go and get a coffee before we head back?" she asked Godber. "The Windjammer Café is round the corner. It's a bit pricey but the food is good."

"I'd rather have a proper Cornish pasty."

"You can get both over the road," she laughed. "Get me one, as well?"

"I'll put it on expenses," Godber said drily, and Tamsyn didn't know if he was joking or not.

"Okay, I just need to get my stuff and I'll meet you over there," Tamsyn said, pointing to a wooden bench overlooking the marina.

She collected her gear and strolled past yachts and sail boats and a few rusting punts, happy to be by the water in the sunshine with a good job well done.

For the first time in too long, Tamsyn began to relax. She leaned back against the sun-warmed bench, closing her eyes and lifting her face to the summer sky. She could hear the soft jingle of rigging in the harbour, and when she opened her eyes again, she had to squint against the glare as sunlight glittered on the water. Godber walked towards her with a pasty in each hand and a grin on his face. He had a voracious appetite and would happily eat all day. Perhaps he'd been a Labrador in a previous life.

Godber was a gentle giant with a crazy sense of humour. But she'd seen the other side of him, too.

Beyond the harbour, a brisk offshore breeze whipped the foam tips of the waves, creating a fine, salty mist which seemed to linger before the next wave followed it in.

Godber joined her, passing over one of the pasties, and parking his considerable bulk on the bench. They both heard it creak ominously, and Tamsyn smiled to herself as Godber muttered something about things not being built to last anymore.

A mobile phone rang, and they both reached for their phones.

"Not mine," said Godber.

Tamsyn looked at her phone's screen which displayed 'withheld number'. She rolled her eyes – she seemed to get one of these calls several times a day.

But just in case, she answered it.

"Hello?"

"PC Poldhu, this is Inspector Walters."

Tamsyn sat up, her back straightening automatically as she heard her police title and the authoritative voice of the woman in charge of all the uniformed officers at Penzance police station.

"Yes, ma'am."

"Where are you right now?"

"I'm in Falmouth, ma'am," she said, glancing at Godber who was frowning.

"You need to come to the station straight away, please, and report to my office."

"Yes, ma'am," she said automatically. "Um, I'm not in uniform because it's my day off."

"That doesn't matter," Inspector Walters said impatiently.

"Can I ask what this is about, ma'am?"

"I'll explain when you come in."

She hung up. Tamsyn took the phone away from her ear, and looked at the blank screen.

"What was that all about?" Godber asked.

"I'm not sure," she said, still frowning at her phone. "That was Inspector Walters – I've hardly ever talked to her – the sergeants do all the daily rotas and briefings."

"I don't like it," said Godber, glancing around suspiciously. "Call Rego, see what he has to say."

"I've got to go straight to the station," Tamsyn continued, puzzled. "She didn't say why, but her voice sounded calm enough. I wonder if there's been a situation – maybe leave has been cancelled..."

"Call Rego," said Godber. "Bugger it! I'll call him."

He pulled out his phone and tried calling DI Rego, but the call went to voicemail.

"Strange," he said. "But then again, the lazy sod is on holiday with his family." He gave Tamsyn a rueful smile. "Well, that's buggered up my Greggs run – I knew I should have bought two pasties for myself." Then he glanced at Tamsyn who still looked worried. "Come on, you have to get going. We'll get a taxi to Porthoustock, then I'll drive you to Penzance, okay?"

"Really? That would be great."

"Nah, it's no problem."

"Thanks, Godber!"

Godber didn't tell her that he was suspicious of this sudden order and he wanted to keep a close eye on her.

The taxi cost an arm and a leg, and Godber moaned the whole time about not being able to claim it on expenses. Holiday traffic was heavy and made it worse, and then it took them over an hour to cover the 27 miles back to Penzance.

Godber parked the Range Rover at the back of the police station, then escorted Tamsyn as far as the door.

"I'll wait outside."

"No need," Tamsyn smiled. "I can walk home from here."

"I'll wait," Godber insisted.

"Okay."

Tamsyn used her key fob to open the station's staff door when she was intercepted by two plainclothes officers.

One of the officers stepped forward immediately.

"Tamsyn Poldhu?"

"Yes?" she said smiling politely, but not recognizing either of the men.

The taller one spoke.

"Tamsyn Poldhu, I am Officer 6943 of Counter Terrorist Command South West, and I am arresting you on suspicion of the threat of action under the Terrorism Act 2006."

"What? No! That's not..."

"You do not have to say anything. But it may harm your defence if you do not mention when questioned something which you later rely on in court. Anything you do say may be given in evidence."

Her smile was slow to disappear because Tamsyn couldn't take in what the officer was saying, only that it was *wrong*.

"What?" she gasped. "No, this is a mistake!"

The man ignored her.

"It is necessary to take you into custody immediately to

obtain evidence by questioning and to allow for a prompt and effective investigation."

Tamsyn could not believe what she was hearing, she was stuck for words, nothing would come out.

The station commander, Inspector Maura Walters, strode down the corridor towards them, her face a stern mask.

"Tamsyn, you are immediately suspended from duty. I need your Warrant card, also your Captor spray, baton, work phone and entry fob. You will be taken from here and interviewed by these officers. *If* you are released from custody, you will not come back into this police station and won't have contact with any officer that works here. Do you understand?"

Tamsyn stood there blinking, confused, uncertain. It was a prank, some sort of joke. But the officers were serious, determined.

"What? N-no!" she managed to stammer at last. "No! This... No! This is a mistake!"

Their expressions didn't change even by the slightest flicker.

"This is a mistake," she said again, her voice shaking. "Ask Inspector Rego! Detective Inspector Rego. Ask him! He'll tell you everything."

She might as well have been talking to the granite cliffs of Land's End.

In shocked silence, she handed over her Warrant card and was escorted to her locker so that her baton and incapacitant spray could be collected.

Tamsyn saw several officers that she recognized and they all watched her, their faces grim and hostile.

One of the plainclothes officers took her arm as she was marched back along the corridor and out to a waiting police van.

"Tamsyn!"

She turned her head as Godber shouted her name, but the officer who had her arm didn't let her pause.

"Don't say anything!" Godber hissed. "Don't talk to anyone, don't trust anyone!"

His eyes narrowed as he glared at her, and all she could do was stare back.

"Tamsyn!" Godber yelled again. "Don't say fuck all until you've spoken to your Fed rep! Nothing! You hear me? I'll call the Federation office now and put them on standby."

The plainclothes officers loaded her like cargo into the van and slammed the door shut. As they walked around to the front, she heard one of them talking into his radio.

"I've just arrested Poldhu."

Not even her first name: just 'Poldhu', as if she were a known criminal.

"Yes, sir," he continued. "We're leaving Penzance now."

She heard them turn on the sirens, and the van began travelling at speed, blue-lighted all of the 115 miles to Exeter, the HQ for Devon & Cornwall Police.

Her body was shaking with cold and fear, and her mind kept somersaulting through the events of the last few days. *This isn't right! It's a mistake! It's all a terrible mistake! I can fix this. I just need to speak to Inspector Rego – he'll tell them, he'll tell them that they've got it all wrong!*

And then other thoughts, other voices began to worm

their way into her mind. It had felt weird, the operation. Why hadn't protocol been followed? Why was there no backup? She'd been told it was covert, that only *she* could help them; only *she* could save the op, the job, the country. But why? Why only her? *I'm just a student officer – why me? Why me? Why me?*

Because you're naïve, the voices replied. *Because you're stupid. Because you trusted the wrong people ... the wrong person.*

Her body was numb.

It's a mistake.

He'll fix it.

It's a mistake.

She nearly wept with relief when she saw the tall silhouette and broad shoulders of DI Rego, as she was brought through the rear entrance of Exeter police station.

"Sir!" she screamed, her voice piercing. "Inspector Rego!" The crowd of officers surrounding him cleared.

Her heart stopped.

He was handcuffed.

Her mind swam and she felt faint. She'd trusted him. He'd promised her...

If he spoke, she couldn't hear the words, but his lips were moving, and she thought he mouthed the words,

"I'm sorry."

CHAPTER 32

Tamsyn had been handcuffed during her training at Middlemoor. She'd even been cautioned and interviewed during role-play, but it hadn't been *this*; this numbing *wrongness*.

In a small room in the custody suite, she was questioned by two detectives – a sergeant and an inspector – neither of whom she knew, although she thought the inspector's surname sounded vaguely familiar, as if she'd read it on a memo.

She'd declined a solicitor and she could see on their faces that they thought it would all be plain-sailing for them. But Tamsyn didn't see how a solicitor could help her. How could she explain to a civilian, about the 'no names, no pack drill' code that was supposed to protect her, that might yet still protect her? She'd been told over and over again by both DI Rego and Godber that she couldn't talk about this to anyone.

She wanted, no, she *needed* to talk to the man she'd trusted. She had to talk to DI Rego. They'd told her that she couldn't; they'd told her that his own interview was being conducted in another room at this exact moment. She wondered what he'd say, or whether he'd say anything at all. She wondered what he'd say about her.

The video camera was switched on.

"The time is 4.15pm on Sunday 31st July 2024 at Exeter Police Station, Detective Inspector Frank Morton and Detective Sergeant Phil Brown attending. Please identify yourself for the purpose of the tape, including your date of birth."

Tamsyn's voice was soft but clear as she spoke.

"Tamsyn Poldhu. My birthday is 10th June 2003."

DS Brown read from his notes without looking at her.

"You have been arrested on suspicion of the threat of action designed to seriously interfere with or seriously to disrupt an electronic system under the Terrorism Act 2006. You do not have to say anything. But it may harm your defence if you do not mention when questioned something which you later rely on in court. Anything you do say may be given in evidence." Finally, he looked up at her. "Do you understand?"

"Yes."

"And you have waived your right to a solicitor."

"Yes," Tamsyn repeated, her voice stronger now. "And I have a short statement to make."

The two men looked surprised, but the DI nodded at her to speak.

"I wish to speak to Detective Inspector Robert Rego..."

"We've already told you..."

Tamsyn ignored the sergeant and spoke over him.

"...and I will only speak to Detective Inspector Rego.

Until I have been able to speak to him *in private*, this will be a 'no comment' interview."

"You do realise that you're in a lot of trouble here," the DI said, learning forwards. "You're looking at a custodial sentence of not less than 14 years. Your DI is looking at life."

Tamsyn's hands were shaking and her mouth was dry. Her nerve was in danger of failing her; she didn't know what to do.

The DI saw her uncertainty and honed in on it like a bloodhound.

"Come on, Tamsyn. Talk to us. I've read your file – you're a good officer. Whatever you've done, I'd be willing to bet it's because Rego told you to do it." He gave her what he thought was an encouraging smile. "This is your chance to give your side of the story."

She knew what he was doing; she knew that he was trying to come over like a friend, and she knew that he'd been trained to do that.

So even though she was terrified, even though she wasn't sure that she was making another terrible mistake, she leaned forward, mirroring his body language.

"No comment."

The two men exchanged a look and the DS took over.

"On Friday 22nd July, you did a dive at the site of the SS *Mohegan*. Why did you choose that location for your dive?"

"No comment." *Novice wreck divers don't choose the location – do your homework!*

"Did you choose that location or Adam Ellis, the dive instructor from Peninsula Diving Club?"

"No comment."

"You recovered something from the *Mohegan* on that dive. Can you tell us what you recovered?"

"No comment." *If you've talked to anyone, done any research at all, you'll know that it was Adam not me who found the drone. Although you probably don't know it was a drone and I'm not going to tell you.*

"On that same dive, you claimed to have spotted the body of a diver. How did you know where the body would be?"

"No comment." *Really? Are you going to ask me 'when did you stop beating your wife?'*

"Who was the diver?"

"No comment." *He had a nice boyfriend.*

"On Monday 25th July, you returned to the site of the *Mohegan* with DI Rego. What was your purpose in going there?"

"No comment." *A really uncomfortable day out with the Rego family: his wife and kids. Oh, and my grandfather who hates my boss because he was arrested by him once – yeah, so much fun.*

"Between midnight of Saturday 30th July and 2am of Sunday 31st July, you returned to the site of the *Mohegan* for a third time in the company of a man we believe to be Richard Beckins, a former officer with Greater Manchester Police."

Tamsyn looked up, engaging for the first time. *Is that your real name, Godber? Nice to meet you.*

"How do you know Mr Beckins?"

"No comment." *He's the DI's friend. I liked him.*

"What were your plans for that evening?"

"No comment." *Well, I was told it was a matter of national security, and I kind of assumed that was to do with keeping Cornwall, or, you know, Britain safe.*

"If nothing illegal took place, please tell me now, because you haven't got anything to hide."

"No. Comment." *I don't know if it was illegal or not. I guess not reporting the accident we saw was wrong. 'Anyone in charge of a ship must report any accidents or incidents to the Marine Accident Investigation'. I could hold my hands up to that, except I wasn't in charge of the op, and I was told not to. Or was that an order? Did Godber ... I mean, Richard Beckins, did he order me not to report it? But then again, 'Police officers should follow police regulations, their police force policies, and orders that are lawful'. Yeah, even if it was an order, it wasn't a lawful one. I think we covered that in training. God, my brain is so messed up.*

"Is there anything you want to tell us in your defence?"

"Yes. I want to speak to DI Rego in private."

"Apart from that?"

Tamsyn bit her lip.

"My first choice is to speak to DI Rego; my second choice is to speak to the Federation rep. Please."

"A Federation representative isn't a lawyer – they don't give legal advice," frowned DI Morton.

"I know, but they do advise on operational policing issues."

Morton's frown increased.

"Are you saying this is about a police operation?"

Tamsyn hesitated, then thought better of answering that.

"No comment."

With a faint sigh of exasperation, DI Morton sat back in his chair and continued questioning Tamsyn for another 25 minutes, but her only words remained,

"No comment."

Finally, DI Morton looked at his wristwatch. "The time by my watch is 16.57, and I'm terminating this interview."

In a different custody suite in another part of the building, DI Rego was being interviewed by his immediate boss, DCI Finch.

"Well, Robert..." the man sighed, then seemed to lose the will to speak.

"I know, boss. I'm sorry."

"It looks to me like you've been running an off-the-books covert op."

"With regret, sir, no comment."

"Who were you working with?"

"No comment."

"You know I can continue questioning you for up to 14 days, don't you?"

Rego nodded, then said, "No comment."

DCI Finch continued to question him, but Rego steadfastly replied, "No comment."

When Finch had asked every question on his list and not received a single answer, he quietly closed the file.

"This is out of my hands now, Robert. I'd hoped that ... well, I'd hoped ... I told ACC Gray that if you talked to anyone, you'd talk to me."

"I know, sir. I'm really sorry."

"I hope you have a good lawyer," said Finch sadly, as he turned off the video recorder.

Rego very much hoped that he wouldn't need a lawyer.

The moment he'd arrived at Penzance station and seen the welcome committee, he made one call to Vikram's burner, and had simply said,

"Code Zero."

He hoped that Vikram came through for him the way he'd promised.

All he had to do now, was wait.

And possibly pray.

CHAPTER 33

Rego was taken back to the cells: his tie, shoelaces, and belt removed; his phone and wristwatch placed in an envelope and retained by the custody sergeant.

The metal door clanged shut behind him, the noise tearing at his nerves.

He stared around the small space, the walls painted a dull grey, and the steel toilet somewhat less than stainless. The air was stale and the place stank of urine and bleach.

Humiliation warred with real concern. Vikram had told him they were taking orders from someone higher up in MI6 – his friend had implied that there was a chain of command. But if the mole hadn't been found, Vikram and whoever he was taking orders from, they wouldn't be prepared to reveal their hand. Especially not for Rego. Which meant that for now, he was on his own.

And the fact that he was currently sitting in a cell contemplating his freedom, career and marriage disappearing down the toilet, it meant that the mole hadn't been found.

He wanted to believe that Vikram was doing what he could, that he was still trying to get Rego released, but so far, it hadn't been enough.

"Come on, Vik," he whispered. "Come on."

He didn't know how much time had passed, maybe a couple of hours? He wondered if Cassie had tried to phone, her annoyance turning to worry when she was still unable to reach him.

Rego could have called her but he had a few shreds of hope left that Vikram would come through. But with every second that he sat in the cell, the shouts of other prisoners ringing in his ears, his hope lessened, like grains of sand slipping through his fingers.

Was time speeding up or slowing down? Rego had no way of knowing. There was no natural light in the cell, just the glare of yellow neon that made his eyes ache.

Every time he heard someone walking past his cell, he prayed that they'd stop at his door, say it was all a mistake and that he was free to go, but the footsteps always continued past, and Rego let out the breath he'd been holding.

He paced the cell, he counted the tiles on the ceiling and the seconds as they passed, he counted the soft beats of his heart, proving that he wasn't finished yet; he even did a hundred sit-ups and fifty press-ups before he gave in to the futility of it all. Then he sat slumped on the narrow bed, his head in his hands.

And when his last splinter of hope, his last certainty that Vikram would come through had shrivelled and died, footsteps rang along the corridor, then stopped outside his cell.

Rego stopped breathing, waiting, praying – and then he heard the loud click of a key in the lock and the door opened.

The custody sergeant was standing there with Rego's boss, DCI Finch.

"Robert, you're being released," said DCI Finch, his voice strained.

"Thank God," Rego muttered. "Sir, I..."

Finch held up his hand.

"Robert, you're an established officer and I regret that matters have come to this, but I have to inform you that you are suspended from duty and have been served with a Regulation 17 notice. The Chief Constable has fast-tracked an Assessment Officer and as you are suspected of a criminal offence, any disciplinary proceedings will take place once that criminal investigation is complete. If you are convicted by a court of an indictable offence, you will then face an Accelerated Misconduct Hearing where you will be put in front of the Chief Constable and sacked with immediate effect."

Rego took a deep breath, but said nothing.

"Dive Supervisor Nathan Tregowan has also been suspended from duty, pending an investigation."

Finch looked down at the folder in his hands and read from preprepared notes.

"In the case of PC Poldhu, as a student officer still within her probationary period, and one who has already raised concerns about her suitability as a police officer, she will be served with a Regulation 13 notice to say that she has failed to get through her probation and the force deems her unsuitable."

"Sir! That's not..."

DCI Finch gave Rego a stern look and shook his head.

"You had your chance to speak, Robert. It's out of my hands." He paused. "Chief Constable Evans has taken a personal interest in your case – these orders come direct from him."

Rego's sudden flame of hope at being released was snuffed out and his despair deepened. Free, but unable to return to the job he loved. Free, but disgraced. Free, but at what price?

"I'm sorry, Robert. There's nothing I can do."

Rego swallowed and nodded slowly.

"Sir, what about PC Poldhu? She was just following my orders. She shouldn't be punished for that. She didn't know..."

Finch shook his head.

"But she didn't do anything wrong!" Rego said, his voice loud with frustration. "She was following *my orders!*"

"And whose orders were you following, Robert?" DCI Finch snapped back. "The Chief Constable cannot, will not..."

Finch clamped his mouth shut, biting back whatever he'd intended to say.

Rego finally understood.

A higher authority than the Chief Constable had ordered Rego's release, and Evans was clearly unhappy about that. So, the Chief Constable needed to have a scapegoat for the embarrassment of having his explicit orders ignored and his seniority trampled all over by MI6. And because there was no way the Chief Constable would be able to find out any further information no matter how long an investigation was conducted.

If Vikram had already done everything he could by getting them released, Rego would still lose his job and maybe face a criminal prosecution. Tamsyn was collateral damage.

"Chief Constable Evans wants to see you before you leave," said Finch. "ACC Gray will be there, too."

"Of course he will," Rego said bitterly.

ACC Gray: the man who'd ordered Rego to stand down from the Kuzma investigation.

Which would just add the icing to a poisonous cake of secrecy and spite.

Finch sighed, patted Rego on the shoulder, then handed him over to the custody sergeant who returned his property with a stony face. Another uniformed officer watched the slow process, then escorted him to the Chief Constable's office.

Rego followed the officer in silence, thoughts crowding his mind: what would he say to Cassie? How could he explain to the kids? God, what would he say to Tamsyn? Her grandparents?

Police stations never truly sleep, but as it was a Sunday and they were in the administrative office building of Devon & Cornwall Police HQ, there were fewer people around to see Rego's humiliation, but there were enough.

Rationally, he knew it was unlikely they had any thoughts about him at all; it was too soon for the gossip to have spread. But still, it felt like everyone was looking at him, giving him second and third glances, whispering as he walked past.

Or maybe I'm being paranoid.

Maybe not.

Just because I'm paranoid, it doesn't mean they aren't out to get me.

Rego smiled grimly to himself.

Or maybe word had gone around, that and the fact that it was rare for the Chief Constable and Assistant Chief Constable to appear on a weekend, people were definitely staring.

And then Rego saw Tamsyn sitting outside the Chief Constable's office.

She looked pale and tired, her hair uncombed and her clothes rumpled. He knew that she'd been held in a cell for the same length of time as him, and he could see what that had done to her. And when Rego saw that her knuckles were white with tension, his guilt grew.

As he approached, she looked up, and it nearly killed him to see the relief on her face, the certainty that her belief in him still lived.

"Hello, Tamsyn. How are you?"

"Oh my God, it's been awful!" she gasped, her voice shaking. "They arrested me! They actually arrested me – for terrorism! I couldn't believe it! That's crazy, right? I was questioned for over an hour. I only said 'no comment' and that I wanted to talk to you, sir. That was the right thing to do, wasn't it?"

"Yes, it was. Well done." Rego's throat was dry.

"But it's all sorted out now, isn't it?" she asked, her bright blue eyes pleading with him to agree.

"Certainly better than it was a couple of hours ago," Rego said, managing a half-smile.

Tamsyn's eyelids fluttered as she took a deep breath, then opened her eyes and smiled.

"Thank you, sir."

Rego felt like the biggest piece of shit on earth.

"Tamsyn, I..." Rego began again then paused, unable to say the words that would take away her last scrap of hope.

"That's okay, sir," she smiled. "At least it will be, now that it's all been sorted out."

He grimaced.

"I'm sorry, but I don't think so. I think we're both about to lose our jobs."

She stared at him in disbelief, her lips moving but no words coming out.

"No!"

"I'm sorry."

"No! That can't be right!"

He had no reply.

"But why?" she begged, her voice breaking. "I don't understand! We didn't do anything wrong!"

Rego wanted to reach out to touch her, but she wrapped her arms around herself tightly, seeming to shrink into herself.

"Tamsyn, just breathe."

Her lips trembled but her gaze was defiant.

"I know you didn't do anything wrong. I *know* you didn't. You were following orders: *my* orders. And I'm going to tell the Chief Constable that." He paused. "The problem is, Tamsyn, that I *wasn't* following orders; in fact, I explicitly ignored a direct order to cease investigating the dead diver."

She stared at him, wounded astonishment, disbelief, and hurt in her expression.

"What do you mean?"

"Exactly what I said. I was told not to investigate any further and that all the files should be turned over to the Secret Intelligence Services."

"Then ... why?"

He wished he could tell her about Vikram and the MI6 shenanigans, but he couldn't. So, he gave her a half-truth.

"At the time, I believed it was the right thing to do."

"Do you still think that?"

He met her gaze. "Yes, I do."

If it makes any difference.

She gave him an uncertain smile.

"Okay then."

Her unswerving belief in him felt like a knife in the gut. He'd have preferred her anger, her disgust, her rage, anything other than her continued trust that he'd make this right.

He promised himself that he would try to reason with the Chief Constable, appeal to the man's better nature – assuming he had one. He would *not* leave that office without making sure that Tamsyn's career was safe. He would do everything in his power to prevent Tamsyn from losing her job or damaging her career.

Although if he was honest, he strongly suspected that nothing he said would make any difference.

I have to try.

This was what he'd risked from the start. He'd walked into it with his eyes open. But Tamsyn hadn't – he'd kept her in the dark, deliberately limiting what she knew and didn't know, dragging her into this murky world of secrets and lies, depending on her help, using her.

But all he'd done was to ruin his own career and also the career of a young woman who would have made a great officer. And that was unforgiveable.

And if he was honest with himself, worrying about Tamsyn took his mind off the fact that he could go to prison. Former police officers didn't do well in prison.

He didn't even know if he'd be charged with Section 5 of the Official Secrets Act 1989 which made it an offence for him, as a Crown Servant, to disclose information specifically covered by the Act. Other officers in similar circumstances had received heavy fines and even custodial sentences. At the very least, he'd be dismissed for gross misconduct.

There was nothing he could say to her.

Nothing he could do. Almost nothing.

I have to try.

He watched in silence as a uniformed Inspector strode past, spoke in muted tones to the assistant, then knocked on the Chief Constable's door and walked inside.

Rego didn't recognise the man but assumed he was the Chief Constable's staff officer. The role was seen as a step on the promotion ladder. The staff officer would attend meetings with Evans, write his speeches, and be a link between Evans and other senior officers or outside organisations. It was a demanding role, but a dogsbody one – Rego knew he'd never want to do a job like that ... then remembered that he'd never have the chance now.

The telephone on the assistant's desk rang and the

woman who answered it, listened, glanced at Rego, then replaced the receiver.

"You may go in now, Detective Inspector Rego."

Tamsyn stood up as well, but the woman waved her back into her seat.

"Just DI Rego," said the assistant.

Tamsyn stared unhappily at Rego. There was nothing he could say that would help, so he just gave her a faint smile.

"See you on the other side, Tamsyn."

"Good luck, sir," she said quietly.

Rego took a deep breath, knocked on the Chief Constable's door, entering when he heard a gruff, "Come!"

Being up against the wall just meant that your back was safe and there was only one good way out. Rego squared his shoulders and mentally prepared to fight his corner and Tamsyn's. It wouldn't make any difference, but it would make him feel better.

Taking a deep breath, he walked into the room where the Chief Constable was sitting behind a large mahogany desk with Charters in front of it. The uniformed inspector was leaning across to see the large computer screen, as they murmured quietly to each other.

Neither man spoke to Rego nor invited him to sit.

Rego stood with his hands clasped behind his back and gazed around him, taking in the walls decorated with photographs of the Chief Constable with various politicians and dignitaries, the largest being one of Evans with the late Queen. Rego recognised photos with Joe Biden, Justin Trudeau, Emmanuel Macron and Angela Merkel – presumably all from the G7 summit back in

2021. But there were no photos of the UK's Prime Minister at the time, Boris Johnson, or Foreign Secretary Liz Truss. *Yeah, not strange at all*, Rego thought grimly. *That's what it's like when you're well out of favour.*

Evans and the uniformed officer were still ignoring him, so Rego took the time to study the rest of the room.

There was a glass-fronted bookcase with a number of heavyweight law books, several of which Rego recognised from his inspector's exams.

To one side, a casual seating area circled a small coffee table for less formal meetings. Rego doubted it would be used for this meeting ... or showdown.

The wall by the window was covered with framed foreign law enforcement memorabilia, including mounted wooden Force crests of the different countries Evans had visited or who had visited him. Rego saw certificates showing courses the Chief Constable had attended in the USA, Canada, Australia and New Zealand – all English-speaking countries. A photo of Evans in an FBI jacket had pride of place.

What kind of man are you? Rego wondered. He'd heard mixed things about the Chief Constable, but knew that it was impossible for any boss to be wholly popular. This was the first time Rego was meeting him – in far from ideal circumstances.

The man himself was dressed in an immaculate uniform with a row of colourful service ribbons which denoted good conduct and long service awards, as well as the King's Police Medal. His epaulettes had crossed tipstaffs in a laurel wreath with one crown, signifying his rank. His dark hair was greying at the temple, and thick glasses had slid down his nose, but his eyes were hard, and chilly waves of disapproval emanated from across the broad desk when he glanced at Rego.

His eyes flicked back down to the screen he was reading, leaving Rego to continue standing in silence.

Rego guessed that Chief Constable Evans and the staff officer were reading his service record.

A moment later, there was another knock on the door and ACC Gray stalked into the room, throwing a withering stare at Rego.

"Ah, Ian! Good to see you," the Chief Constable said, shaking the other man's hand warmly, a greeting in stark contrast to how Rego had been received. "Have a seat while John and I finish this."

"Good to see you too, sir, John," Gray responded, glaring at Rego again. "In the circumstances."

The Chief Constable and the staff officer finished reading whatever was on the screen, then the younger man took a seat next to ACC Gray and pulled out a pen and writing pad, ready to take notes.

Evans steepled his fingers together, peering up at Rego.

"Yes, the circumstances. Very unfortunate circumstances. Well, here it is." And he paused. "These are the facts of the case: on Friday the 22nd of July, a body was recovered approximately one mile off the coast of Porthoustock in 100 feet of water. The following day, a *post-mortem* was to be performed by Dr Manners, Home Office Forensic Pathologist. This did not take place, as officers from the Secret Intelligence Services notified me of their interest in the case and their decision to take it over as a matter of National Security, a decision which was conveyed to you by ACC Gray. Am I correct so far, Detective Inspector Rego?"

"Yes, sir," said Rego crisply.

"This order you then disobeyed by starting your own unauthorised covert operation into the death of the victim. You misled, withheld information from, obfuscated and lied to intelligence officers and Naval officers at Culdrose; you illegally used personnel and resources from Devon & Cornwall Police to continue your activities, endangering the lives of Sergeant Nathan Tregowan and Police Constable Tamsyn Poldhu, a student officer. Further, you illegally shared sensitive information about the security of this country with several civilians. Good God, man!" the Chief Constable shouted, slamming his fist on the desk. "I was called by Culdrose's base commander to tell me what one of my officers had been up to! He wanted to know what was going on? So do I! What were you thinking? Or were you thinking at all?"

"Permission to speak, sir!"

"Denied."

"Sergeant Tregowan and Constable Poldhu were following my orders, sir," Rego said hurriedly. "They shouldn't be..."

"Do not speak when I am speaking!" the Chief Constable roared. "This insubordination, this direct and wilful disobeying of an order pertaining to national security, this is not something I can write up with a stern talking-to or a few days of unpaid leave. And the reason, the *only* reason that you're not being kept in custody is because I have been advised that it could lead to this matter becoming more widely known within the force – disclosure of your activities would be prejudicial to national security. The investigation will be undertaken by a specialist team appointed by me. The disobedience was of a most egregious, dangerous, even treasonous nature, and as a minimum you should expect to make a career change immediately, but I will personally ensure that you are prosecuted to the full extent allowable by law." He leaned back in his chair, making an effort to contain his fury as Rego stared at a space to the left of the Chief Constable's head. "The serious nature of your offence, conduct which was carried out with a purpose prejudicial to the safety of His Majesty's government and the United Kingdom, constitutes a clear and serious breach of the Standards of Professional Behaviour – so serious as to justify dismissal. Furthermore..."

The Chief Constable didn't finish the sentence because he was interrupted when his office door opened without warning and a tall, gangly man in a Barbour jacket strolled into the room.

"Who the hell are you?"

"Good afternoon, Chief Constable Evans," the man smiled affably. "The name's Guy Barker. I've just popped down from Vauxhall Cross. Oh, and Sir Edward sends his regards."

Rego tensed. Another spook?

Barker's eyes roamed around the room, glancing off ACC Gray, and settling on Rego. "Ah, Detective Inspector Rego, how nice to meet the man I've been hearing so much about. Our friend Vikram asked to be remembered to you." He smiled benignly.

Hope roared to life inside Rego's chest, but he didn't

dare believe what he was hearing – and it seemed as though the Chief Constable felt the same.

"What the hell is going on here?" he bellowed, confusion, annoyance and irritation in his voice.

"Do forgive me interrupting, Chief Constable," Barker said, his smile still in place but his gaze unwavering. "It has come to our attention that DI Rego might have got into a bit of bother over this unpleasant Ukrainian business, but we feel that it would be better all round if the case were closed as quietly as possible. No one needs an internal investigation or inquiry bringing up the bodies, so to speak."

He leaned casually against the wall his arms crossed, surveying the room, ensuring he had everyone's undivided attention before he continued.

"It really wouldn't be advisable for you to take any course of action that would undermine the public's belief in our invulnerability, Chief Constable. I'm sure you understand that no one would want to escalate a situation that could cause serious embarrassment to His Majesty's Government: *Semper occultus*." He smiled. "Of course, that's only my advice and ultimately, it's your call, but I have to say, Rego here has done a remarkable job. We really are terribly grateful."

The Chief Constable frowned at the intruder, steepling his fingers together.

"You're from MI6?"

"Well, technically we're the Secret Intelligence Service, but what's a name between friends? After all, we're all on the same team, wouldn't you agree, Chief Constable?"

Rego stared at Barker critically. The man was clearly doing his best impression of a 'rupert' with his jolly-hockeysticks style of talking, but there was no mistaking the confident coolness of his gaze or the soft threat in his voice.

"The thing is, Chief Constable," Barker continued amiably, "your officer has done a great service for our country. Of course," he added, "not that we could ever broadcast the fact, so no medals for you, old chum, although you have won our unceasing gratitude." His eyes fastened on Rego. "Perhaps there's something else you'd like?"

Rego's mind raced as a smile started to spread across his face, but he had to think fast.

"Richard Beckins: I couldn't have done it without him. He should be immune from prosecution."

"Of course," Barker said smoothly. "Already taken care of. Anything else?"

"Nate Tregowan..."

"...will be back on duty with a clean record."

"Nate Tregowan's dive boat was badly damaged on the op," Rego hinted.

"I assume he has insurance," Barker replied, raising one eyebrow.

"I'm sure he has – but he'll also have to pay the excess and increased premiums."

"Noted," Barker said, neither agreeing nor disagreeing. "I suppose you think he should be promoted, too."

Rego realised that Barker was dropping a broad hint. He inclined his head to one side as he thought about it.

"Diving is Nate's life so I don't think he'd want to be promoted out of an operational role, but I think he could do with a change from diving in cold, muddy waters. Maybe some training in the Caribbean would be motivational."

"Novel idea," Barker said. "I don't see why not."

Rego rushed on, hoping his unbelievable luck was going to hold.

"PC Poldhu is waiting outside. I'm told she's been served with a Regulation 13 – but she's a good officer and she was only following my orders."

"Well, we wouldn't want to lose an officer with her potential, but perhaps she's a little inexperienced to be promoted just yet," Barker said with a small smile, and Rego had the distinct impression that the man was laughing at him – or at the Chief Constable.

"She'd be very interested in attending a training course with the Underwater Search Unit at Plymouth," said Rego, ignoring Barker's quiet sarcasm.

"I think that can be arranged. Anything else?"

Rego nodded slowly. "My family are down on holiday and I've been working non-stop since they arrived. I'd like to have two weeks paid leave in addition to my annual allowance to get back in my wife's good books. And two weeks additional leave for PC Poldhu and Dive Supervisor Nate Tregowan, as well. After that, I'd just like to get back to work."

Barker met his gaze with a wry smile, nodded, then turned to Chief Constable Evans.

"And of course, Chief Constable, His Majesty's government – and Sir Edward in particular – we are very grateful to you for your astute support. Very grateful indeed. Let's just say these things are not forgotten when it comes to the New Year Honours List." He glanced at ACC

Gray. "And, of course, we're awfully grateful to your esteemed second in command."

"I see," said Chief Constable Evans, his mouth a thin line of annoyance as understanding flared in his eyes. "Well, we do have a very good team down here. I'm glad to say that my officers go above and beyond in the performance of their duties."

"Ah yes, leading by example," said Barker, bowing his head.

Rego's lips twitched with a smile but he managed to maintain his composure.

"And as we are of one mind on that," Barker continued, "we thought that honouring PC Poldhu with an award from the Royal Humane Society would be a small way to thank her for her involvement."

The Chief Constable clearly had no clue what Barker was talking about so Rego filled him in quickly.

"On the same day that PC Poldhu discovered the body of the dead diver, she assisted her diving instructor, Adam Ellis, from depth to the surface after he was attacked by a conger eel. His finger was nearly severed and he was close to passing out from shock. It was PC Poldhu's first wreck dive, sir, and she didn't panic. Without her, I believe Ellis would have drowned."

Evans stared at Rego appraisingly. "I see."

Gray seemed to be the last to catch up, then he nodded grudgingly.

"We should do a press release and mention the Ukrainian diver has been identified, too. That would be..."

"I think *not*," Barker said sharply, his hail-fellow-well-met persona vanishing. "Certain persons are never to be mentioned outside this office."

"Of course not," Evans agreed, throwing the Assistant Chief Constable a scornful look.

ACC Gray turned puce and clamped his lips firmly shut.

"Marvellous," said Barker, clapping his hands, his smile reappearing. "So, all charges dropped and wiped from your records – no need to mention it again. Ever."

He reached out his hand for the staff officer's notepad, and with a quick glance at the Chief Constable, it was handed over without further comment. Barker tore out the top two pages and handed it back.

"Well then, I'll leave it all in your capable hands, Chief Constable. It's back to the Big Smoke for me. You're so lucky living in such a beautiful part of the world," and he strolled out, utterly at ease.

The room was heavy with silence as Chief Constable Evans exhaled slowly, turning his gaze towards Rego, but it was ACC Gray who spoke.

"You seem to lead a charmed existence, Detective Inspector Rego. I hope it lasts."

An indecipherable expression passed over Evans' face as he glanced at his second-in-command.

"You took risks, Rego," the Chief Constable conceded at last. "Both personal and professional. But as has so recently been explained to us," and here he glanced at Gray, "you have been of great service to your country. Well done."

"Thank you, sir."

Evans paused, a glimmer of humour in his chilly expression. "Don't do it again."

"No, sir."

"And I'll be in touch about PC Poldhu's award," he said, raising an eyebrow. "So best not to mention it generally, although you may inform her."

"Understood, sir."

"Good. Well ... thank you for your time, Inspector. Dismissed."

"Thank you, sir," said Rego, standing abruptly and almost sprinting to the door in case the Chief Constable changed his mind.

Tamsyn's eyes widened at the huge smile on his face as he left the office.

"Good news," said Rego, grinning from ear to ear. "We're off the hook!"

"What do you mean, sir?"

"All charges dropped and our records are squeaky clean."

EPILOGUE

Rego sat on the park bench, appreciating the shade as the lunchtime temperature rose steadily. Several families were enjoying picnics, and a group of kids kicked a football across the grass, using their jumpers for goalposts.

It was the first day of August and the summer stretched ahead, promising beach walks and wild swimming and lazy days in the sunshine – or more probably rain, cool temperatures, busy shops and bored kids, but a man could dream. Cassie had agreed to stay for the whole summer and arranged with her employers to work from the cottage, and she'd also helped to find Patricia a small room behind the Admiral Benbow pub whose motto made Rego smile:

> *To err is human, to arr is pirate.*

His career was back on track, and both the Chief Constable and ACC Gray had decided to endorse Rego, taking their cue from the man who called himself 'Guy

Barker' and from a phone call that the Chief Constable had received from the Cabinet Office. Rego wasn't privy to that conversation, but Vikram had assured him that it had taken place.

He'd also spoken to Tamsyn again and promised to attend her medal ceremony, although that wouldn't be for months. He was glad to hear that she was heading off to the Boardmasters international surfing competition and festival at Newquay. Mostly, he was glad she'd recovered from everything he'd put her through.

He frowned at the thought. So many secrets, so much to hide. And the man who should have been punished had died nearly two years ago.

Rego saw Jameson in the distance, walking at a steady pace, neither slowly nor quickly, as if knowing there'd be no good news to rush towards.

Vikram had spoken to his bosses and given Rego permission to tell Jameson the truth about Kuzma, although the drone and its consequences were not to be mentioned.

Jameson sat down on the bench his hands resting loosely in his lap.

"I was surprised to hear from you, Detective Inspector Rego."

"I would have called sooner," Rego said carefully, "but I can't tell you everything – some of it is classified."

"I guessed as much," Jameson sighed, his knee beginning to jiggle with anxiety. "I'm sorry, I can't sit here. Can we go for a walk in the park, Inspector?"

"Sure," said Rego. "It's a nice day."

"Is it?"

They walked past the tennis courts into a quieter part of the large park where the palms were tall and cast cooling shadows.

"Do you know what happened to Freddie?"

There was no point trying to sugarcoat it, so Rego plunged right in.

"Fedir Kuzma wasn't his real name and he wasn't Ukrainian."

Jameson drew in a shuddering breath but didn't speak.

"We believe that he was Russian..." Rego went on.

"You mean...?" Jameson gasped, freezing mid-step. "Oh, my God! I can't believe it! I can't believe it! Are you sure?"

"We're sure he wasn't Ukrainian. We have strong evidence that he was trying to download data from the underwater cables to intercept encrypted messages between the UK and the US."

"The questions he kept asking me..." Jameson looked ill.

"We recovered the laptop that was stolen from your room..."

"Who? Who took it?"

"I can't tell you that, Mr Jameson. I *can* tell you that person is no longer a threat to our security."

"And this person, did they kill Freddie?"

"No. We believe that the Ukrainians suspected him and when he met with his UK contact, they became convinced that he was a spy."

"So, they told someone and ... and *we* had him killed?" Jameson asked, his voice rising in shock and disbelief.

"No, we weren't aware of Kuzma until we recovered his body. It's our belief that a person or persons unknown deliberately sabotaged his dive computer and cylinders."

Jameson rubbed his hands over his face.

"The Ukrainians killed him?"

Rego frowned.

"I don't have proof that I could take to court, but yes, that's what we believe."

Jameson lowered his head and wiped his eyes with his fingers.

"I thought he might be a spy, but I thought he was on *our* side. Was anything about him real? Did he even have a sister?"

Rego shook his head.

"The address from his so-called sister went to their foreign intelligence, an SVR factory. It seems likely that when Kuzma disappeared, they tried to find out what had happened to him. They may have even thought he'd defected. When they couldn't contact him and there was no trace, they thought they'd see if you knew what had happened to their agent ... maybe even recruit you." Rego paused. "Kuzma did ask you to share classified intelligence, didn't he?"

Jameson closed his eyes and nodded.

"Yeah, but I didn't do it. I already told you. Even though he said it would help the Ukrainian cause." He shuddered. "I was too scared. He kept asking me, but I kept saying no." He opened his eyes. "I'm not a traitor, Inspector. You do believe me, don't you?"

Rego nodded.

"If I didn't believe you, we wouldn't be here having this conversation now."

He didn't add that Jameson, his phone, laptop and work computer had been thoroughly examined for any intel leaks – there was nothing.

Jameson shook his head, trying to take in everything that he'd learned about the man he thought he knew.

"He didn't deserve to die like that," he said quietly. "Alone, in the sea, drowning. Even if he wasn't who he said he was, he was still murdered, Inspector. And you're saying that no one will ever be charged?"

"I can't see that happening, no."

"It's not right!"

What could Rego tell him? That was the system, the process. You gathered evidence, you looked at the facts, and if the evidentiary results didn't pass the CPS threshold, there would be no prosecution.

"I can only guess how hard this is," said Rego. "But not every crime can be prosecuted, and not every prosecution results in a conviction. Even then, not every conviction leads to jail time. In this case..." he paused. "In this case, there is no case. It's officially closed, recorded as an accident."

And in this case, no governmental willingness to pursue a prosecution.

"So, that's it?"

He nodded, and Jameson threw him a look of rage and despair.

Rego had worked on a number of murder cases, and he knew that most MIT detectives had at least one case that was never solved. The price of being a police officer was to carry a list of names, people, places, crimes in his head that stopped him from sleeping at night.

But to Jameson, he had nothing left to say, and it was several seconds before the man spoke again.

"Do people at work know about Freddie? And me?" he asked hesitantly.

"Yes, a few: Sergeant Bladen, Corporal Campbell, and the base commander, Captain Irwin."

Jameson curled his lip.

"Pretty much everyone that matters then. I'm not sure I even care anymore." He took a deep breath and stared up at the endless blue sky. "I've decided: I'm leaving the Royal Fleet Auxiliary."

"Is that what you want?"

Jameson closed his eyes, and Rego waited, unwilling to break the man's thoughts or meditation or his need to draw a line under this part of his life.

Finally, Jameson looked down and shook his head slowly.

"What I want doesn't exist."

Rego didn't have a response for that.

"Where will you go?"

"It turns out I have very transferrable skills in the private sector," Jameson replied with a small smile.

Rego nodded and held out his hand.

"Well, good luck. I hope it works out for you."

"Yeah. Me, too." Jameson paused. "Do you know a young woman officer, Tamsyn Pol— something?"

"Yes, I know Tamsyn."

"She saved my life."

"I heard."

Jameson's eyes tightened.

"Could you say ... could you tell her ... hell, I don't even know if I wanted to be saved ... but could you say thank you ... I think."

"Maybe I'll just tell her the 'thanks' part," Rego said.

Jameson shrugged, then turned and walked away without another word, his hands in his pockets, his head bowed.

Rego watched until he disappeared out of sight. He wondered if Jameson would be one of the ones who made it. He hoped so.

His phone rang and he pulled it out see that it was his DS calling.

"Afternoon, Tom – please don't tell me there's anything urgent because if I work another day while I'm supposed to be on leave, my wife is going to serve me with divorce papers."

"I'm sorry, sir," Stevens said quickly, "but I thought you'd want to know. The Albanian organised crime boss who nearly killed Tamsyn earlier this year..."

"Besnik Domi? What about him?"

"He's been arrested in Tirana and is being extradited. He'll be in the UK in a couple of days."

Rego's skin prickled. This was *his* case, his first case as an inspector. Two people had been murdered; Tamsyn and her grandfather had nearly died – and now Rego would have the chance to face the murderer in court.

"Thanks, Tom," he said. "I'll be at the office in ten minutes."

THE END

<u>Author's Note</u>

On the day that the first draft of this manuscript was completed, Tobias Ellwood MP wrote,

"As warfare evolves into the realms of cyber and space, the importance of safeguarding our digital infrastructure has become paramount as the defence of our territorial borders ... there are difficult conversations about the formation of drone brigades, cyber-attack responses, and the downing of satellite networks that need to be had today rather than after such an event takes place."

DEAD RECKONING – Cornish Crime #3

When Besnik Domi, the feared enforcer for organized crime gang the Hellbanianz, is extradited back to Britain, PC Tamsyn Poldhu has to face the man who tore her family apart, and DI Rego has to make sure that the case against the killer is watertight.

The evidence that will convict Domi is strong, but when threats are made against both their families, Tamsyn and Rego have to choose: justice or vengeance.

Coming 1.3.25

WHAT TO READ NEXT...

DEAD RECKONING – A Cornish Crime Thriller #3

When Besnik Domi, the feared enforcer for organised crime gang the Hellbanianz, is extradited to the UK, Tamsyn has to face the man who tore her family apart. Detective Inspector Rego has to make sure that the case against the killer is watertight.

But the Domi brothers have a long reach, and when threats are made against Tamsyn's and Rego's families, they have to make a choice.

And it might not be justice.

Read chapter 1 now...

www.berrickford.com

THE CORNISH CRIME THRILLER SERIES
SAMPLE CHAPTERS

There are four books in this police procedural crime fiction series so far, with more planned. Each standalone story features Police Constable Tamsyn Poldhu and Detective Inspector Robert Rego, along with a cast of recurring characters, all set in the beautiful seaside county of Cornwall.

Read the blurbs and sample chapters from each book.

Book #1 DEAD WATER

Book #2 DEAD MAN'S DIVE

Book #3 DEAD RECKONING

Book #4 DEAD SHORE

www.berrickford.com

ACKNOWLEDGMENTS

To DS Dave Stamp (rtd) for information on diving the wreck of SS *Mohegan*, as well as supplying lots of technical information.

To Emily Humphreys for background info and hot chocolate.

To Ben Daddow, Royal Navy Clearance Diver for giving me a good way to kill off Kuzma. Good luck to him and his young family as they sail around the world, perhaps forever.

To Bob Williams, underwater engineer and search specialist

To Kamla Millson, for borrowing her name and for the proofreading

To Peggy Moerman, proofreader extraordinaire

To Stone's Reef for supplying the hot chocolate, and Sisu for the motivational brownies.

Thanks to Andrea Rego for lending her and Ozzie's names to the story; for all things Cornish, including 'dear of 'im'; and for explaining the magical feeling of diving down to the seabed and staring up through crystal clear waters to the sky.

To Sharkfin Media for the great website and all things techy.

And last but never least, to Coby Llewelyn: reader, editor, friend – as always.

FORENSIC FILE

In each edition of my monthly newsletter, I'll cover a topic of interest from the forensic files.

Topics covered so far:

Fingerprints
More correctly called 'finger ridges', these are formed on a foetus by six months, due to the movement of amniotic fluid, and even the fingerprints of twins aren't identical.

Digi dogs
Search dogs have been trained to locate drugs or explosives, but they can also be trained specifically to sniff out technology such as laptops, mobile phones, USB sticks and even SIM cards. First trialled in the UK by Devon & Cornwall Police, with assistance from the FBI.

Drones
At the beginning of 2023, more than 400 drones were

FORENSIC FILE

used in police forces across the UK. Drones are being trialled in remote rural areas: 'Drone as First Responder'.

Police Divers

How do divers work in murky or pitch-black underwater conditions? What precautions do divers have to make when working with Explosive Ordnance?

Learn more on my website and sign up for the monthly newsletter www.berrickford.com

Printed in Dunstable, United Kingdom